SMALL ACTS OF MERCY

EMMA SALISBURY

BLOODHOUND
BOOKS

First published in 2026 by Bloodhound Books.

www.bloodhoundbooks.com

Print ISBN: 978-1917705660

To my wonderful family, always.

"Sometimes you don't survive whole, you just survive in part..."

—Toni Morrison

CHAPTER ONE

The scream coming from the neighbouring room makes me flinch.

'Mercy?'

The use of my name snaps me back into the room. I nod to show that I'm listening, stretch my mouth into a smile.

'This is a real opportunity for you, Mercy.' Liam Douglas, my solicitor, looks at me expectantly. 'One that I urge you to grab with both hands.'

I imagine grabbing his head with both hands and blowing a big fat raspberry on the top of it. He's too young to be bald, it ages him. Makes him look as though the best years of his life are already behind him. Mind you, I should talk.

The wailing coming from next door gets louder. I feel a shiver run through me as my gaze flits to the wall separating me and the poor cow beyond it.

'If you convince the panel you're ready, you'll be let out on licence.' Liam's bushy eyebrows meet in the middle as he frowns, at odds with his shiny scalp that glistens under the strip lighting above us. I study the shape of his head beneath his pallid skin and think of the sound a skull makes when it shatters.

'You do *want* to go home?' he demands when I don't respond, as though there can only be one right answer.

'Of course I want to go home, but what's the point in that?' I say defiantly. 'Wanting gets you nowhere. I mean, it's not like I haven't tried.' For the last few weeks, I've racked my brain over what I could say this time around that would be any more persuasive to the previous two parole hearings I've attended.

What lies I'd have to tell.

'Sometimes you have to know when to throw in the towel,' I say with finality. I feel the disappointment coming off him in waves. I can barely bring myself to look at him.

'I'll give you time to think about it.' He tosses his paperwork into his briefcase before getting to his feet. 'Give me a call if you change your mind,' he tells me, then he's gone.

As I step into the corridor to return to my cell, the door to the neighbouring visitation room opens. I increase my pace, causing the prison officer who's chaperoning me to bark, 'Where's the fire?' I stop outside the doorway, peering into the room like a driver rubbernecking a pile-up on the motorway. It's strange how compelling it is to watch as someone else's life is blown apart. To observe their horror in grotesque fascination. *Stop!* I shake my head, remind myself that misery isn't a contest. I remember how I felt when the world I'd worked so hard to build came crashing down.

What I had to do to put it right.

The room is kitted out identically to the one I've just left: empty apart from a bolted down table and two chairs either side of it. A woman from my block is slumped on one of them.

'I've got no time for this nonsense, get up or I'm putting you on report!' The PO with her is trying to pull her to her feet.

Officer Frame is sour-faced and mean with it. One of those people who equates wearing a uniform with power.

'What's happened?' I call out.

The woman holds her head in her hands but she lifts it at the sound of a sympathetic voice. She looks at me, her eyes flickering in recognition. 'They've taken my kids, Mercy, they've taken my fuckin' kids!'

I don't know her, but I've seen her around. I help out at the welcome desk when the newbies arrive. Peer support is the proper name for my role; means I help the first-timers settle in. On those days I wear a yellow *Here to Help* vest over my sweatshirt and give them a guided tour of the induction hall, like an HR manager showing new recruits around the shop floor. In truth, these women are too bewildered or spaced out to take anything in that I tell them. All they want to know is that their children are safe, that their mothers will cope with the extra mouths to feed. I hand out their welcome packs, answering any questions I can. Consequently, they all know me even though I couldn't pick any of them out in a line up. Oh, the irony.

The woman searches my face for kindness. Her own face is a map of worry lines but close up, I can see she's much younger than me, late-twenties at most, with cropped brown hair and a tiny butterfly tattoo on the side of her neck. I try to pluck her name from the endless line of women that traipse through Fairmile's heavy air-locked doors and it comes to me at once. 'Debbie?' I say to her, but she's already dropped her gaze. She stares straight ahead as though picturing the future without her children in it.

Officer Frame glares in my direction. I wonder what's happened in her life that's bent her out of shape, why she chooses to take it out on the lame ducks around her. 'Jog on!' she yaps.

Being a peer support helper affords me privileges with some

of the prison officers, but not all. Some see me as a mediator, to others I'm a threat. An agitator. Too big for my boots. Each one of them is correct.

I was interviewed for the post, even though it's voluntary. They don't let just anyone wear that yellow vest, you know. I had to demonstrate that I'm respectful to others, empathetic and, above all else, clean. I regard Officer Frame and wonder what criteria was used to assess how suitable she was for her role. If needling and prodding the vulnerable are desired traits, then she has them in spades.

I turn to the PO who escorted me to my meeting with my solicitor. Officer Woods is a decent sort, doesn't wind folk up for the sake of it.

'Mercy helps out at the welcome desk,' she reminds her colleague, giving her the chance to change tack without losing face.

'Whatever!' Frame responds. She makes a wafting motion with her hand, giving me permission to enter.

I move slowly to where Debbie's sitting and drop down on my haunches so I'm in her line of vision. There's a sense of desperation about her that resonates. *I feel it, sister*, I want to tell her. 'Let's get you back to your pad,' I say instead, then more quietly when she doesn't move, 'Not worth giving them a sideshow.' It doesn't pay to wear your grief in here, too many folk to weaponize it then use it against you. I give her hand a quick squeeze to show her I'm on her side. She hauls in a breath and pushes herself to her feet.

'About fuckin' time,' mutters Frame, shooing her out of the room.

'I'll look in on you later,' I call after her, but she's gone.

Vonnie has the kettle on, there are two plastic mugs beside it, an herbal teabag in each. 'What did your brief have to say, then?' she asks as I flop onto my bunk.

I shrug. 'Same as usual.'

The kettle boils and clicks itself off. Vonnie pours hot water into both mugs. She knows not to push, that if I've got something I want to share with her then I'll come out and say it, otherwise it's a case of mind your own beeswax. We've been pad-mates for eighteen months. I struck lucky with her, some would say. Others with longer memories might claim her luck ran out the day she moved in with me.

It isn't easy sharing a box room with a stranger. There's no such thing as personal space in prison. Our cell is three metres by two and has a metal toilet in one corner. Every piss, shit and tampon change is carried out in full view of your pad-mate, but after a while you stop noticing. If you want to survive in here, you leave modesty at the door.

'Get your laughing gear round that,' she says, handing me my mug. She pulls a packet of biscuits from her shelf, lobs it onto my bunk before picking up her own mug. We sit side by side. She takes two biscuits from the pack and offers me one, which I take.

'You lost more weight?' I ask her, keen to steer the conversation away from my lawyer's visit.

Vonnie is too tall and too thin. What she gains in height she loses in self-confidence. She stoops so that no one will notice her. When you first see her, you think she's looking for something she's dropped when what she's really doing is avoiding your eye. She's a serial shoplifter. She does it to pay for her boyfriend's drugs, only she's not very good at it, hence this is her third stint inside. Vonnie takes my observation as a compliment. 'I'm watching what I eat.' The biscuit she's holding is covered in cheap waxy chocolate. She demolishes it in two mouthfuls.

'I can see that,' I tease her, poking her in the ribs when her face drops.

'I don't want Wayne thinking I've let myself go.'

Wayne is pasty-faced with lank hair. It clings to his scalp on visiting days like he's run a marathon rather than walked the five hundred yards from the bus stop to the visitor centre. I get it. Beauty is in the eye of the beholder.

'There's no danger of that, you're a stunner,' I remind her. It's true. Even in here she manages to keep her herself looking nice. Shoulder-length wavy hair frames her angular face, setting off large green eyes, which when they look at you are mesmerising. You hear about women who don't recognise their beauty, Vonnie is one of them. Her face flushes. She's about to contradict me, the way women do when someone gives them a compliment, but I throw her a look. *Take it.*

As we sip our tea, my eyes sweep along the photos on the wall beside our bunks. Photos of the lives we've left behind. We've arranged them so our loved ones are the last thing we see at night and the first thing we see every morning: me, with my siblings Hope and Clem; Vonnie and her pasty-faced Wayne.

Vonnie rests her mug on her knees and turns to face me. God knows what she sees in Wayne, why so many women with potential settle for feckless men.

'What if I can't hack it?'

Her release date is looming and already she's in a tailspin. She's been asking this question on a loop for the last few days.

'It'll be better this time,' I tell her, though it'll only really be better if she says goodbye to Wayne.

Vonnie is one of those people whose glass is half empty. If there's a choice between believing one of two things – both of which there is evidence for – she always chooses the one that makes her feel bad. Nothing works out for her. Everyone's life is better than hers. Prison is a relief because she's finally found her tribe. She takes out two more biscuits and passes one to me. I take it and place it on the sink. 'I'll save it for later,' I tell her.

'Suit yourself.' She pops hers into her mouth and chews vigorously. I realise then that the tea she made wasn't for me to unburden myself about my solicitor's visit, but for her. She's building up to something. I take another sip of my drink and wait. It's not like I'm pressed for time.

'Wayne says he's going to give up the gear.'

'That's a good thing, isn't it?'

She looks at me sceptically. She's so used to viewing the world from a place of deficit that positivity feels foreign to her, the same way people on the outside can't imagine being locked up, I suppose.

'He promised he'd pack it in the last time I was in here. Time before that, too, if I'm keeping score.'

'So what does that tell you?' I ask, hopeful she'll finally see the light and send him packing.

Mashed biscuit has lodged along the front of her teeth. She picks at it with her finger before using what's left in her mug as a mouth rinse, swallowing the loosened debris in one gulp. 'That I need to stop getting my hopes up. That way, when he falls off the wagon again I won't be disappointed.'

I stifle a sigh.

Vonnie's mouth turns down at the edges. 'I went out with a fella a few times, years back, who was really nice.'

'What happened?'

'I had to pack it in. It felt wrong. It freaked me out when he showed up when he said he would. There's got to be a catch, right?'

I gape at her. With a mindset like that, no wonder the Waynes of this world thrive.

'All I want is to get home. Get back to how things were,' she says.

'You sure that's what you want, Von? Sounds to me like you're harking after something that doesn't exist.'

Vonnie ponders this. 'It wasn't all bad.'

'Wasn't it?' I recall her previous stints in here. Her vow never to return. 'Nostalgia makes liars of us all.'

'I'm used to him,' she admits. 'Guess I'm a creature of habit.'

'We all are to some extent, especially while we're stuck in here...' I reason. Wayne promising to clean up his act then failing isn't the problem, it's Vonnie's constant acceptance. '...but once you leave, you're allowed to choose a better life, you know.'

Vonnie looks at me, unconvinced.

'You know it's a thing, don't you?' I tell her. 'Cherophobia. It's an irrational fear of being happy.'

Her eyes brighten as though I've bestowed her with lavish praise. 'I've got a phobia,' she says, smiling. 'I fucking knew it!'

'You've got to let it go, girl,' I tell her. 'Start leaning into the joy.'

I stand, place my mug beside the kettle and wrap my biscuit in a strip of toilet paper. I slip it into the pocket of my jogging bottoms and grab my yellow helper's vest from my dirty washing pile.

'I'm going for a wander,' I tell Vonnie, but she's stopped listening.

'Chero-pho-bia,' she says, trying it out for size.

Fairmile prison is divided into five house blocks. An induction block that sounds better than it is, where the newbies are housed when they first arrive; a medical block; punishment block; and house blocks four and five where everyone eventually ends up, whether short or mid-term sentenced prisoners, or those serving long-term sentences, or life, like me. There are two floors to each, and residents – as the governor refers to us on the prison service website, as though staying here is optional – socialise in the central areas.

'May the Lord have Mercy on your soul!' bellows a gaunt-looking woman when I pass through the social area for our block. It's a running joke, and has been for the last sixteen years, since we both arrived here as wet-nosed runts, green in every way imaginable. Tanya's inside for killing her pimp, and for that she gets to say what she pleases.

The social area comprises a grubby settee and several cushion-backed chairs alongside a mini kitchen equipped with a kettle and toaster. It's a place to gravitate to when the four walls of your cell – or your pad-mate – feel like they're closing in on you. I acknowledge Tanya with a nod, declining her offer to join her and her cronies with a wave of my hand.

A young woman hops from foot to foot impatiently by the toaster, raking long nails through hair that was once blonde but now sports a colour block of auburn.

'Come and join us,' she says when she catches my eye.

'Another time, Lola, I'm on my way to see someone,' I tell her, waving my vest like it's a life raft.

Lola's mouth forms a pout but she thinks better of it. One of the perks of being a convicted killer is other inmates think twice about getting on my wrong side.

I slow down as I approach the next row of cells, unsure which one is Debbie's, until I hear her cries echo along the corridor. A crowd of inmates are starting to gather. They step aside quickly to let me pass, eager to find out what all the fuss is about. Officer Frame, the PO who'd escorted Debbie to her legal visit this morning, stomps along the polished floor, coming to a halt outside her cell door at the same time as me. A dirty sanitary towel blocks the hatch, stopping anyone from looking in to check on her.

'I'VE HAD E-FUCKING-NOUGH OF THIS!' Frame yells, reaching for her keys.

'Why did you lock her in? It's association time,' I demand. Inmates are allowed to move freely around the wing during association time. It coincides with when our meals are served, giving us an opportunity to have company while we eat, company which in Debbie's case would have provided a welcome distraction.

Frame's eyes are cold and penetrating. 'She was acting up. Not that it's any of your business.' She mutters insults under her breath: 'Dirty whores, the lot of you. Waste of taxpayers' money. Shouldn't be allowed to breed.'

I lean in close. *Fuck you*, I mouth.

Frame turns and glowers in my direction.

I glower back.

The cries coming from the other side of the door get louder, interspersed with low, inconsolable moans.

'What's wrong with Debs?' one of the women calls out, breaking our stand-off.

'She's had some bad news,' I answer. 'I just want to check she's all right.' I keep my gaze on Frame but shift my head slightly: *Your move.*

Frame lifts her radio to speak into it, then thinks better of it when another PO appears on the landing. 'Let Mercy have a word,' the officer urges Frame. 'See if she can't talk some sense into her.'

Frame turns to me grudgingly before unlocking the cell door. She takes a step back.

'Knock yourself out, *Oprah*, you've got five minutes.'

I slip on my yellow vest before I go in.

Debbie is lying on her bunk, limp. Her eyes are closed from exhaustion. She's done with crying but not done with being sad. She senses a presence and stiffens. 'It's only me,' I say to reassure her. I perch on the edge of her bunk and wait her out. Around us, the sound of women's chatter permeates the walls. It takes a while to get used to the white noise of prison. The clang of metal on metal as the doors and gates open and close and keys turn in locks. The rattle of food trolleys as they are pushed to and from the kitchen to each house block and back. It's hard to find a quiet place.

There's a crackle of radio and heavy footsteps as officers run to an emergency somewhere on the wing – this constant noise is the reason the prison doctor dishes out so many sleeping pills. Eventually she pushes herself into a sitting position, cradling her arms around her knees. Bloodshot eyes peer at me beneath swollen lids. A trail of snot perches on her upper lip. She wants to be heard but no one is listening. In here, when bad news is delivered you're expected to get on with it. After all, you're a criminal, you relinquish the right to compassion the moment you arrive through those heavy prison gates. Absorb it and move on.

'Do you have a tissue?' she asks meekly.

'I can do better than that.' I reach into my pocket and pull out the toilet paper covered biscuit. The sight of it makes her cry again but then she laughs, takes it and blows her nose. She bites into the chocolate coating and closes her eyes. I wait until she's finished eating.

'Is this your first stretch?' I ask her.

'What?' Her eyes snap open. Creases form along her brow as she scowls at me, at the indignity of my question.

'You'd be surprised,' I respond, holding my hands up. This

isn't the first rodeo for many of the women at Fairmile. It stands to reason, if on release you return to the same life you had before, and more pointedly, the same man, then back you will come.

Debs' face is conflicted. I've disappointed her but right now I'm all she's got.

'Do you want to talk about it?' I ask.

She shakes her head. This morning's news has knocked the wind from her. Today she needs kindness.

'Would you like to see the chaplain?' I ask.

She makes a sound like a tyre losing air. 'Christ, *no.*' Her answer is firm.

I look at the sanitary towel blocking the viewing hatch. She'll be marked down as a suicide risk and if the POs can't check on her like they're supposed to, they'll have to keep entering her cell, which will hack them off no end. 'Mind if I take that down?'

'Oh God, I'll do it!' she says, red-faced. She moves to the door, peeling back the dirty pad from the glass before rolling it up and throwing it into a bin. 'I saw someone do it last week, thought I'd give it a go,' she explains.

'You'll see a lot of things while you're in here. Not many of them are worth copying.'

She lowers her head. 'I suppose not.'

A thud on the door tells me my time is up. 'I've got to go.' I get to my feet. 'It'll be crap for a while but it'll get better eventually,' I add, meaning every word. Most unpleasant things require a period of acclimatisation. I show her how to control her breathing if she starts to hyperventilate, how to distract herself by focusing on something in her cell that she can see and touch. Her gaze falls on a photo of her children Blu-Tacked to the wall and she looks as though she might cry again. There'll be many more tears, but I don't tell her that. Nor do I tell her that going into care was the making of me. Given where I'm standing, I can understand that would take some believing.

'If you ever want to talk...' I look at her and pull at my vest. 'Not like I'm hard to find.'

The door swings open and Officer Frame tells me she'll take it from here.

My cell is empty when I return. Vonnie craves company the same way I avoid it. She'll be on the periphery of a group somewhere, boasting about her newly discovered condition.

Perhaps seeking Debs out wasn't one of my better ideas, I think as I slump back against the wall and blow out a breath. There are days when such proximity to sorrow is overwhelming and right now, I feel wrung out. My solicitor dangling the 'P' word in front of me earlier hasn't helped. I find the whole damn process of parole unnerving. The panel hearing is intrusive; complete strangers deep diving into the darkest corners of your character while you demonstrate your remorse, like a criminal justice version of *Show and Tell*. And for what? To be turned down again and again?

'*You are taking this seriously, aren't you?*' My lawyer's question chimes in my ears. It's hard not to get caught up in his enthusiasm, not to feel that glimmer of hope that one day I'll leave here and slot back into the life I left behind. It's easy to get carried away by it, but then I remember the truth I've held back, a secret buried so deep it's become a part of me. A toxic tumour, heavy like a stone. I don't deserve to ever be released.

I slow my breathing down, extend my outbreaths, my eyes skimming over my scant belongings as I seek reassurance from the familiar: washed out clothing and threadbare towels; cheap toiletries and junk food ordered from the prison's online store.

My gaze settles on the photo of me, Hope and Clem, pinned to the wall beside my bunk. I lean forward to touch it reverently, my finger running over the huddled outline of the three of us, preserved in time. How naïve we were, laughing into the camera like it was our God-given right, blissfully unaware that this would be the last photograph of us taken together. Hope claims if she'd known she'd have made more of an effort with her appearance, put some lippy on, or tied her hair back so the wind wasn't blowing it across her face. Clem reckons he'd have shaved that morning if he'd known his patchy stubble was to be captured for eternity. As for me, if I'd had one single iota of what was coming round the corner, I wouldn't have been laughing at all.

I set about tidying the cell for the second time today, lining up our belongings in the order that I like them. Luckily for me, Vonnie doesn't baulk if I straighten her cutlery or turn her mug so the handle's pointing the same direction as mine. My shoulders feel tight as I appraise my handiwork; a ball of dread forming in my stomach reminds me that I'm not done yet. Anxiously I lift both mattresses and look underneath them, dropping down onto my haunches to peer under the table where the kettle sits, then the chairs either side of it. I run my fingers along the back of the heating pipes, glance quickly under the shelves. I feel myself relax as the tension leaves my body. I straighten myself, satisfied everything is as it should be.

I move over to the sink. To the chipped mirror above it. Take a long, hard look at the face staring back at me. I was a head turner once; eyes the colour of dark chocolate, coiled black curls that refused to be tamed.

Knock yourself out, Oprah...

Sixteen years on and the person in the mirror has sallow skin and eye bags, a scar I prefer not to talk about and unkempt frizz that sits on my head like an ill-fitting helmet. It's me but not me. I step away from the mirror, preferring the memory of who I was before I came here, to the reality of who I am now.

I can barely remember what my life had been like before Fairmile's gates slammed shut behind me sixteen years ago. Had I been happy? Or had I wasted my days fussing over trivial things, petty worries that pale into insignificance when compared to life in here?

I've worked hard to obliterate the details of the day my world turned upside down. All I have left are the brackets of the day. Waking up that morning mentally checking through my to-do list. Going to sleep that night charged with murder.

CHAPTER TWO

'Knock knock!'

The voice behind the door is high-pitched and excitable and can only belong to one person. I mock sigh, regretting my decision to leave the door open pending Vonnie's return.

'Come on in, Lola,' I call out, filling the kettle for want of something to do.

'What was all that fuss about, then?' she demands. News of Debs' meltdown is obviously doing the rounds. She pushes the cell door to, sensing the information might be sensitive.

'I wondered how long it would take for you to come knocking.' I keep my back to her.

'What else is there to do in 'ere? C'mon, Mercy, spill.' She flops onto my bunk, like a doe-eyed teen wanting the gossip on her latest crush. 'You know you want to,' she coaxes, grinning. Her head bounces as she speaks, her face making occasional twitches. Some people find it impossible to be still.

I blow out another breath. Debbie's situation will become common knowledge soon enough due to a combination of her neediness and the prison grapevine. Even so. I spoon instant coffee into two mugs while I deliberate. Being in Lola's orbit always makes me crave caffeine.

'I don't know much,' I tell her truthfully, 'but this morning she found out she'd lost custody of her kids.'

Lola's grin collapses. 'That's awful.' She falls silent as she considers this, but there's something about the way her shoulders droop that catches my attention. She looks troubled.

'What's it to you?' I pour boiling water into the mugs, adding a splash of milk before handing one to her.

She studies the contents of her drink before lifting her gaze to meet mine. This isn't the Lola who strutted into the induction block for the first time eighteen months ago following an alcohol-fuelled brawl. Who left two months later swearing never to return, only to become one of Fairmile's frequent fliers. She's the drama queen of this block, living her life at crisis level, one calamity after another. *That* Lola is flighty and unpredictable; the life and soul of the party or the neighbour from hell, depending on which side of the dividing wall you happen to be occupying when she's on a bender. This Lola is hesitant, reserved. Not sure of herself one little bit.

'Come on, then,' I say to her, wondering whether one of Vonnie's biscuits would give her the sugar rush she so obviously needs but I give my head a wobble. Rule number one if you want your life inside to be harmonious: never take your pad-mate's possessions, however well intentioned. Even though I could lay Vonnie out if I wanted to, I'd never disrespect her stuff.

'If there's something you want to get off your chest then spit it out,' I tell her, not bothering to sugar-coat my words. 'This is my cell, not the welcome desk, I'm not on duty now.'

This gives her the focus she needs. She lifts her chin and looks at me defiantly. 'I've got a kid, Mercy. A little boy. He's four.'

My eyebrows lift in surprise. 'Well you're a dark horse. How come you've never mentioned him before?' I know it's hypocritical of me, expecting full disclosure while I keep myself closed off. I don't claim to be perfect.

Lola shrugs, swiping at the corner of her eye with her sleeve.

'Where is he now?' I ask her, wondering if he's had to go into foster care while she's in here. That would explain her reaction.

'He lives with my parents,' she says matter-of-factly. 'I was young when I had him. Made sense that Mum and Dad take care of him.' She looks away as she says this. Places her coffee on the table untouched.

'I was fifteen when he was born,' she adds, second guessing my next question.

That's practically middle-aged on the sink estate where I spent my childhood. Only Lola doesn't hail from anywhere like that. She grew up in a wealthy Cheshire suburb, enjoying the trappings that came with it. A detached home with stables. Family holidays in Tuscany. In Lola's cell there's a photo of a pony beside her bunk, but no son.

Her privileged upbringing made her a target during her first stint in here. Her fresh face and breathy manner a permanent reminder that she wasn't like the other women who came through Fairmile's doors. They resented her confidence and her honey-coloured hair. The opportunities she squandered to end up in the same place as them anyway. I had to step in once, when the sniping turned ugly. Since then every time she's back she follows me around like a stray I can't quite shake off.

'These things happen,' I say, the familiar pang reminding me that actually, they don't, not to everyone. 'There's no reason for you to keep quiet about him if you don't want to.' This admission would make her less of a princess, make her relatable to the others on the wing. The girl everyone thought was so prim and proper wasn't quite so squeaky clean after all.

Lola tugs at a tendril of hair, wrapping and unwrapping it around her fingers. 'I don't think my parents would like that. They're raising Danny as their own. Said it would give me a chance to make something of myself.'

'Sounds reasonable, if that's what you want.' I pause. '*Is* that what you want?' I ask when she doesn't respond. I wait a beat. 'And what about the baby's father?'

'He was never really on the scene,' she says quickly. She hasn't fully answered my question but I decide against pressing for more.

'Do you see much of Danny?'

Her smile slips away. 'It hasn't been easy, what with me getting into trouble all the time. My parents said it would be easier if I moved out. They reckon it isn't healthy, him growing up around a drunk.'

My nod is slow as I consider this. 'Have you discussed what will happen in the future?'

Lola looks at me quizzically. 'What do you mean?'

'There might come a time when you want to take responsibility for his care. When you feel more able to. Have you talked with your parents about what will happen then?'

'Mum says I'm not fit to be a mother, that it's better for all of us if Danny's brought up thinking I'm his sister. I'm not exactly proving her wrong, am I?' she says defensively when she sees my expression. 'Look at my last attempt at getting my life back on track. Evicted from the hostel I'd been released to because I was caught having a drink.'

'It *was* a dry house, Lola,' I remind her.

'I know, I know!'

'If you knew it was a dry house, why did you drink?'

'It was someone's birthday and no one had asked me before.

I wanted to join in.' She flaps her fingers every time she comes up with an excuse, like a butterfly looking for a safe place to land. Her previous release had been conditional upon her staying sober. Breaching that condition means she's been recalled to Fairmile for twenty-eight days.

'How did your parents take it when they heard you'd been recalled?'

She moves her head slowly from side to side, mouth downturned. 'Nothing I do shocks them anymore. There was a time when they were livid at everything I did. When I saddled them with a baby, when my drinking spiralled, landing me in all sorts of scrapes which they kept trying to bail me out of. Dad wangled a job for me to train as a veterinary nurse with one of his golf club friends a couple of years back, which I lost when I received my first custodial sentence. It's been mortifying for them,' she admits. 'Things were never easy between us and now I've made everything so much worse. I don't think Mum's ever really forgiven me.'

'I'm sure she will in time. You need to start getting your shit together, though.' My tone is serious. 'You can't carry on like this, Lola.'

'Don't I know it,' she agrees. She eyes me shyly. 'I wish you were my mum, Mercy. Did you never want kids?'

The look I throw at her tells her she's overstepped the mark and she visibly pales. 'We've talked about boundaries before,' I caution her.

'Sorry!' she says, recovering. 'Forget I said anything!'

'Forget what?' says Tanya, appearing in the doorway without bothering to knock.

'Nothing,' I say quickly. 'What is this? Party at mine?'

Tanya's brought her own mug and a teabag so it isn't a flying visit. I put the kettle back on and set about making her a drink.

'Why was the new girl making all that racket?' she asks me.

'They're taking her kids away.' Lola relishes being the first to impart news.

Tanya frowns as she hands me her mug. She's rake thin, like a head on a stick. All spindly arms and legs. A recovering addict, her pimp got her hooked on a cocktail of heroin and crack. It took her years to get clean, then a locum doc in here prescribed pregabalin for her anxiety. Like heroin, it's hugely addictive. She's working with the detox team to come off that now. Her hand shakes when she reaches for the mug I've filled for her. 'That's tough,' she says, flopping down onto the bunk beside Lola. 'Then again, who wants mothers like us?'

Tanya's kids were taken from her because she couldn't give up the drugs and she wouldn't give up her man. Fast forward a year and the cheating scumbag had long gone, unlike her habit, which was costing her £200 a day. She sold her possessions and when they ran out, she started selling her body. She killed her pimp when he attacked her for not bringing in enough money to cover his 'costs'.

She writes to her kids but they don't reply. She's asked them to visit but they don't want to know. They're adults now but the crater that formed when they went into care has never closed.

I fix Tanya with a look as I pull out a chair and sit down. 'You won't make their lives better by punishing yourself. Get properly clean and I'm sure they'll want to get to know you.'

'You're right,' she says in the tone I've become used to. There are so many obstacles in the way of turning her life around it's exhausting for her to acknowledge them. It's not just about getting clean and finding a place to live and a job that doesn't result in frequent STIs. Her drug addiction has scarred her. Her front teeth are gone, the rest are rotten, worn down to ugly stumps. Getting clean on its own will not change her life or the way people see her. She needs extensive dental surgery to fill out her face and a month in the sun to lose that pallor. I smile at her with all the encouragement I can muster. At least with no pimp to go back to, she stands a chance of making her own decisions when she eventually gets out. It's something.

'How did it go with your brief?' she asks me, changing the subject.

I shrug. 'He seems to think it's worth another shot at parole.'

'And so he should. Men like Gary Walsh are a waste of oxygen.'

'You can't say that out loud, Tan!' I berate her, cracking my first grin in a long time, albeit an exasperated one.

'Seriously, Mercy, you've done your time.' She pauses to take a sip of her tea. 'What you did was a form of pest control rather than murder.'

'The courts didn't quite see it as that, funnily enough,' I remind her.

'More fool them.'

'I bet if it happened today you'd only get half the sentence you've already served,' Lola chimes out of loyalty.

The cell is hot and stuffy and I feel like my space is being invaded. A flash of anger overtakes me. 'I got the right sentence for the crime I committed!' I bark. 'The only bit I have a problem with is having to make out to the parole board I'm sorry I killed him, when I'm not!'

Lola's eyes widen.

'She didn't mean anything by it, did you, doll?' Tanya soothes, patting her shoulder.

Lola regards me and I her. She knows that I'm sorry but also knows better than to expect me to say it. She attempts small talk and I join in to show there's no hard feelings. When she stands, claiming it's time to return to her cell, I don't try and stop her. Tanya lingers after she's gone, in no hurry to leave. 'What's got you all bent out of shape?' she asks.

'I'm not.' My tone is defiant.

Tanya looks at me shrewdly. 'My mistake. There was me thinking you're worried that this parole hearing will go the same way as the other two.'

'Oh, I'm confident that won't happen.'

'Why not?'

'Because I'm not going to bother this time, that's why.' I fix her with a look. 'And before you start, just remember where the last two applications for parole got me.'

Tanya shakes her head in frustration. 'They can't hold that drug bust against you forever, doll. It was the reason they turned down your first application but they can't use the same reason again.'

Our cells are turned over – or spun, as it's called in here – every once in a while, the governor's feeble attempt at controlling the use of drugs. My gaze drops to the mattress Tanya's sitting on. Where officers carrying out a routine drug sweep found a block of heroin wedged beneath it. No one cared that it wasn't mine, that I hadn't known it was there and had no idea who it belonged to, all the usual clichés trotted out by the guilty and innocent alike so much so that it's become background noise.

'I'm only paid up to here,' the male PO commented when he found it, turning his hand sideways as he positioned it below his chin. 'And from where I'm standing, you're in breach of the rules.'

I wasn't sharing a cell at that time, had no one to back me up, or to blame.

The idea that someone had planted heroin in my cell seemed preposterous to my own ears. When you're in prison your world becomes small. Things you wouldn't normally give a toss about start to matter. Some inmates resent it when they see me striding across the landing to the induction block, when all they've got to look forward to is three steps to the cell door and back if they're lucky. It gets up their nose that I'm doing something they're not, but even so, this wasn't an act of spite. I don't move around in the kind of circles where 'fitting someone up' if you have a disagreement is considered the answer. Of course, the governor just smiled when I said *that*. The kind of smile she saves for the deluded. Her report to the parole board was concise. Class A drugs had been found in my cell, which I claimed to have no knowledge of. It was the first thing the panel asked me about when the hearing began, and it kind of went downhill from there.

It's the reason I check my cell every time I return to it. Like the saying goes, 'Fool me once, shame on you; fool me twice...' Well, I'm nobody's idiot.

'You'll be all right this time, doll,' Tanya assures me. 'Lightning doesn't strike twice.'

I smile at her the way the governor smiled at me. 'I hope you're right,' I tell her, grateful she doesn't mention the reason they turned me down the second time.

CHAPTER THREE

I spend weekday mornings donning my yellow vest, helping out at the welcome desk in the induction block. 'Don't know why you bother,' Vonnie says to me each time I leave. She's said it for so long it's become a ritual, the equivalent of *Have a good day*, if we were on the outside.

Working in the induction block gives me certain privileges. In prison, no one can move unescorted between blocks except when 'Movement' is called. During this time inmates can move freely, once they've been counted out and back in. My yellow vest elevates my status, suggests I can be trusted to walk from A to B without breaching security. I take my time, savouring each step.

There was no such thing as the welcome desk, or an induction block for that matter, when the sweatbox that brought me to Fairmile pulled up inside the prison gates sixteen years ago. I remember being led, blinking, from the rear of the court building, along with another newly convicted prisoner. The woman's steps were uneven as we moved towards our transport, as though she was traversing a rocky terrain rather than crossing tarmac. We regarded each other warily before climbing into separate cages in the back of the prison van. It was obvious she was coming down from something. Her eyes were glazed, her hair was matted and greasy, her skin a patchwork of infected rashes. Even in her confused state she must have registered the fear etched on my own face, the tremor in my hand as I hoisted myself into the metal cage. 'You'll be fine, doll,' she said, her words running into each other so they came out *yullbeefinedoll.* 'Just another day in paradise.' Some people have the capacity to surprise you. I'd written her off as nothing more than a junkie yet she'd reached out to me, hadn't written me off quite so easily.

The drive to Fairmile seemed to take ages but was unlikely to have been more than an hour. Long enough for me to contemplate the choices I'd made that had resulted in the life sentence I'd been given. To wonder how far back I'd need to go into my past to rewrite my story. Like that was even a possibility.

Back then the prison 'processing' room resembled an enforced labour camp. Utilitarian décor, grey walls lined with posters warning us of the dangers of drugs and unprotected sex. The passenger I'd shared the ride over with was pale and clammy when she stepped out of the van. She told me her name was Tanya before yelling to see the doctor, her face contorted in pain as her body went into withdrawal.

'There's no one on duty,' the PO informed her before summoning us for a strip search. 'Keep the racket down overnight and you can see the doc tomorrow.'

'It'll be okay,' I told her as she was led away to sweat it out in her cell, my voice feeble and lacking the assurance of her earlier affirmation.

Today's induction block and welcome desk have been recent additions, along with brightly coloured walls and posters offering drug treatment courses, programmes for victims of domestic violence, and opportunities for training. I can't help but wonder if more of these interventions were made available on the outside that maybe there'd be fewer women needing them in here.

I stand by the desk with the other volunteers. We've been given our clipboards and await the new arrivals like airport holiday reps waiting for the next batch of tourists to fly in.

First timers are easy to pick out amongst the motley crew that make their way towards us. They arrive in a state of shock, their lawyers' assurances that a custodial sentence was unlikely still ringing in their ears. Once they've been searched and their mental health assessed, they make their way along the slow-moving service line like diners at a buffet no one wants to eat. Next of kin forms are processed, then their clothing is sorted out, before they're sent over to me for their welcome pack. I hand out white string bags containing a mug, plastic cutlery, sanitary products, knickers, a couple of tracksuits, tea, coffee and a hairbrush. It's nothing but it's everything. If they've come from police custody via the courts, they'll only have the clothes they were wearing when they were detained. I smile at each bewildered face encouragingly, letting them know I'll see them in a little while for their orientation.

The induction area is kitted out like a training room. The women sit at tables facing me and a line of staff as different aspects of prison life are explained to them. They give the hall manager their full attention, but they're tired and overwhelmed. They start to fidget when a worker from a visiting charity introduces herself, then switch off completely when it's the chaplain's turn. I'm like the warm-up act but in reverse. They follow my every word as I tell them how to order their food, get a healthcare appointment and order their canteen, which is like a virtual grocery store except it doesn't sell booze or fags. Deliveries arrive weekly in sealed plastic bags and the canteen trolley being pushed along the landing is the highlight of the week.

Unlike the male prison system, very few women's prisons are separated into categories dependent upon the crime that's been committed, Category A being the most severe. Most female prisoners are lumped together: murderers and shoplifters, benefit cheats and paedophiles. One big happy fucked-up family.

I'm about to take them on their tour of the induction block when a woman in a tailored suit approaches me to ask if she can have a word. Dr North is in today to carry out mental health assessments and anything else the prison can throw at her. Swallowing down apprehension, I ask one of the other volunteers to take over from me before following the doc to her consultation room.

A line of women stand in the corridor waiting to be seen by her, some holding small plastic pots of urine. It's not just to test for drugs. For some poor cows it's when they learn they've picked up an infection, or the extra weight they've been carrying isn't down to food.

Dr North unlocks her office and ushers me in before closing the door behind us.

'Looks like you're busy,' I say to her, gesturing to the women beyond the door.

The look she gives me says she's not letting me off the hook that easily. 'They can wait. I've been hoping to see you. Considering you're down here most mornings our paths have barely crossed.'

Only because I've seen her coming first. 'It gets so busy down here, you know how it is.' I throw my arms wide in a *what can you do?* gesture.

'Take a seat, Mercy,' she says, waiting for me to sit in the chair beside her desk before dropping onto her own, which she angles so that she's facing me. She runs her palms down the front of her trousers until her hands rest on her knees. She searches my face for something. I keep it neutral.

'How've you been?' she asks.

'Living the dream,' I tell her.

Dr North nods as though she thought I'd say that. Her gaze drops to my arms, which are covered by my T-shirt's long sleeves. There's something in her expression that makes me uneasy. Before I can work out what it is, there's a commotion outside, two women shouting at each other. She's distracted momentarily, then when it doesn't sound like it's escalating, she carries on. 'How are you getting on today?'

I blow out a breath. Maybe the commotion will remind her there's a queue of women to get through, that now isn't the time to go off-piste with someone who doesn't have an appointment. I grab the opportunity to play it down. 'Newbies can be hard work but there's nothing I haven't seen before.' I incline my head towards the corridor and the training area beyond. 'Everyone thinks their problems are unique, yet they're so depressingly similar. Like the saying goes, behind every incarcerated woman is a man who wrong-footed her.'

Dr North seems disappointed by this. 'I've had a letter from the psychologist you were referred to.'

Her words catch me unawares, like an elbow to the gut. I try to keep my face in neutral, wait her out. She gives me a look that says she's onto me but she'll play along if she has to. The disagreement outside picks up once more. 'Dyke' and 'skank' permeate the walls. A male officer's voice booms along the corridor telling the women to calm down, which has the opposite effect. 'DON'T TELL ME TO FUCKING CALM DOWN!' screams one. 'THAT'S PATRONISING, THAT IS!' yells the other.

We share a smile.

Dr North isn't easily distracted. 'You were supposed to make a follow-up appointment with her.'

Outside, the prison officer is radioing for backup. 'They're clucking their tits off, mad bitches!'

I recognise the whining voice. Despite only being in his forties, Johnny Daynes is an officer from a bygone era. I've heard his colleagues complain about him: he's handsy with the women officers, belligerent with the men. They can't ignore his call for backup but they'll make him wait.

The din outside has gone up several decibels. 'Sorry, doc, I didn't catch that,' I lie.

Dr North's gaze sweeps over me, reminding me of my class teacher at school on the days I was able to make it in. 'Does the prospect of parole frighten you?' she asks.

I narrow my eyes. 'Has my solicitor put you up to this?'

'Sorry?' Her eyes crease in confusion but before she can continue, a deafening blast comes over the air, signalling a freeze on movement. When this happens it means everyone must stay where they are while officers respond and clear the scene. My shoulders dip. Dr North can't see anyone else while the freeze is on. I'm in her crosshairs now and we both know it.

'How's your wrist?'

My hand moves instinctively to check my sleeve hasn't ridden up my arm, though we both know it's not the scar she wants to inspect but the reason that it's there. 'It's fine.' I bite down on the inside of my cheek.

I cut myself once, just to see what it was like. Whether it lived up to the hype that some of the self-harmers in here were claiming. Only I got carried away, cutting too deep and too long, and next minute I'm bleeding out, only I don't call for help. It was as though my morbid curiosity had kicked in and I wanted to see what would happen next. Vonnie got such a fright when she found me.

They threw me in the psych ward. I'm due a follow-up appointment, which I keep putting off, only it looks like I've run out of excuses. I wouldn't mind but it was all for nothing. The pain of the razor blade cutting into my flesh was supposed to alleviate the fucked-up feeling in my brain, only it didn't so I'm back to square one. This time, though, under the microscope of a head shrink.

'Thank God I came back when I did,' Vonnie kept saying over and over for weeks afterwards. I did my best to look suitably grateful.

'The psychologist wants to explore whether it's the fear of release that caused your relapse,' Dr North says.

'Relapse?' I narrow my eyes, confused. Relapse suggests a regression. A backward step. A return to troubling ways. 'What else have I done to cause concern?' I wonder what they can dredge up against me to make their point.

What they've discovered.

'There was that incident the year before last...' Her words trail off so that I can make the connection.

'What?' I sit forward in my seat. 'You're kidding me, right?' I shake my head as I try to make sense of it. 'I was beaten half to death by a psychotic prisoner...' My words fall away as I wait for her to say something, but she doesn't. Why do I feel like I'm walking into a trap?

'I ended up in hospital,' I say lamely.

'Alice Maltby was in a coma for several days.' Her words feel like a slap.

The incident, albeit terrifying at the time, achieved two things: Maltby was transferred to a maximum-security hospital, removing the tension that had settled on the prison following her arrival. Unfortunately it also stymied any chance I had of parole that year.

'Most residents would have been upset at the prospect of

their release being scuppered,' Dr North adds. She states it matter-of-factly, the inference being I must have been more upset about it than I made out, hence the wrist cutting incident, even though that happened much later. Either that, or I have a deep-rooted dread of being reunited with my family, hence the wrist cutting incident.

'I'm beginning to understand how the witches felt,' I mutter.

The all-clear siren rings out, meaning the freeze on movement has been lifted and I'm able to make my escape. I get to my feet even though Dr North's in no hurry to end our conversation. I move to the door.

'I can't ignore the psychologist's request,' she informs me. 'Particularly in light of your admission to the psychiatric ward.'

'It was only for one night,' I say, exasperated.

'You never completed your assessment. I can't sign you off until you do.' She lets that settle. It's a condition that anyone volunteering in the induction block has been approved as fit to work. She smiles. The doc's got style, I'll give her that. If she hadn't gone into medicine she'd have a lucrative career in extortion. She opens the consultation room diary and skims along the entries. 'I can make an appointment for you this Friday at 1.30pm. How does that sound?'

'I may need to shuffle a few things round,' I say stubbornly, 'but I guess it'll work.'

It's dinner hall association. We have half an hour to collect our meal tray from the kitchen hatch and eat it. I'd stayed away at lunchtime and now my stomach's rumbling with hunger. I carry my tray to the table Tanya and I commandeered during our first week here and have gravitated to ever since. Different faces have joined us over the years. Short termers counting their days until release, whole lifers who've since transferred to other prisons. We're the old guard now, maintaining our position as others come and go, like giant rocks in a turbulent ocean.

'Where were you at lunchtime?' Tanya asks.

'I wasn't hungry,' I answer.

She thinks I can't see the look she shares with Vonnie and Lola. That when Lola opens her mouth to say something she nudges her to keep quiet.

'Christ, if you've got something to say, spit it out!' I tell them without looking up. I focus on the lumps in my shepherd's pie, mashing them out with my fork.

'You *have* been a bit quiet,' Vonnie says. Her voice is hesitant, as though she's betraying my trust. After all, how we are behind those closed doors is nobody's damned business. I throw her a look but there's no malice in her face, only concern.

'I just wanted some time to myself,' I say to them, summoning a smile. 'Got a lot on my mind.'

'Want to talk about it?' Lola asks, leaning forward. She wasn't here when I hurt myself, she doesn't understand why the others are treading on eggshells.

'The doc says I need to go back to that psychologist if I want to keep working at the welcome desk.'

'She can't do that!' shrieks Lola automatically, then she frowns. 'Why do you need to see a psychologist anyway?'

'None of your fucking beeswax,' says Tanya.

'Just go along with it,' reasons Vonnie. 'I mean, you love that job, don't you?'

I suck air through my teeth. Love's a strong word. Admittedly the freedom to leave my cell every morning keeps me sane; the thought of being cooped up for twenty hours a day like the others doesn't bear thinking about. 'I only started volunteering because I heard it'd look good on my parole application. Fat lot of good it's done,' I grumble.

'It's a reason to keep it going though, isn't it?' says Vonnie.

Tanya regards me shrewdly. 'You don't want anything to get in the way of your parole, do you, doll?'

I don't want to get into my discussion with Liam. If I admit to the others I'm considering not applying for it, they'll think I've lost the plot.

'I suppose a bit of therapy never hurt anyone,' Lola adds for good measure.

'Depends what you need to get off your chest,' I tell her.

They all stare back at me, unable to tell if I'm joking.

'Hi, Mercy.' Debbie stands at our table holding her tray. 'Any chance I can have a word?'

This is the moment where I should invite her to join us so we can finish our meal before finding somewhere private to talk. I guess she's ready to unload. Unfortunately, I'm not ready to hear it. I pull at my sweatshirt. 'In case it's slipped your attention I ain't wearing my fucking vest right now, so get lost!'

The table falls silent. Debbie's face crumples as she hurries away.

'Maybe seeing this quack wouldn't be so bad after all,' Tanya says, giving me the beady eye.

I return to my cell before the end of association time. I can't bear the looks the others are giving me and any chance of small talk has flown through the bars on the landing's high windows. Admittedly, I snapped at Debbie, yet they're acting as though I'm single-handedly responsible for taking her children away.

I go through the motions of checking everything is where it should be: *cutlery, mugs, mattress, table. Chairs, heating pipes, shelves,* before crawling onto my bunk and screwing my eyes shut. Dr North cornering me like that has churned up images

I've worked so hard to block out but now they come into focus, unbidden.

My night on the psych ward following my return from hospital. I was kept on constant observation, which meant that a PO sat outside my cell for twenty-four hours, checking on me through the hatch in the door. If the white noise of prison is hard to get used to, then the commotion along that stretch of corridor is impossible. My head throbbed with the tortuous screams of women begging for meds, their family, to see a doctor, to go back to the main wing as it was all a misunderstanding; ranting assurances that they were perfectly fine and no longer needed to be held against their will. The constant racket of plastic cups banged against cell doors and the threat of what would happen if someone didn't come RIGHT NOW. It wasn't just the noise that made me feel like I was in a horror film; the alternating stench of shit and bleach as a woman in the next cell defecated on the floor before smearing it on the walls turned my stomach. Prison is bad enough but this was the closest I'd come to hell. I vowed I'd never go back.

My eyes snap open. Dr North's words have rattled me. If I want to keep doing the only thing that keeps me sane in here, I need to persuade the prison psychologist that I'm not mad.

That what I did to myself, Alice Maltby – and Gary Walsh, for that matter – were merely blips on an otherwise unblemished character.

I might as well give up now.

CHAPTER FOUR

Vonnie stands in front of the mirror, preening. I watch as she teases each strand of hair into position so that it frames her face just so.

'Christ's sake, Von, I didn't spend as much time as you getting ready on my wedding day.'

She pauses mid-air as she studies me in the mirror. I've overshared and she's wondering if she can acknowledge what I've said by asking a question. I tip my head at her to show it's okay.

'I didn't know you were married!' she says. 'I mean, you've never mentioned anyone in all the time we've been padded up. I'm guessing it didn't work out.'

I shrug. 'In a manner of speaking, no it didn't.'

'So, what happened?' She keeps her back to me, though her gaze in the mirror has latched onto mine, the loose strands of hair forgotten about.

'I was young, and lonely. My kid brother and sister had been adopted by this couple, only there was no room for me... I didn't care,' I add, refusing her pity. 'I was glad Clem and Hope had stability in their lives.'

'But what about you?'

'I lived in a children's home until I was sixteen, before moving into a council flat. I suppose I felt a bit displaced. I ran wild, married the first man who told me I was special, not realising it was a phrase he was trying out for size.' It seemed exciting at first. Billy took care of me in a way I'd never experienced before; the low bar making him look better than he was.

I'd worn a white mini dress I'd bought from a charity shop. Hope's mum put ringlets in her daughter's hair. Clem wore a waistcoat and a bow tie he'd borrowed from his new dad. We celebrated with fish and chips, which we ate in the registry office car park while we waited for their new parents to take them home.

'Is this the happiest day of your life?' Hope had asked. I'd nodded, ignoring the hollow feeling in my chest.

'So what happened?' Not content with speaking to my reflection, Vonnie turns to face me. We'll need to leave in a minute to go to the visitor centre and she knows this isn't a conversation I'll want to continue once we step outside.

'No great mystery,' I admit. 'I was young, he was a dick. Or rather, he couldn't keep his in his pants.' The me of today would not have stayed with him. I gave him five years of my life to sort himself out and in return he gave me chlamydia. I had no idea, of course; I was naïve in the ways of the world. We'd been trying for a baby and when I failed to get pregnant my doctor referred me to a specialist who explained my tubes were irreversibly scarred. He called a nurse into the consulting room to sit with me while he explained what had caused it. That night I packed Billy's bags and left them in the hall for when he got home. At least he had the grace not to put up a fight. He wanted kids, he told me. No point sticking around if they weren't in our future.

'We got divorced when I was twenty-one,' I tell Vonnie. We

lived in the same town and I'd catch myself looking at him if we crossed paths in the street and try to imagine what others could see, without the burden of everything I knew about him. 'He's remarried now.' He must have got himself treated because I heard through the grapevine he has a couple of kids. He lives a good life with his family, proof that there is no such thing as karma.

'It's not too late,' Vonnie says, as though if I'm really lucky, someone like Wayne will sweep me off my feet. She's trying to be positive so I let it lie. The cell door opens and the PO escorting us to the visitor centre calls out our names.

'Hang on a minute,' I say as I pat my hair down in the mirror before joining Vonnie on the landing.

Vonnie isn't so easily pleased. 'Do I look all right?' she whispers, despite all her preening.

'A million fucking dollars, girl,' I tell her. 'Don't you forget that.'

Clem sits solemn-faced at the table he's been assigned, searching for me along the line of women filing into the room. When he catches my eye, he raises his hand in greeting like we're in a swanky wine bar and he's motioning me over to a table he's bagged.

I acknowledge him with a nod. We're not from demonstrative stock and we've been apart for so long we've no terms of reference for how 'extra' siblings are supposed to interact; what level of affection is deemed appropriate. Hope is his twin, the other half of his soul. They have a way of communicating, a synergy, that's exclusive to them. I'd often feel, when I was with them both, that I was on the outside looking in.

Clem looks ill at ease amongst the visitors. He's quieter, takes up less space than the other men in the room. With his soft brown curls and delicate features, he inherited his looks from our father's gene pool. Thankfully they're the only traits passed down to him. He's grown into a kind, even-tempered man who goes out of his way to avoid conflict. I guess our old man's bad shit stopped with me.

He admits he feels awkward joining the queue that forms outside the family centre come visiting time, waiting to place personal items in trays that run through a scanner before lifting arms, hair and tongues for the body searches and pat downs. 'All the tedium of going through airport security,' he laments often enough, 'without the prospect of two weeks in the sun at the end of it.' He hates the slow pace as they move from one air-locked room to another, the oppressive heat pumping from the vents in the ceiling. Despite the fact the two-dozen people jammed into the enclosed space are there for the same reason – someone they care about is serving a custodial sentence – he can't bring himself to engage in the conversations going on around him. It's hard for the relatives. Although they're free to come and go as they please, they serve their own sentence. They're the ones who are left to explain our absence, who see blame rather than compassion etched on the faces of the people they tell. They feel they have no right to their sadness; their grief is heavy and hard to navigate. Whilst our presence here fills them with shame, they miss us, knowing the public will despise them for it.

'Sis,' he says.

I flop into the chair opposite and flash him my *It's a Wonderful Life* smile. Across from us in the play area children pull out manky toys from a toy box. Prison to them is as normal as going to the supermarket.

'How come Hope couldn't make it?' I ask.

'She had to ferry the girls to some party.'

'Another one?'

He shrugs. 'Guess they're that age, any excuse for a manicure and a sleepover. Both high as kites, you know what they're like.'

Except I don't. Hope was pregnant with them when I was sentenced. Apart from when they were babies and she'd bring them in strapped into their double buggy, I haven't been in the same room as my twin nieces for years. Clem looks away, embarrassed by his clumsiness.

'I can imagine, though,' I say hurriedly, to make him feel better.

He turns his attention back to me. 'She sends her apologies,' he says brightly, but I'm not sure he means it.

They take it in turn to see me, like I'm a burden to be shared equally. Hope has missed three of her 'turns', citing her daughters' social lives, meaning that Clem's been here six visits in a row. Unless he's won the Nobel prize since he was last here, he'll have nothing new to tell me. I save him the tedium of regurgitating his daily routine. 'I've some news,' I tell him tentatively. 'My solicitor wants to put in an application for parole.'

Clem's nod is slow. 'Again?'

'It's been two years since my last hearing!' I remind him, stung. It doesn't matter that I've practically told Liam that I don't want to bother, that's not the point. It's one thing for me to have cold feet, but what's Clem's excuse?

'No, seriously, that's great,' he says, though his eyes say something else entirely.

'What is it?' I ask.

'Nothing...'

I wait him out.

'It's just that...'

Not nothing, then.

'...it's probably not worth getting ahead of ourselves this time,' he states.

I look at him sharply. 'In case what? In case I do something to screw it up?'

Clem looks away, embarrassed. 'That's not what I'm saying.'

It's exactly what he's saying and we both know it. My earlier ambivalence dissolves in a fit of pique. I want this release because he thinks I won't get it.

On the next table Vonnie sits across from Wayne. Out of a million sperm I can't believe he swam the fastest and didn't get lost. He's regaling her with some story or other and she's staring at him rapt, like the feminist movement never happened. All she needs is a lace fan to cool herself down before she swoons.

'It wasn't my fault that I was turned down last time,' I remind Clem.

'You were involved in a fight.'

I eye him suspiciously. 'Have you been talking to the doc?'

He narrows his eyes. 'No, should I?'

I huff out a sigh. 'For your information, I didn't get involved in a fight, I fought off an attacker. That's a seismic difference in behaviour.' An image of Alice Maltby passes in front of my eyes.

Clem's gaze is cold. 'If you say so.'

Him treating me like this flips me over the edge. 'For God's sake!' I bang my hand on the table causing two POs to look in my direction.

'You've always been hot-headed. It wouldn't be the first time your impulsiveness has got the better of you, would it?' He eyes me steadily, daring me to contradict him.

I feel a trickle of unease as I wonder what's got into him. Whether he'll ever let our past go.

'How's business?' I ask, moving the conversation along.

'Fine.'

'The bar's keeping busy? You were worried about the nightclub that opened–'

'It's a different crowd. We're good.'

'They didn't poach any of the staff away, then?'

'I'd have told you if they had. Don't worry, your investment's safe.'

I lean across the table and stare him down. Make a point of keeping my voice low. 'It's more than an investment, Clem, it's *my* business.'

I own the bar Clem runs in my absence. Hope works there too; she studied bookkeeping at night school and now does the accounts. They both live above the bar in the flat that I bought for us all, where I hoped we'd settle once they'd left their adopted home.

Before things turned out the way they did.

Clem's body seems to deflate. His shoulders dip as he looks at me shame-faced. 'I'm sorry, sis, it's just this place. It gets to me every time.'

'At least you can leave,' I quip.

On the neighbouring table Wayne's voice has risen above the melee of the room. 'Are you stupid?' he snipes, causing Vonnie's shoulders to lift up to her ears.

'Don't you and her share a cell?' Clem asks.

'We do,' I say, hoping this is the moment that Vonnie sees Wayne for what he is.

Clem merely goes through the motions for the remainder of his visit. Each time I take a step forward, he makes a hasty retreat, barely able to look me in the eye. He visibly relaxes when the clock on the wall shows our half-hour is up.

'Visiting is over, everyone, please!' calls one of the POs.

I get to my feet, reluctant for our time together to end on a sour note. 'I don't mind seeing your ugly mug, bro, but tell Hope if she isn't sitting in that seat this time next week, she'll get her backside kicked.' It's the closest I get to admitting how I feel about them.

The corner of Clem's mouth flickers in response and I try to shake off my earlier unease as I turn to join the procession back to our block, but it's impossible. I catch Clem's eye and his slow blink gives him away.

He's hiding something.

CHAPTER FIVE

Cutlery, mugs, mattress, table. Chairs, heating pipes, shelves. The cell feels claustrophobic after being in the visitor centre. Clem's expression as I joined the line returning to our block has left me on edge. Whatever's troubling him got the better of him in that unguarded moment. I'd have given anything to run back and ask him what's wrong. 'Get a shift on,' Officer Frame had growled, leaving me no option but to file out with the rest of the women. With the cell audit complete, I slump into a chair, grateful for the distraction when Vonnie stomps in, her face dark like a storm's brewing.

'How's love's young dream?' I ask. Immersing myself in her problems will stop me fretting over mine.

Vonnie tuts. 'Wayne isn't half doing my head in. Maybe I should have turned while I had the opportunity. Try before you buy and all that.'

Unlike in male prisons where homophobia is rife, lots of women have sex with each other while locked up and no one bats an eyelid. *Being gay for the stay*, is its Sunday name. It's something to do.

'Not too late,' I tell her. 'Though don't look at me, I haven't the energy or the inclination. My bits dried up years ago.'

Vonnie throws back her head and laughs. 'Not if you found the right person.'

I give her the beady eye. 'And who says I'm looking?' I smile to soften my words. 'Now, are you going to tell me what your beef is with Wayne or are you going to do your usual trick and wait until lights out to start analysing your love life?' I lean against the cell wall with my arms folded while she climbs up to the top bunk. She lies on her side facing me, propping herself up on her elbow.

'You remember how he said he wants to get clean, right?'

'Yes.'

'Well, he's now been offered this really cheap gear. Reckons it'd be a shame to miss out on the opportunity just because he's decided to go on the wagon.'

'So it's the prospect of getting off his face at bargain basement prices that's floating his boat?' I ask her, incredulous.

'No.' She shakes her head as though she can't believe what she's about to say. 'He's going to sell it.'

I frown at her. 'I didn't realise he was a dealer.' A dealer with a habit. *Dragons' Den* would tear him to pieces.

'He isn't. But *his* dealer reckons he'll be good at it.'

'And what's it got to do with him?' I ask, though I can see where this is going.

'It's his dealer who's selling the cheap gear. Claims he's offering him a once in a lifetime opportunity.'

'Which he's got to pay for up front.'

'Yeah, but–'

'At a mutually beneficial discount,' I finish for her.

'I suppose.'

I nod to show that I've kept up. 'Can Wayne afford this one-time only deal?' I ask.

'His dealer has offered to lend him the money to help get him set up.'

'Why doesn't that surprise me?' I pause to make it look like I've really considered what she's told me. 'You know it's bollocks, don't you?' I say eventually. 'That this is pyramid selling, junkie-style. The interest rate on that part of the deal will be extortionate and no matter how hard Wayne works he'll never pay off his debt.'

'That's what I said to him.'

'His dealer's setting him up. You don't give a drug addict keys to the kingdom and expect it to still be standing when you return.'

'I said that to him as well. Well, near enough.'

'Was that the point where he called you stupid?'

Vonnie's neck flushes red. 'You heard him then.'

'We were on the next table,' I remind her.

Her face falls. 'I don't know, Mercy. It was bad enough when he announced he was going clean, but selling drugs is a whole different ball game.'

'There *is* an element of the fox guarding the hen house,' I admit. I look at her troubled face and vow she's not going to follow in my footsteps and waste her best years on a man who doesn't deserve her. The question is, how do I make her see sense without saying something that has her running to defend him?

I tell her more about my relationship with Billy. About the way he lied so convincingly that I was forever doubting myself, believing his word over what my instinct was telling me. It's called gaslighting now, but back then I knew it by the heaviness in my heart, by the constant suspicion that I chose to ignore. 'Don't get me wrong,' I conclude, 'most relationships rely on compromise, and it isn't unusual for one partner to do most of the heavy lifting. But if you're forced to put up with something you can't forgive, it'll eat away at you like acid.'

'Did Billy call you stupid?'

'He said I was difficult. It's what men say when they want women to stop being themselves.'

'I stop being me when I'm not in here,' Vonnie admits. 'On the outside, Wayne'll say something mean to me and I'll not respond, then spend the rest of the day thinking of all the things I wish I'd said back to him.'

'You need to ask yourself if that's how you want to live your life.'

'I suppose.'

Vonnie looks thoughtful for a moment, then her eyes light up as though she's remembered something. 'Looked like you and your Clem were going toe to toe for a moment back there,' she remarks.

I blow out a breath. 'Yeah, he was really grinding my gears at one point.' I regard Vonnie and consider what I've already shared with her today, then decide in for a penny. 'Clem's never forgiven me for not doing more to be kept with them when they were put up for adoption.' Now I've said it out loud I can understand the enormity of it. How it must have felt to be separated from the only constant in their lives. 'We were living in the children's home at this point. Our mother was dead and our father ran off without a backward glance. Our social worker said she'd try and find a home for us, then took me to one side and quietly explained what she really meant: cute little twins would be snapped up in no time, even brown ones, but it could take years for someone to come along who'd consider a gangly pre-teen as well. By that time, Clem and Hope would be older and not quite so appealing. Including me in the package seriously limited their opportunities.'

'She had no right to say that! What a position to put you in.'

Vonnie's indignant and I'm grateful to her. Even though it felt unfair at the time, I had no one in my corner looking out for me. I accepted it because that was just the way things were. All I cared about was the twins. As long as they were cared for, I knew I'd be okay. I could look after myself.

I shrug off her concern. 'Maybe not, but desperate times require desperate measures. Once I got my head around the fact I was keeping them from finding their forever home, I started acting up a bit on purpose, making it easier for prospective parents to reject me because of my delinquency rather than the fact that I didn't fit in with their image of a picture-perfect family. The problem was, Clem and Hope didn't understand why I kept getting into bother. I could hardly tell them, could I? They'd have ended up resenting their new family.'

I remember Clem's folded arms and sour face as they were driven away from the children's home by their new parents. The couple had made it clear they didn't want me. I'd made it clear that suited me just fine.

'Your siblings probably thought you were trying to spoil their chance of adoption too,' remarks Vonnie.

I look at her. I'd never thought of it like that.

The sound of cell doors opening signifies it's evening association time. 'Think I'll stretch my legs,' I say, getting to my feet. 'You coming?'

Vonnie shakes her head. 'I need to think things through about Wayne. The bellend isn't capable of doing anything by himself. I ended up in here because he had me stealing to feed his habit. What will he expect me to do once he starts dealing?'

'I think we both know the answer to that.' I pause in the doorway. 'You're not asking for too much, Von. You're just asking the wrong person.' I cross my fingers behind my back and hope she makes the right decision.

Debbie's sitting on one of the foam-backed chairs in the social area, nursing her mug. She's blowing across the top of it when sees me and looks away quickly, but I can tell from the way she tenses that I'm in her peripheral vision. I move to where she's sitting and crouch down, the same way I had the other day in the legal visits room.

'How are you, Debs?' I say to the side of her head.

'Well, I'm up and not crying,' she says.

'That's good.'

She turns her head to face me. 'Are you sure we're able to have this conversation? What with you not wearing your Wonder Woman costume or whatever the hell else it is that you need to put on to make you civil.' She challenges me with a look and I hold my hands in the air. Guilty as charged.

'Look, I'm sorry about yesterday. I had a lot going on, though I had no right to take it out on you. Can we start over?'

Her face floods with relief as she nods. 'I'd like that. I could do with a friend right now.'

I move over to the chair beside her, ease into it with a mock groan.

Debs is studying me. I pick at a thread of cotton that's worked loose on the arm of the chair. Wait for the inevitable question.

'What are you in for, Mercy?'

I blink away the image of Gary Walsh's broken head.

'There's a rule on this block,' I tell her as my gaze locks onto hers. 'You don't tell anyone about why you're here unless you want to. They've stripped everything else away from us, we're entitled to keep our past buried, if we choose.'

Her mouth turns down at the edges. 'Makes no odds to me who I tell. I've not done anything wrong.'

I keep my cynicism in check; prison is full of people who claim the world is against them and their presence here is evidence of an ongoing conspiracy.

'I'll tell you what I'm in for,' she adds, as though she knows what I'm thinking, 'but first I need to tell you what led to it.' She puts her mug on the floor, draws her feet up onto the chair and wraps her arms around her knees. When she speaks next, it's like she's offering up a part of herself she normally keeps hidden.

'My ex used to hit me.' Her head dips momentarily with the shame of it and I wonder why women habitually shoulder the blame when men beat them. Why we're conditioned to look inwards, find reason where there's none to be found.

'I kept quiet about it for a long time because I felt so ashamed,' she says in answer to my unasked question. 'I had a successful career when I met Ed. I worked in marketing. I loved my job and I was damn good at it too. Colleagues turned to me for answers. They knew I was someone who got things done. To admit to them... about what was going on... and see them look at me with pity. I couldn't bear it.'

'It's the pity that turns you into a victim,' I say quietly.

She looks at me in surprise. 'Yes! That's exactly what it does.' She moves her body to face me, 'How–?'

'Carry on,' I interrupt, nodding to show she has my full attention.

Shrugging, she returns to her original position. 'I gave up work when I had the kids – Ed's idea, not mine. He said I'd have my hands full, when what he really meant was that his demands wouldn't drop just because there were little ones to consider, and I'd need every spare minute to keep on the right side of his temper.'

She looks up at the barred windows above us, as though imagining the ordered world beyond these disordered walls.

Then, just as suddenly, she's back in the room, as though she's been released from a hypnotist's spell.

'Life's funny, isn't it?' Her mouth is the closest to a smile since I've joined her.

I rub the base of my neck with my hand. I've never understood that phrase. Never felt it touched the sides of what people really mean, which is as far removed from funny ha ha as you can get. 'How so?'

'I never thought I'd become one of "those" women. You know, a battered wife. I expected more for myself.' Her eyes latch onto mine again, refusing to let go. 'Anyway, it got so bad he ended up serving time for it.' She huffs out a sigh. 'While he was inside, I went back to work, found a new place for me and the kids to live. For the first time in ages our future looked good.' Her smile widens at the memory. The fact we are having this conversation in jail tells me this isn't how her story ends. I encourage her with a nod.

'After his release he applied for joint custody even though the kids are terrified of him. They used to hear the things he did to me, witnessed a lot of them too. They're getting bigger now; I worry what Ed will do if he loses his temper with them and I'm not there to protect them – or at least provide a distraction. I couldn't take that risk so I applied to the family court, who appointed a solicitor to review our situation.'

'Sounds reasonable.'

'You'd think so, wouldn't you?' She makes a sound like a laugh but there's no mirth in it. It's the sound a desperate person makes before they kick away the chair. I glance at her wrists but they are clear.

'This court appointed *solicitor*,' her voice takes on a bitter edge, 'decided, after one half-hour meeting, that Ed isn't a risk to our children. This exact same solicitor who wasn't prepared to sit in a room with him on his own because he made him feel uncomfortable, recommended unsupervised visits with our children. How can that be right?'

I shake my head at the absurdity of it. 'I don't know.'

She rubs at her temples. 'He's wrapped the authorities around his little finger. Painted me as a manipulative bitch who wants to keep the kids away from their father. My youngest clung to me every time he came to pick them up. I had to watch him drag her away from me, crying. They returned from one visit with injuries. Bruising above my son's eye and finger marks on my daughter's cheek. They refused to say what happened but it looked like he'd assaulted them. I should know, they were identical to the bruises he used to leave on me. I reported it to their social worker and they raised it with the court, but the ruling was the same. He was deemed to be no threat. Hardly a surprise. By the time the case was called he'd submitted a plausible excuse for their bruising which the kids were too scared to contradict. So the court pointed the blame at me, claiming I was alienating them from their dad. I started refusing to let him take them when he came to the house, and I ended up back in court. He claimed I was instilling false beliefs in them, abusing them emotionally. I was summoned to court to answer to the charges and *suddenly I'm the criminal*. I couldn't take it anymore. I...' She pauses as though she's run out of steam but her eyes are scanning the space in between us, sifting what she can reveal to keep my sympathy.

'No judgement here,' I tell her.

'I did a stupid thing, Mercy.' She takes a breath. 'I started posting the things he'd done to me online. I know, I know...' She holds her hands up to shield her face, she can barely look me in the eye. 'I was angry. I wasn't thinking. All I saw was the injustice of my situation and the fact that everyone seemed to be listening to him and ignoring me.'

'Life's a bastard like that. Everyone's a hero in their own story,' I sympathise.

Debs takes a breath. 'I've been jailed for Contempt of Court because I breached reporting restrictions. I've been sentenced to nine months.'

I let out a low whistle. 'We've all done things in the heat of the moment, Debs. Don't ask...' I say when she looks at me. I wait for her to continue.

'After I was sentenced, Ed applied for the kids to live with him and I was informed yesterday that it's been approved. Now he's been given custody I'll have to apply for supervised contact when I'm released. I've lost them, haven't I?'

I can sense the scream that's building inside her. I reach out tentatively and place my hand on her shoulder. 'Jesus, Debs, I've no idea. What does your lawyer reckon?'

'I can't afford one. My family helped at first but that was only able to stretch so far. I don't qualify for legal aid because I'm working, yet there's no way I can afford those kind of fees on top of everything else.' She looks at me as the reality dawns on her. 'That's my job gone up in smoke too, isn't it?'

Her question is rhetorical. I can see from the slump in her shoulders she knows the answer.

'I never even got to explain to my kids what happened. The hearing took place while they were at school. I dropped them off in the morning fully expecting to be waiting for them at the end of the day. I keep ringing my ex to ask if I can speak to them on the phone but he won't put them on.'

I think for a moment. Even if, with her changed employment status, she qualifies for legal aid, the application process is known to drag on. Doesn't bode well for those kids, going by the sound of her ex. 'I could talk to my lawyer. See if he'd be willing to speak to you. I can't promise anything, mind.'

She looks at me gratefully. 'There was a time when I'd have

been too proud to accept anyone's help, especially in a place like this. But when it involves your kids, you'd do anything, wouldn't you?'

I stare at her numbly and nod.

The buzzer sounds, announcing the end of association time. We get to our feet. 'Will you be okay?' I ask her.

'Got no choice, have I?' she says.

We start to move in the direction of our respective cells.

'Mercy...' she says.

'Chop, chop!' calls out Officer Woods, clapping her hands. The atmosphere's lighter, a lot less threatening when she's in charge of rounding us up. We show our appreciation by dawdling.

'...I know you said there's a rule about not having to say why we're here...'

'You want me to tell you what I'm in for?' I finish for her. I wave at Officer Woods to say I won't be long. She chunners and marches off in a different direction.

Debs' nod is hesitant. She wants to know but is worried about how it'll affect our friendship.

'I'm in for killing the man who used to batter my sister,' I tell her before walking away.

I've a feeling our friendship will be just fine.

In the spirit of pushing my luck, I ask Officer Woods for a favour.

'You've got five minutes before Officer Frame comes on shift,' she grumbles in response. 'If she finds you, you're not to let on that I looked the other way.'

I use the landing phone to call my lawyer. He works for

himself, so he's well used to out of hours calls from ne'er do wells. He answers on the third ring. 'Liam Douglas,' he barks.

'Hope I'm not interrupting *supper*?' I tease him.

'Is everything all right, Mercy?' His voice softens, as though of all the clients he has in jail, I'm the one he's least irritated by.

I fill him in as quickly as I can. 'There's a new girl on the block who's in a bit of bother with the family courts–'

'Then she'll need a lawyer who specialises in family law,' he says tartly.

'You don't say, Einstein, I'd worked that much out for myself. Only she's broke and the whole legal aid process is a minefield...'

I hear a sharp intake of breath down the line that sounds like he's drawing on a cigarette. He told me he'd quit smoking years ago. I suppose everyone needs to blow off steam.

'...and I wondered if you'd be able to have a word with her next time you're here.'

An exhale this time, that goes all the way to his shoes. Or will it be slippers, this time of evening?

'I'm flattered you think I'm so multi-talented,' he says eventually, dragging out his response. 'Only, I've no reason to return any time soon, have I? Unless you've changed your mind about not submitting your parole application?'

I detect the hope in his voice and feel bad that I'm letting him down. 'I spoke to my brother and even he thinks it's hopeless.'

'Really? That doesn't sound like him.'

'I know. Something's off at home, I can feel it. I don't know what,' I say in answer to the question he's about to ask, 'but Clem's been acting weird and I haven't seen hide nor hair of Hope in weeks.'

'Have you spoken to them about it?'

'You don't have proper conversations with your family when

you're in prison, Liam.' Every exchange is stilted, reduced to a welfare check with appropriate responses, the kind of conversation you have with passersby or strangers at a bus stop: *How are you? I'm fine. And you? Same.* There's little time for meaningful discussion, no privacy to allow for anything more.

'So that's it, you're giving up?'

'It's not about giving up. It's about being realistic. Hope and Clem have their own lives and I've got mine. They've obviously moved on and I should let them.'

'I think you're making a huge mistake, Mercy.'

'At least it's mine to make.' I sigh into the phone. 'Look, there's something else. The prison doc wants me to go back to that psychologist, Stacey Sheridan. She thinks I'm still rattled by what happened with Alice Maltby.'

A pause. 'Are you?'

'No way! What happened with that psycho is firmly in the past. I don't think about it at all.'

'That's good, then.'

Officer Frame spots me by the phone and bellows my name. 'Get in your hovel now or I'm putting you on report!'

'I need to go!' I say quickly before she can make good on her threat. 'Can I tell the new girl you'll speak to her?'

'I'll think about it,' he says before ending the call.

'Mercy, are you awake?'

Vonnie needs to improve her sense of timing. She said nothing while I changed into my T-shirt and shorts, put away my dirty washing, and brushed my teeth. She'll have heard me crawl into my bunk, tap the photo on my wall to say goodnight to it before I give in to tiredness and pull my blanket over my shoulders. It's as though she's been waiting for me to close my eyes before calling out my name. She's some girl.

'Mercy?' she repeats.

'What is it?' I try to make my voice sound sleepy but it falls on deaf ears.

'I've come to a decision. I'm going to break up with Wayne when he visits next week.'

'You could have saved that breaking news until tomorrow. I wouldn't have minded,' I tell her.

'I wanted to put your mind at ease. I know you worry about us.'

I open my eyes. 'Us?'

'Me, Lola and Tanya. We're like a family, aren't we?'

'Christ, you're nothing like *my* family.'

She giggles. 'You know what I mean.'

I suppose I do. We have each other's backs while we try to make the best of our bad situation. What doesn't kill you makes you stronger, and all that. Though in jail, you have to be careful who you say *that* to.

I'm flattered that she values my judgement. I move onto my back so that I'm looking up at her bunk. 'You could send Wayne a text if you'd rather. I can have a word with Magda if you like?' Although we have access to landlines on each landing and a few cells have started to be kitted out with them, you can only call numbers previously approved, or 'whitelisted' on your phone card, and there's no facility for sending texts. Magda, a Ukrainian holed up on the other landing, hires out mobile phones smuggled in illegally that she gets her cronies to hide, charging inmates for every message they send. I'm sure she'd be flexible on the price if I had a word.

'No thanks, I don't like where they hide them.'

'They slip condoms over them, Von, you wouldn't have a clue if she didn't call them her fanny phones.'

'Nah,' she says eventually. 'Wayne deserves to be told face to face.'

I detect the anger in her tone and like it. 'Yeah, he does. Just make sure I've got a ringside seat when you do it.'

She laughs nervously, and I know I'll need to keep an eye on her this week so she doesn't lose her resolve.

'Von...?' I say into the darkness.

'Yeah?'

'You're doing the right thing, you know. You can't shrink yourself to make someone else happy.' Then I breathe heavily so she thinks I've fallen asleep.

The uneasy feeling I had earlier about Clem returns. I feel bad thinking this but he definitely looked shifty at the end of his visit. I'll call him tomorrow, see if I can't get to the bottom of what's troubling him. I take three calming breaths. There's no point fretting about it, not when there are other, far more pressing, reasons to stress out about, I remind myself. Like my upcoming appointment with the prison psychologist, and the lies I'll have to tell to keep her onside.

CHAPTER SIX

I'm returning from my morning stint at the induction block when a familiar voice shouts out its usual greeting: 'May the Lord have Mercy on your soul!'

I look behind me to see Tanya being led away from the visitation area. It isn't family visiting time so she must have set up a meeting with her lawyer. I slow my pace so that she can catch up with me. The PO escorting her is an accommodating sort, won't mind me tagging along with them until I get to my cell. It's another hour until lunchtime association, so crossing paths with her like this is an unexpected bonus. Her face clouds over as she draws near. 'What's up with you?' she asks, giving me the once-over.

'You know me, Tan, everything's peachy.'

'You might want to tell your face that.' She gives me the side-eye.

'Just another day in paradise,' I respond using her go-to phrase to lighten the mood.

'Anyway, enough about you,' she gushes. 'My brief reckons I can apply for parole too. According to the tariff set when I was sentenced, I'm eligible so long as I show how sorry I am.' She does a little happy dance, yanking the chain that joins her wrist to the officer's. It's not lost on me how thrilled she is, despite not having a job, home, or anything remotely resembling a family to go back to once she leaves here. She's repaid her debt to society; her conscience is clear. If only I could say the same.

'I'm so happy for you, Tan, you deserve it.'

'I've got to convince the panel yet, though it should be a doddle. I mean, not a single person has mourned that sick motherfucker since I sliced him open.'

'You might want to work on your contrition,' I tell her, smiling. Her stricken face tells me how much this means. 'You'll be fine. Go in there and sock it to 'em. Remember what I always say when I need to give myself a pep talk?'

'Tits and teeth,' Tanya parrots, shooting me a look. 'Though that's easier said than done for some of us.' She pushes her tongue through the space where her front teeth should be to make her point. We laugh so loud the PO barks at us to give it a rest.

It's strange, I never expected to laugh in this place after losing my freedom. The new world I found myself in was dark and lacking and I couldn't see what pleasure there was to be had in it. I'd made my bed; I had to learn to lie down and get on with it.

I remember bumping into Tanya on our second day in Fairmile. She was being taken to the medical block; at least the prison officers had kept their promise. She shuffled along the landing like a geriatric, her face glistening with greasy liquid at the effort. She raised a shaking hand in my direction. 'It's my sweatbox twinnie!' she called out, flashing me a toothless grin. I looked into her dilated pupils and smiled.

'What's your name?' she asked me.

I told her.

'May the Lord have Mercy on your soul!' she boomed,

fanning her skeleton arms wide, fingers quivering. I blinked. Caught a glimpse of something white clamped beneath her thumb. I took a step to one side to let her pass, filing it away under *None of my damned business*.

Later, she explained that she'd been prescribed a dose of methadone every morning. Known as liquid handcuffs, the green opioid had to be consumed in the medical block. 'Only, twenty-four hours is a long time to wait for your next fix,' she informed me, matter-of-factly. The white thing concealed in her hand was a tampon she'd cut in half, which she'd hide in her mouth before drinking the prescribed amount – this was her way of splitting the dose in two. I caught myself laughing at her ingenuity. Laughter wasn't off limits as I'd feared, all I had to do was adjust my mindset. Even though she was eventually caught, this classic Tanya hustle is still referenced by the POs and nurses in the block.

The prospect of Tanya's release is momentous. I push away thoughts of what it will be like to be stuck in here without her. Dwelling on that now won't serve any purpose. Instead, I try to think of something special I can do for her that'll mark the occasion.

'Mercy?' Tanya is staring at me, serious-faced. I must have lapsed into silence. Or was that relapsed?

'Are you sure everything's okay?' We've reached my cell and the PO is unclipping the master key from his belt to unlock my door. 'I thought you'd be pleased for me. You know what this means, don't you?'

I give her a blank look.

'Wakey, wakey!' she says, prodding me in the arm. 'If you get your parole the same time I get mine, we could both be on the outside in a couple of months! Imagine that!'

Something in my face gives me away as she peers at me closely. 'You really aren't yourself today, are you, doll?'

'It's not that, Tan.' I can't lie to her. I can't get her hopes up over something that's never going to happen. I brace myself in readiness for her reaction. 'I told my solicitor not to bother putting in my application.'

Tanya recoils as though I've slapped her. 'Are you out of your mind?'

I shrug. 'Probably, which is why I'm better off staying in here.'

'Take this up later, ladies, I'm due a break,' the PO barks, ushering me inside before locking the door behind me.

'We're not finished, Mercy!' Tanya shouts as she's led back to her cell.

I lean against the door and let out a breath. Vonnie looks up from the magazine she's reading. I can tell from her face that she's heard every word.

'Save it!' I snap, throwing myself onto my bunk and switching on the TV.

When the bell rings out for lunchtime association, I make a beeline for the landing phone. I need to find out what's going on with Clem. He can be a touchy so and so at times but something about yesterday's visit just felt off. The prospect of Tanya leaving gives me the excuse I need. I've spent the last hour obsessing at the thought of being left in here without her, but that isn't enough to make me change my mind. I got my hopes up so high the last two times I applied for parole that when it was turned down, I was devastated. I can't put myself through all that again. If Tanya gets hers, I'll be pleased for her, she deserves it, but she'll have to go for it without me. She might be mad at me right now but she'll get over it, especially once she's on the outside. I've been thinking about what I can do to mark the occasion for her, something special to ease her transition, and for that I need Clem's help.

Usually Hope answers the phone when I call home. Clem's normally downstairs in the bar while she does all the paperwork from a makeshift office in the flat upstairs. I'm thrown momentarily when Clem's solemn voice answers. He sounds surprised to get a call from me, so soon after his visit.

'I thought you'd be in the bar,' I say to him breezily.

'I was on my way down,' he says gruffly. 'I can't stay on long.'

He must realise how cold that sounds because he clears his throat and apologises. 'Sorry, sis, it's been one of those mornings.'

'It's okay, Clem, I get it, I won't be on long. Are you still looking after that account I asked you to set up for me?'

'Course I am. Every month I make a deposit like we agreed. The business is turning a tidy profit, it's only right that you get your share.'

'I'll need to liquidate some of it soon. That going to be a problem?'

'Whatever you want, sis, don't worry.'

I tell him what I need it for. That I'll get the details of where he's to send it as soon as I can. I get the sense he's trying to bring the call to an end but I'm not ready yet. I haven't even started on asking him what's wrong but it's clear that as far as he's concerned, we're done. 'While I'm on you can put Hope on the line,' I tell him. 'She can make up for swerving me yesterday.' He agrees reluctantly and following a muffled conversation, Hope comes on the line. 'Hey, big sis,' she says in her usual upbeat way before filling me in on what her and the girls have been up to.

When I end the call, I'm glad that I'd made it. Clem still doesn't sound like his usual self but it's been great chatting with

Hope. I make a mental note to ask her what's going on with him when she next comes in to visit.

The atmosphere around the lunch table is light-hearted, despite the mac and cheese slopped onto our trays tasting like regurgitated rubber. Vonnie has announced that she's breaking up with Wayne. The others make a fuss of her, giving her advice on how to do the deed.

'Pretend you're Alan Sugar,' says Lola. *'You're dumped!'* she booms, imitating the famous businessman's stance at the end of each episode of *The Apprentice*.

'If you're feeling bad about it, you can always start a fight and let him dump you,' Tanya points out. We share a look and never one to bear grudges, she winks.

'Where's the fun in that?' says Vonnie and we all laugh.

Debs saunters up to our table once she's been served at the hatch. She asks me whether Wonder Woman is in the building, causing the others to look on with caution.

'No, but her better looking half-sister is,' I quip and invite her to join us. Relieved that I haven't kicked off again, the women shuffle round to make room for her.

'Welcome to the only hotel in Manchester that's always 100 per cent full,' Tanya greets her.

Debs is happy to talk freely about the reason she's here and the women give her their full attention.

'Bastards,' says Lola once Debs has finished.

'Every last one of 'em,' Tanya agrees.

A band of broken sisters ready to take another under their wing.

I tell Debs about my phone call with Liam. That I've asked him to meet with her next time he's in.

'Thanks, Mercy,' she says gratefully.

'He hasn't agreed to it yet,' I warn her. 'He's in a bit of a tailspin because I've told him I don't want to apply for parole.'

'She already knows what I think!' grumbles Tanya when the others fall silent. I feel their eyes on me as they weigh their responses carefully.

'You're bound to be scared,' says Vonnie.

'The thought of leaving here must seem daunting after all these years,' reasons Debs.

'Hello? She's off her rocker if she doesn't give it a try!' Tanya states for good measure. So much for letting things go.

'Why are you all shaming her for saying she doesn't want it? The reason we're all here is because we did something we should have said *no* to,' Lola says quietly and everyone looks at her. 'Just sayin',' she adds when Vonnie tuts.

'Can we change the subject? Whether I apply for parole or not isn't up for discussion, so please, just leave it,' I tell them.

'Your choice, I suppose.' Tanya shrugs, her demeanour signalling to the others to give it a rest.

I move the conversation back to Debs. 'I was thinking. I could put a good word in for you in the induction block,' I tell her. 'There's a job going making up those welcome packs.' She needs to be kept busy; helping other women in the worse moments of their lives might make her believe she can get through this.

'Pays three pounds a day if you're up for it,' Tanya informs her.

'Yeah, why not?' she says, then looks around guiltily. 'Don't any of you want to go for it, though?'

'Shoplifters aren't allowed to apply,' Vonnie tells her.

'I was caught trying to slip miniature bottles of hooch into the packs,' admits Lola.

'They don't trust me round tampons anymore,' Tanya confesses, causing everyone to crease up.

Officer Frame is on lunchtime duty. She must have been listening to our conversation because she fixes Tanya with a look. 'Best go back to what you're good at then, blow jobs and turning tricks.'

Tanya's grin slips momentarily as she gives Frame the once-over. 'It must be so hard to be you,' she says.

'Shut it, baghead,' sneers Frame.

'There's no need for that,' Tanya snaps, holding her ground. She leans forward, shoulders raised, hands clenched into fists as though gearing up for a fight.

'Just leave it, eh?' I say to her, putting my hand on her arm. 'We can do without any grief from her.' Tanya needs to let it go and I know just the thing to distract her. 'I was going to save this until later, but now's as good a time as any.' I lead her away from the table to give us some privacy.

'What is it?' she asks, all serious. 'Don't tell me you're going to shank her? I mean, if you really don't want parole, you've got nothing to lose.'

I shake my head at her. 'Thanks but I'll give that a pass, I think. No, this is much more exciting...'

A shadow falls across her face, swift, like a cloud blocking out the sun. Good things don't come our way often. It's best not to hope for them. I lean into her ear and tell her what I have planned.

Her face is a picture. 'FUCK ME, GIRL, TURKEY TEETH!' she shrieks, causing everyone in the dining hall to look over. She jumps up and down on the spot, does another one of her happy dances.

'She's only gone and ordered Turkey teeth for when I get my parole!' she tells the others excitedly as she runs back to our table, leaving me in her wake. I don't think I've seen her move so fast in all our years at Fairmile.

'It's my brother Clem who's doing all the arranging,' I tell them as we sit down. 'So everything'll be ready for when you leave.' I smile at Tanya and she grins back.

Debs is looking across the dining table at me, confused. 'What are Turkey teeth?' she asks.

I fill her in. 'It'd be great for Tanya to get her smile back but you know how expensive cosmetic dental treatment is. There's loads of clinics abroad that offer cut-price deals. They throw in two weeks' holiday as part of the package, too. I remembered my brother talking about a clinic in Turkey that some of the punters at our bar swear by.'

'I can't believe it!' Tanya shakes her head. 'I'm going to look normal again.'

'You're going to look better than normal,' says Lola. 'You're going to have a smile like those celebrities on TV.'

'Imagine that,' says Vonnie.

Tanya reaches for my hand and gives it a squeeze. 'Wouldn't it be amazing if you changed your mind about your parole and we went to Turkey together?'

Vonnie laughs nervously as my brow shoots into my hairline. 'Fucking unbelievable,' I mutter.

CHAPTER SEVEN

I'm late back from the induction block. Now there's no reason for me to dodge Dr North, I'm happy to stay longer at the welcome desk helping the newbies settle in. I'm not exactly wild about crossing paths with the doc, but I get the impression that now she's booked me in for a psych appointment her work is done.

As I enter our block, I can see Tanya and the girls are seated in the social area. Lola waves frantically for me to join them. Vonnie gestures towards the Pot Noodle she's holding and fills the kettle with boiling water when I nod.

'Remember Alice Maltby?' I ask suddenly as I join them, causing everyone but Debs to gawp in my direction.

'How can anyone forget a child killer?' mutters Tanya.

Lola visibly shudders. 'She had a little one the same age as my Danny, didn't she?'

'I didn't know you had a kid,' says Debs.

'What?' splutters Tanya. 'Wait a minute, am I missing something here?'

'If you are, you're not on your own,' says Vonnie.

They stare at Lola, mystified. I look on as she tells them about her teenage pregnancy and the son her parents are bringing up as their own. The women cluck around her, patting her back and stroking her arm in turn.

'The fact that you're talking about him... does this mean you want him to live with you when you leave here?' I ask her.

Lola nods. 'I've thought about nothing else since I spoke to you. I know it'll take time. I'll have to tell him who I am first and he'll need to get used to the idea, but yes, I want him with me.'

'Hang on, you knew?' Tanya splutters as she stares at me.

I spread my hands wide. 'What can I say? It's like the confessional in my cell, only without the threat of eternal damnation.'

I turn back to Lola. 'Danny'll be fine. I survived my messed-up childhood,' I tell her. It was what came after that was my undoing.

Tanya regards me with narrowed eyes. 'Anyway, why are you dredging up Alice Maltby after all this time?'

'That name rings a bell,' says Debs, joining in, her face a picture of concentration. 'Hang on,' she says slowly, her face clearing as it dawns on her. 'Wasn't she the woman in all the papers? She set fire to her house while her kids were asleep?'

'That's the one,' I confirm.

'Five beautiful kids,' says Tanya. 'She wanted to start over with some fella she'd met in Ibiza. Reckoned the kids were holding her back.'

The public had been full of sympathy when the tragedy first made the news. Front page images of her standing outside the burnt-out property clutching a teddy bear went viral. The back door of the family home had been jemmied open and petrol had been poured around the ground floor before being set alight. Well-meaning strangers held vigils and set up a crowd funding page to help with the funeral costs. The police conducted a very visible manhunt to track down the perpetrators of this terrible atrocity. Politicians used it as an opportunity to spout rhetoric about cracking down on crime. Far right groups used it as an opportunity to stir up tension, pointing a finger at a nearby hostel for asylum seekers. Maltby's ex-husband had been set upon by self-appointed vigilantes and had to be moved to an undisclosed location. Then the post-mortem report sent everyone reeling. Lab results confirmed that each child had been heavily sedated before they'd been put to bed that night. The country had been in uproar. Those same red-faced politicians put pressure on the courts to sentence her to prison rather than to a psychiatric unit, which they saw as a vote-losing soft option, so she ended up at Fairmile.

As my pad-mate.

'They should never have put you in that situation,' says Tanya vehemently. 'The bitch should have been put in the seg.'

Fairmile doesn't have a vulnerable prisoners' unit, known as a VPU, where nonces and child killers normally serve out their sentences. The next best thing the governor could have done with Maltby was put her in segregation, referred to as the seg. It's mainly used as a punishment block and the threat of it is enough to make most of us keep in line, but it would have kept her out of the prison glare. According to the prison officers, the governor was reluctant to feed Maltby's notoriety and reckoned the best way to avoid that was to put her in the main block. The fact that it was a disaster waiting to happen was the one thing that united prison staff and inmates alike.

I was working in the induction block the day she arrived. There'd been a police escort assigned to the sweatbox bringing her in, but it hadn't put off the crowds waiting outside the rear of the crown court. Rumour had it that it had taken two POs the rest of the day to hose off the caked-on eggs and dog turds that had been lobbed at it as it passed by.

Her arrival was like the opposite of a royal visit. The induction block fell silent as she was escorted inside, the expression on the faces of the welcome desk staff, cold and hard.

All eyes were trained on her, soaking up her appearance, consigning it to memory so we could compare notes later. All any of us knew about her up to this point was the evil caricature portrayed in the press. In truth, she looked no different from any other prisoner. She was heavy-set, five foot two at most, long dark hair she left loose despite the hairband she wore around her wrist. What struck me about her was how ordinary she looked. She was the kind of woman you'd chat to at the supermarket checkout while you waited in line, then forgot all about when you were done. The kind you didn't really notice. Unassuming. Unremarkable. Inconspicuous. Until she tucked her kids into bed before setting their home on fire.

Crimes like hers, where the murder of a child was involved, affected everyone. The staff moved about her on auto-pilot, spewing out instructions, all the while unable or unwilling to meet her eye. As she moved along the line towards me for my string bag of goodies, I felt her gaze seek me out and I looked up, momentarily locking eyes with her. I thought of the babies I'd been unable to have and the children she'd sacrificed for a man not worthy of them and I knew I had the opportunity, right in that moment, to harm her. We are all one misfired impulse away from madness – that's the reason I'm here, after all – and I'll not lie, I entertained the idea for several seconds.

It was she who broke the silence first. 'Where do I go next?' Her voice was calm, polite. Her eyes devoid of tears.

Hell. You'll go to Hell, I wanted to say but instead I pointed her towards the medical block. We'd been briefed that she wouldn't be attending the standard induction meet and greet session. There was concern that once the reality of what she had done kicked in, she'd be at risk of serious self-harm. Instead of staying in the induction block she was to be placed on the psych ward, which provided twenty-four-hour supervision. I had yet to discover the horror of that place, so had looked on dispassionately as I'd replied.

Two days later I was taken to see the governor, a treat usually saved for those facing a reprimand for breaking prison rules. The last time I'd had the pleasure of spending time in her company was following drug-gate – the block of heroin that had mysteriously found its way into my cell.

'Hello, Mercy,' she'd said, stretching her mouth into something that resembled a smile.

I'd frowned in response, her use of my first name putting me on alert. She invited me to sit and I did as I was told, aware I'd never been invited to do so before. Inmates normally stand when presented to the governor, like misbehaving pupils sent to the headteacher.

Jeanette Cassidy was slender with short hair feathered around her face, a hint of grey showing through blonde highlights. She wore plain studs in her ears. Everything about her was efficient and unfussy. Even her nails, which were short and varnish-free. A simple pendant hung in the V of her white blouse. Her suit was high-end fashion chain. The type of store that wraps each purchase in tissue before placing it in a fancy paper bag. She looked demure but I knew her to be ruthless. This was her third prison. Second as governor. With 800 inmates, Fairmile was twice the size of her previous post. She had a lot to prove.

The only window in the room was behind her, looking out onto the prison estate and the dual carriageway beyond it. The walls were adorned with certificates and a photograph of her shaking hands with a minor royal. A glass cabinet displayed trophies for women's rugby union, hockey, prison service team photos beside them. It didn't surprise me that she captained both teams. Governor Cassidy liked to win and she didn't tire of showing it.

Her smile grew wider though it had yet to make it to her eyes. 'Apart from the unfortunate incident eighteen months ago, you've had an exemplary record during your time here,' she commented, an acknowledgement woefully missing from her previous report to the parole board. According to her then, I'd breached prison rules then lied about doing so, any mention of my exemplary record left at the door.

'I'm advised that the women in your block respect you. You've become quite a role model, in many ways.' Another testimonial missing from that report, or rather character assassination, to give it its proper name.

I remained silent. She hadn't asked a question at that point, though I suspected one was coming. I also suspected it was going to be framed in a way that limited the response I could give.

'The senior management team feels Alice Maltby would benefit from sharing a cell with a resident who can be trusted to keep an eye out for her. And after much consideration, I think that resident is you.'

She looked at me as though that was the part where I was supposed to say thank you, as though a great honour had been bestowed upon me rather than a poisoned chalice.

I'd looked at her askance. 'So you want me to babysit a ticking time bomb?' I clarified, so there was no confusion. Just because she was shafting me didn't mean I had to bend over and take it in silence.

'I wouldn't put it quite like that,' she breezed. 'In fact, this may prove to be beneficial to everyone concerned.'

I raised an eyebrow in anticipation. I couldn't wait to hear *this*.

'Maltby's presence here has the potential to be unsettling for many residents.'

I searched her face for any trace of irony but there was none.

'Whilst under your watchful eye, she has an opportunity to integrate into the prison community without threat, so a sensible resident, able to keep their eye on her in the short term would be a good thing.'

'Short term?' I seized on the bait she was obviously dangling.

Governor Cassidy eyeballed me. 'I see you have another opportunity for parole coming up. A statement from me recognising your sense of citizenship is certain to go a long way.'

There it was. The prospect of freedom if I babysat a child killer. Governor Cassidy looked on, pleased with herself. 'Do we have a deal?'

How could I refuse? Ignoring every alarm bell that sounded in my head, every nerve in my body that warned me against it, I said yes.

'The governor stitched you up good and proper,' Tanya comments, bringing me back to the present. 'Damned if you said yes, damned if you said no.'

'Not like anyone says no to the governor,' Vonnie reasons.

'You must have wondered what kind of weirdo you were getting holed up with when they put you in with me,' I say to her, even more appreciative of her friendship. Vonnie had been put in with me once the spectre of Maltby had died down.

Vonnie's already shaking her head. 'No way, Tanya put me straight,' she says. 'Besides, everyone was talking about the danger you'd been in. About how she'd held you hostage. That must have been terrifying.'

'I'd have freaked out,' comments Lola.

'You freak out about everything,' Tanya scoffs, pursing her lips.

Lola grins and flicks her the middle finger.

'Yet again the dealers were behind it,' adds Tanya, raising her voice so it can be heard across the room, where Magda and her cohort sit. 'If the governor wanted to blame someone it should have been them. It was the gear they sold her that turned her psychotic.'

A couple of Magda's lap dogs glare in our direction, but a look from me has them swivelling back in their seats.

'She already had problems, Tan,' I remind her.

Alice Maltby will be the main topic of conversation for the remainder of association time, but by morning the others will have forgotten her. For me, there's no such reprieve; she's lived rent-free in my head for the past two years, ever since our worlds collided in the induction block. I knew in that moment that something about her was off. What I didn't know, had no inkling whatsoever about, was that *something* was me.

I head back to our landing ahead of the others. Today's the last day in the month to order our canteen and though she hasn't asked me to, I'll order a Pot Noodle to replace the one Vonnie gave me. I've got time to fill out an order form and hand it in if I hurry.

Back in my cell I run through my checking ritual: *cutlery, mugs, mattress, table. Chairs, heating pipes, shelves.* But instead of reassurance, I feel a trickle of alarm.

Something is wrong.

My eyes dart frantically over every surface, but I can't put my finger on what's causing my pulse to race and my heart to thud loudly in my chest. A wave of anxiety rises inside me, making me struggle to catch my breath. I can't make sense of it. The cell looks the same as it did when I left earlier; there's no obvious sign of disturbance. Everything is where it should be.

Then I realise it isn't.

CHAPTER EIGHT

The photo beside my bunk is missing.

The picture of me, Hope and Clem before the world conspired against us, has gone. I touch the place where it's supposed to be in case my eyes are playing tricks on me. They're not. Instead of the silkiness of a glossy Polaroid, my fingers graze over decades' worth of peeling paint. I stare at the small square of wall that's paler than the area surrounding it, feel the line of sticky residue where tape had secured it in place. There's no sign of it on the floor and the tackiness on the wall confirms my suspicion. The photo hasn't fallen anywhere, someone's taken it.

'What's up?'

I spin round at the sound of Vonnie's voice. 'Did you move my photo?' I ask, hoping there's a simple explanation.

Her face screws up as she tries to work out what I'm asking her. I point to the expanse of wall beside my bunk. The achingly empty expanse where my photograph should be. She follows the trajectory of my finger and her mouth opens in surprise. She looks back at me curiously. 'What? No way, why would I?'

'I don't fucking know why, Von, a joke, maybe?'

'I'm not that stupid, Mercy, here, let me help you look for it.' She moves towards my bunk and lifts my pillow and blanket and pulls out the mattress.

'It isn't there, I've done all that! You know what I'm like every time I come in here!' I say impatiently.

'Even so, two sets of eyes are better than one,' she responds, her eyes scouring the floor. She glances quickly at Wayne's photo to check it's still there and even though she's going to dump him, her face floods with relief.

'Just stop!' I bellow. 'It isn't here!' My voice must have carried along the corridor as Tanya appears in the doorway flanked by Lola and Debs.

'Is everything all right?' Lola asks.

'Does it LOOK it?' I yell. I point to the empty space on my wall and turn to them. 'Did any of you take it?' I demand.

'Course we didn't, doll, what d'you take us for?' says Tanya, hurt.

I pace the floor, which isn't easy with this lot in the cell. 'Someone's taken it, Tan.' I can feel my blood pressure rising. I keep glancing at the wall, in case the photo magically appears, which is pathetic and desperate, I know, but right now that's all I've got.

'Can you get your family to send another one in?' Debs asks.

'It was a Polaroid,' Tanya informs her. 'There isn't another one.'

'Get them to send in a different one then.'

I round on her. 'That was the last photo taken of us together! Do you not understand what that means? There isn't another *last photo*. Only a photo before the last photo and that isn't the same!' I huff out a sigh. 'You've only been here five minutes, you don't understand.'

'Photos are like lucky charms in here,' Tanya explains.

'Especially for us lifers. The reason the universe behaves itself is down to every precious picture and the wishes we make when we look at them. Once you put your photos up you can't take them down, it's bad luck.'

'I need it back,' I say simply.

'You need to work out who's got it first, doll,' Tanya replies. 'My money's on Magda.'

I shake my head in frustration. 'Magda's got no beef with me, Tan. She's got no reason to do this.'

'Well someone's got it in for you,' Tanya states.

'What about one of the screws?' asks Vonnie.

'I've rubbed Frame up the wrong way a couple of times,' I say, frowning. I think back to our stand-off outside Debs' cell. 'She's petty minded enough to want to get back at me.'

'That Frame is an evil bitch,' says Tanya. 'I wouldn't put it past her to do something like this, just to wind you up.'

'Well it worked then,' I reply, pushing through them to step onto the landing.

'Mercy, wait!' Tanya chimes after me but I don't look back. I won't sleep without that photo and whoever's stolen it really wants to mess with my head. It makes sense that Frame's behind this, she thrives on conflict, would think nothing of goading an inmate, especially when she's the one with the upper hand.

I find her sitting behind the desk at the POs' station eating a bar of chocolate while flicking through a magazine. Two wall-mounted CCTV cameras point at the desk and the landing either side of it; it's one of the safest places to be on the block. She looks up as I approach. Is it my imagination or can I detect the flicker of a smile?

'YOU'VE BEEN IN MY CELL!' I yell at her.

She stares at me head on. 'I had reason to believe you were harbouring a banned substance.' At least she doesn't deny it.

I glare at her. 'Oh yeah? Care to elaborate?'

'I heard on the grapevine you were fancying yourself as a bit of a spice girl.'

I start to laugh. I turn to Tanya, who's caught up with me and has been following our conversation. Her eyes caution me to tread carefully.

'That can't be right,' she reasons on my behalf, 'everyone knows Mercy doesn't do drugs.'

Frame looks pleased with herself. 'Apart from that time–'

'When I was set up,' I finish for her. 'The heroin wasn't mine.'

She shrugs. 'Whatever.'

I jerk my thumb in the direction of my cell. 'Nothing's been moved. Just my photo. Why did you take it?'

'I needed to get it swabbed for banned substances. You lot think you can run rings round us, getting your visitors to smuggle in nasal sprays laced with spice, well you can think again!'

Spice is a lab-made drug that mimics the effects of cannabis. It's often sprayed onto clothing or paper that's then cut up and smoked. It's for this reason letters and cards sent to us are opened by the staff at the front desk and photocopied – we get the photocopy, never the original. To get around this, enterprising dealers get customised nasal sprays smuggled in and charge their punters 'per spray'. It's why so many library books in here end up with missing pages, why self-help leaflets left on reception don't last two minutes.

'Yeah but that's got nothing to do with Mercy, though!' Tanya persists, earning an evil glower from Frame.

'Do you seriously think I'd let anyone near my photo with that stuff?' I'm careful not to lean over the desk in case it comes over as aggressive on the CCTV. 'Just give me my photo back and we'll call it quits,' I add, keeping my anger in check. No matter which way I turn I'm in full view of the security cameras and Frame knows this. She's had her fun, if she hands the photo back, I'm happy to call it a day.

I watch as she shoves a meaty hand into the breast pocket of her shirt and pulls out two strips of paper that she places on top of the desk. I blink as I look down at them. The strips of paper are actually my photograph, torn in two.

'Oops.' She sniggers as I stare at the pieces before picking them up. The photo hasn't been ripped in half, more a two thirds/one third split. Clem and I in one piece, Hope in the other.

I stare down at our faces, unable to speak. I swallow but my throat feels dry. I curl my fingers around the remnants of my broken family and back away.

Tanya, done with being nice, squares her shoulders. 'I always suspected you were a cunt,' she snarls at Frame, 'and that,' she makes a jabbing motion with her finger towards the desecrated photo in my hand, 'proves I was right.'

Tanya walks back with me to my cell. 'Someone needs to sort her out, good and proper. She's unhinged. Good job you're not superstitious, eh, doll?'

Lola is sitting with Vonnie on her bunk. They look at me expectantly as I walk in the door but I'm guessing Tanya is making wide eyes at them behind me, warning them to keep quiet. They climb down and make their way towards me tentatively but I sidestep them and drop onto my bunk.

'It's not as bad as it looks,' Tanya says. 'Bit of glue and it'll be right as rain. Don't go reading things into it that aren't there.'

Lola gasps at the torn strips of Polaroid as I place them on my pillow.

'If you can't say anything positive, doll, don't say anything at all,' Tanya hisses as she manhandles her out of the door. 'You okay?' she mouths at me and when I blink my eyes are moist.

She means well but this isn't something I can be jollied out of. A darkness descends on me as my brain goes into overdrive. As my thumb traces the jagged edge that runs the length of Hope's body I don't see an act of cruelty.

I see an omen.

CHAPTER NINE

Visiting days are a double-edged sword. In one way they keep us going, an all-important contact with family and friends who knew us before the incident that sent our lives spiralling. These people care about our welfare; to them we're nothing like the others we're locked up with, which is a tad delusional, I know, like parents blaming the way their child turned out on mixing with the wrong crowd, never believing their child *was* the wrong crowd.

I stand in front of the mirror rubbing body lotion into my face, wiping the excess over my hair. I'm wearing a sweatshirt Hope bought for me a couple of Christmases ago. The sweatshirt is flattering, despite the fact most of the colours have washed out of it. I wear it to show her I'm taking care of myself, that she doesn't need to worry about me. That I'm good.

I've done well to get any time in front of the mirror the way Vonnie's been carrying on. Today Wayne's getting the big heave-ho and she's been in a constant state of indecision, veering between not making any effort with her appearance – to show Wayne she no longer cares what he thinks – to going all out – to show him what he'll be missing. Vonnie forgets how great she looks when she's not even trying but when she opts for the latter there's a part of me that enjoys the spite of it.

At the sound of our door being unlocked I steal a glance at her. 'No second thoughts?' I ask.

'Nah, be glad when it's done so I can get on with the rest of my life.'

I could hug her but instead we bump fists, last thing either of us want to do is smudge her make-up.

We step onto the landing but when I look across to Lola's cell, she isn't standing outside waiting to be taken to the visitor centre along with us. Her mum's due to visit today, with Danny.

'Hold on,' I say to Officer Woods who's about to escort us. 'Lola's supposed to be coming too. She's got a visitor today.' I've never had any trouble with this PO and she doesn't let me down now. She calls over to the officer escorting Lola's side of the landing. Unfortunately, it's Office Frame.

'What the fuck has it got to do with you?' Frame shouts at me when Officer Woods explains why she's querying Lola's absence. She doesn't wait for my response. 'Silly cow's refusing to leave her cell, I'm not wasting my time persuading her.'

Officer Woods looks at me as if to say *there's your answer*.

'Can I go and speak to her?' I ask. 'There's no way she'd miss this without a good reason.'

Officer Woods isn't convinced and if she isn't, then I've got no chance of persuading Officer Frame to change her mind.

'Her mum's bringing her little boy in. It's his birthday,' I lie. 'There's no way she'd miss that. Please?'

'You'll be holding back the others, which doesn't seem fair.'

'I'll be quick,' I promise.

'I don't mind, honestly,' Vonnie pipes up, loyally. The women from the neighbouring cells shrug their indifference, the promise of seeing their loved ones a close second to the reality of it.

'Quick as you can, then,' says Woods, shrugging at Frame's wide-armed *what the hell* gesture.

I walk across the landing, nodding at Frame as though me going to speak to Lola had been her idea. She unlocks the cell door grudgingly, muttering, 'If you ask me, the little bastard's better off without a drunken jailbird for a mother.'

I clench my fists, keep them down by my side. The door clicks unlocked and, not one to make anything easy, Frame pulls it open just a fraction and holds it so I have to slip in sideways.

'Don't keep me waiting,' she grunts.

'Fuck you very much,' I say quietly as I step inside.

Frame makes a point of locking the door behind me in response.

Lola has curled herself into a ball on her bunk and her face is buried into her pillow. At the sound of the door shutting, she turns her head. Two large panda eyes stare up at me. I nod towards the door and the gobshite waiting on us. 'Not sure her lift goes all the way to the top floor, know what I'm saying?' I say to minimise the sting of her words.

'She's right though, isn't she? It's what Mum keeps telling me. I rang her this morning to check she was bringing Danny in but she told me Dad's taking him out instead. Can you believe that?'

'Perhaps they thought it would be too much for him. I suppose you've got to trust their judgement given they're the ones with him most of the time.'

'Trust them? I'll never trust either of them as long as I live.' She's about to burrow her face back into her pillow when I place a hand on her shoulder. 'Get off me!' she says, pushing my hand away with force.

I back away from her bunk to give her the space she needs. 'Lola, what is it?' I ask.

She turns away from me so that I'm looking at the back of

her head. We don't have long. Frame would love an excuse for me to miss my visit and there's no way I'm handing her a reason on a plate. If Lola wants to be alone right now, I'll have to leave her to get on with it.

'Nobody's going to make you do anything you don't want to do, Lola. If you can't cope with seeing your mum, that's fine. I wanted to check you were okay, that's all.'

Lola turns and pushes herself up into a sitting position, her eyes seeking out mine. 'Do your emotions ever make you feel out of control?'

I throw her a look. 'I'm serving a life sentence for murder, you idiot, what do you think?'

That raises a smile. 'It's how I feel right now,' she adds, wiping her nose on the sleeve of her jumper. 'Like my body's made up of thousands of atoms whirling around me ready to explode. That one wrong word will set them all off.' She blows out a breath. 'It's better that I don't see Mum today. She's not as nice as she makes out and I don't think I can deal with that right now.'

'Then don't. Look, I need to go, but how about I come back and see you later? Check how you're getting on?'

Lola nods gratefully. 'Who's coming to see you today, your brother or your sister?'

'Hope's actually gracing me with her presence for a change. I don't know what's got into that girl lately but showing her face round here has become as rare as hens' teeth.'

'I love it when she comes,' gushes Lola. 'She always brings a dose of glamour to the visitors' room.'

I bite the inside of my cheek. Lola means well but her words are a stark reminder of everything that I'm not. I was the looker once, Hope nothing more than a gangly teen, but now the situation has reversed. Her tight curls have been relaxed over the years, resulting in a sleek bob that sits on her shoulders, accentuating glossy red lips and her trademark matching nails. On visiting days she sits poised in the visitors' room, her clear brown eyes fixed on the security door while she waits for me, oblivious to the admiring glances sent her way. It's never made her conceited. As she's fond of saying, her looks brought Gary Walsh into her life and look how that turned out. A wry smile forms on my lips at the memory of that and I realise how much I'm looking forward to seeing her.

'Guess we all need a touch of that,' I say to Lola, banging on the cell door for Frame to let me out.

'What was wrong with Lola?' Vonnie asks as we make our way out of our block to join the procession heading towards the visitor centre.

'Her mum won't bring Danny in to see her. Sounds like she's been pushing a lot of her buttons recently and today was the last straw.'

'She's only in for a month,' Vonnie reasons. 'A couple more weeks and she'll be able to see him when she wants.'

'That's the problem. Her folks have claimed him as their own – admittedly it suited her at first but she regrets that now – she's scared they're trying to edge her out of his life. It can't be easy. I said I'd look in on her later.'

Vonnie's only half listening now we've entered the visitor centre, her eyes already scanning for Wayne amongst the seated congregation of friends and family members. A dopey figure waving from the back of the room catches her attention and she reluctantly waves back. 'Wish me luck,' she mutters, before heading in his direction.

I survey the rest of the room with a prickle of unease. Hope's glowing skin and glossy hair make her stand out from any crowd but I can't see her anywhere. Has there been some mistake? Did the welfare officer get the date of her visit wrong or, more likely, I think irritably, has she bailed on me again? All around me inmates are settling into chairs opposite their loved ones; the decibel level in the room has risen several notches. The women from my block are seated at various tables; I'm the only one left standing, trying hard not to look as worried as I feel. I turn to Officer Woods. 'Where's my visitor?'

She looks towards a raised platform where two POs sit and watch over the proceedings. One gets to his feet and makes his way over to us. He's so tall and straight it looks as though he has an ironing board up the back of his shirt. Jack Murdoch is the most senior officer in the room. 'Mercy Reid?' he says, checking the prison number I recite for him against the details on the clipboard he's holding. 'You're to come with me.'

'Are you coming as well?' I ask Officer Woods, suddenly in need of a familiar face, but she shakes her head. She'll have to cover the desk while Murdoch escorts me to wherever I'm being taken – they can't risk a mutiny. 'What's going on?' I ask him, but he's striding ahead of me and either doesn't hear or doesn't want to reply. All I know is that we're making our way towards a set of doors at the other end of the hall, which lead to a corridor of much smaller rooms where inmates are taken to meet with solicitors or social workers, where personal matters are discussed in private. My heart lurches. Why does Hope need to speak to me in private? Is Hope even here? What if I'm being taken to a private room because a police officer's waiting to speak to me? What if this police officer needs to speak to me because something awful has happened to Hope?

There's a commotion close to me as an angry voice lets loose a volley of expletives. A dozen heads turn in Wayne's direction as he lurches to his feet. 'Crazy bitch! I always suspected you were a lezzer anyway!' he shouts at Vonnie before two POs grip him by the arms and propel him towards the exit.

Vonnie catches my eye, her mouth forming an 'O' shape when she sees where I'm being taken. 'Everything okay, Mercy?' she calls out but I don't have time to answer. Officer Murdoch unlocks the door and steps into the corridor, gesturing for me to follow. He does this in silence, his solemn face sending my anxiety into overdrive. Once he's locked the door behind him, he moves to one of the private visitation rooms and opens it. Rather than chivvy me along, he stands outside the door and waits, and that's when I realise that it's the room Debs was in last week when her world came crashing down. I don't want to go in there but I know I've got no choice. I slow my pace, dragging my heels to stretch out every moment, every second, every nano-second, because I know beyond a shadow of doubt that when I enter that room everything will change.

CHAPTER TEN

I join Officer Murdoch in the doorway and peer into the room.

The person seated at the only table is Hope. Only it isn't Hope, not as I know her. Sunken eyes stare at me from a hollowed-out face. A wisp of hair peeks out from a woollen beanie hat and the baggy top she's wearing fails to conceal the skeleton-like frame beneath it. Her manicured nails tapping on the tabletop are the only part of her I recognise.

'I've been dreading this,' she admits, as the ground beneath my feet falls away.

I move unsteadily to the table and lower myself into the seat opposite.

'What the hell, Hope?' My voice comes out in a whisper. The door closes behind me and when I look round, Officer Murdoch has gone. He's watching through the window that looks into the room, I turn my back to him.

Hope dips her head. Her neck looks so fragile, like it could snap in two. 'We phoned the prison and asked if there was somewhere I could speak to you in private... I wanted to be the one to tell you, Mercy.' She sees the look on my face but doesn't try to reassure me. I grip the edge of the table for support.

'There's no easy way to tell someone you're dying.'

I try to swallow but my mouth has gone dry.

'I wanted to wait,' she says quickly. 'I wanted to give you *good* news. That I'd had cancer and I'd beaten it. It's what people say, isn't it, like it's an Olympic event that they need to go into training for. I didn't want to tell you until the scary bit was behind me and I'd been given the all-clear. It's why I swore Clem to secrecy. I mean, why worry you if we didn't need to?'

'I'm your family, I could have helped.'

'Not from here you can't! You knowing wouldn't have achieved anything.' She pauses. 'Lying to you is taking its toll on Clem, he was never very good at hiding his feelings, was he? Even now he's sat in the car park fretting about what you'll think of him for keeping you in the dark.' She smiles, but it quickly falls away. 'And now, well, the situation has changed. Things have moved on...'

I listen as she tries to fill me in on her condition but my head is spinning, it's so much to take in. She talks about weight loss that she was pleased with at first, then, coupled with going to the loo a lot and passing blood she went to see her GP. 'One colonoscopy later, I'm staring at a consultant who tells me I've got a large tumour. He booked me in for an operation the following week.'

'When was this?' I ask, trying to process what I'm hearing.

She looks sheepish. 'It was when I told you I'd booked a holiday with the girls.' She reaches for my hand across the table. 'Please don't feel bad, Clem's been with me every step of the way. He's been brilliant.' Which makes me feel worse, not better. I'm the older sibling, it's my role to take charge, look after them in the absence of our parents, the way it's always been. Hope gives my hand a squeeze as though I've spoken aloud. 'I hoped the surgery would do the trick, that I'd be right as rain in no time... Only it didn't work out that way. The cancer was more aggressive than feared and I started on a course of chemotherapy–'

'Which is why you couldn't visit,' I finish for her. And why Clem was so jumpy.

'I reacted badly to the treatment each time; he hated leaving me.'

My head is reeling as I try to take in what she's telling me, what she's really trying to say. Even so, I need her to spell it out for me.

'How are you now?' I ask, already knowing the answer, dreading it all the same.

'A new scan shows the cancer has spread to my other organs. There's nothing more they can do for me, Mercy. The doctors' conversations have moved away from treatment to about doing what they can to keep me comfortable.'

I cough out a sob. I can't begin to imagine how Hope feels. She looks done in. 'I've got parole coming up.' The words come out unbidden. 'I can help you. Help with the girls...'

'Clem told me. He's worried how I'll take it if you're turned down again.'

'Tell him not to worry. My solicitor reckons I've got a strong case this time.' It's not quite how Liam put it but it does the trick. The worry lines on Hope's face ease.

'Remember when I was expecting and we used to talk about what it'd be like with the babies?' she asks.

I nod.

'I always wanted you to be a big part of their lives.'

'I'm sorry it didn't work out that way.'

'I wish I'd never met Gary!' she spits.

'Yeah, well, that was down to me too, wasn't it? Anyway, you'd never have had those lovely girls if you hadn't met him, and you don't regret them, do you?'

'Not for a minute. Oh, Mercy, I'm not ready to leave them

but I've got no say in it, have I? They're only sixteen; you and I both did stupid things at that age. You got together with Billy; I got together with Gary. I need to know you're going to be there for my girls, stop them making the mistakes we made. You've served your sentence, surely it's time for you to come home?'

I take one look at my dying sister and make a pact with myself that I'll be there for her no matter what it takes. I nod as though my life depends on it. 'Of course I'll be there, for you and for them. I've never let you down, Hope, and I don't intend to start now.'

It's the only answer I can give, even though the odds are stacked against me making good on it.

CHAPTER ELEVEN

Officer Murdoch escorts me back to my block. He takes his time, making small talk, which flies over my head; something about a caravan in Tenby where he used to take his kids, where he plans to take his grandkids once they're better behaved. It's a one-way conversation to distract me from the thoughts racing round in my head. He doesn't mention Hope, or the reason she came, instead he tells me that he was transferred here six months ago from a prison down south. 'My wife's staying put, though. We've got family living close by and in three years I'll be eligible for my pension.' I get the impression the job move wasn't his doing. I suppose being here feels like a sentence to him, of sorts. When we get to my block, he takes me to the hall manager's office, tells me to take a seat. The office is empty, which seems to please him. He makes me a sweet tea then lifts the desk phone from its cradle, uses his index finger to press the button for an outside line before handing it to me. 'Call whoever you want, you've got five minutes,' he says before stepping outside.

I lie back on my bunk and close my eyes as I run through my conversation with Liam. Within an hour of my call, he brought the paperwork needed to lodge my application for parole. He'd kept the original forms, he told me, all that was needed was my signature. He warned me that Hope's condition doesn't change things. 'She's not your dependent, Mercy,' he'd said gravely, 'and Clem is there providing support.'

'He's running the business on his own now, he can't look after the girls as well!' I'd responded.

'I'm just saying it how the panel will see it,' he warned.

'I don't care how the panel see it; the fact is my sister needs me and I really need to be there for her,' I'd persisted. 'Are you sure there isn't anything you can do from your end?'

'Of course you want to be there and of course Hope wants you with them, but her condition doesn't give you a magic pass. I know it's tough but you're going to have to go into that panel hearing and prove you're ready for release, just like anybody else. Do you think you can do that?'

'I've got no choice,' I'd said, resigned.

'Then I'll do everything I can to get the hearing scheduled soon.' Liam's voice was measured but his caution was justified, given my previous performances in front of the panel.

I open my eyes. If there ever was a time in my life when I felt everything and nothing all at the same time, it's now. I feel helpless. I'm desperate to go home so I can look after Hope and give my nieces a chance to get to know me before the inevitable happens. Hope may have weeks, or months, her doctors won't commit. I hope Liam can pull whatever strings he needs to get a panel assembled quickly to consider my application, but beyond that there's little I can do.

'You up yet?' Vonnie's head appears round the cell door. When I grunt a reply, she pushes the door wide and steps in.

'I've brought you a sandwich. You didn't eat anything yesterday but you need to get something inside you.'

I push myself into a sitting position. She hands me a triangular carton and a plastic bottle of orange. I rip open the carton and bite into the cheese and ham sandwich, surprised at how hungry I am.

'Tanya was going to pop in and see you but she's gone to check on Lola. She's been holed up in her pad too.'

I cover my mouth with my hand. 'Oh God, I told her I'd check on her after my visit from Hope.'

'It's okay, me and Debs went to see her to let her know what's going on. She knows you've got a lot on your plate.'

'I haven't though, really, have I? Not like I can do much from here.'

Vonnie's smile is sympathetic. 'Won't stop you worrying though, will it?'

Her gaze drops onto the torn photo that I now keep beside my pillow. I reach for it, tracing the rough edges with my finger. 'It was taken not long after we found out Hope was expecting,' I say to her, recalling happier times. 'I was so excited I cleared out the box room straight away so that it could be turned into a nursery. We'd just got home after spending the morning choosing paint when I asked Gary to take it. We'd taken loads of him and Hope earlier in the day but I wanted a photo taken with my siblings, the three of us together.' It strikes me that soon there won't be three of us anymore, that I was right, the torn photo was a harbinger of doom. I push that thought as far away as it will go.

I throw my sandwich wrapper and empty juice bottle in the bin and get to my feet.

'Where do you think you're off to?' Vonnie's gone all Mother Hen on me, which feels weird but I let it go.

'There's not much I can do for Hope right now but there might be something I can do for Lola.'

Vonnie looks at me, incredulous. 'The only place you're going is to the medical block. Your appointment with the psychologist is in half an hour, or had you forgotten?'

I can't believe something that had been weighing so heavily on me has completely slipped my mind.

'And if you don't mind me saying, you might want to freshen up,' Vonnie adds, wrinkling her nose.

I look down at my slept-in clothing and set about making myself presentable, pulling clean clothes from the cupboard and swilling my face and underarms with water.

'That's better,' Vonnie says, giving me the once-over when I'm done.

I might look ready but that doesn't stop a wave of anxiety threaten to engulf me. The consequences of me not getting Stacey Sheridan onside are huge now that my application for parole is going ahead.

What Liam said earlier, about Hope's condition not changing anything, is wrong.

It changes everything.

CHAPTER TWELVE

As I head towards the medical block, I try to shake off my apprehension at seeing the psychologist again. It's not that Stacey Sheridan's intimidating, she's more stealth-like than that. I've always believed that people with true power seldom need to display it and Stacey has an uncanny way of making you feel at ease before she slips inside your head, the same way a photographer distracts a child with a puppet before taking their picture.

'C'mon, girl, tits and teeth,' I mutter. All I have to do is keep my mouth shut and appear amenable and everything will be fine.

The waiting room is crammed full of women waiting to be seen by the nurse on shift. As Dr North isn't in today, there'll be no prescriptions given out, it'll either be treat and street or admit them for a night on the ward if their condition merits it. I keep my head down as I move towards a row of chairs closest to the consultation room, I'm friendly with a lot of the staff on this wing through my peer support role and don't want them to know I'm here as a patient. If any of them see me, they don't let on.

Officer Daynes strolls in. It's shift changeover time and he swaps places with a bored looking PO standing guard outside the treatment room. He says something to her, causing her face to harden but she bites back a reply. He leans against the wall, leering as she stomps away. He's a mediocre man convinced he's irresistible to women. He's sporting a bruise on his cheek and I hope it's from the fracas a couple of days ago. His hair is normally shorn but hasn't been lately. It's grown back uneven in places, merging with his facial stubble, giving him the appearance of a human porcupine.

He sees me sitting on my own and wanders over. 'What are you doing here?' His tone's sharp, like I'm up to no good and he's caught me in the act. I look from him to the consultation room door in the hope he can read the subtext.

'Cat got your tongue?' he demands. We eye each other steadily. It isn't just his female colleagues that he tries it on with, he's handsy with inmates too. My rite of passage was in a blind spot on the stairwell. He grabbed my left breast and in response I squeezed his balls so tight he spent the remainder of his shift walking lopsided.

'I've got an appointment,' I tell him.

'The doc's not in today,' he informs me. He looks smug, the way people do when they think they're telling you something you're not smart enough to have worked out.

'I'm aware of that.'

He folds fat arms across his chest as he looks me up and down. He wears a thick gold band on his wedding finger and I wonder what ordeal his wife endured in the past for her to think he's all she deserves.

'You're not allowed over here without permission.'

'I'm waiting for Ms Sheridan.'

'The psychiatrist?'

'She's a psychologist,' I correct him.

'Same thing.'

I let it go. There's nothing to be gained in getting on his wrong side other than a night in the punishment block if I really go to town on him. I think of Mum's response when I told her she shouldn't leave needles where the twins could reach them: *No one likes a smart-arse.*

He's staring at me as though trying to work something out, then his face clears. 'I'd forgotten you'd tried to top yourself.' He sniggers.

I'm about to put him straight – some things you just can't let go – when the consultation room door opens and a woman wearing a smart blouse and navy trousers stands in the doorway.

'Hello, Mercy,' she says, ushering me in.

'I'd better get back and clear your cell of any sharp implements,' porcupine face says in a low voice in case Sheridan hears and reports him to the governor.

'Off you fuck, then,' I reply, not caring who's listening.

Stacey Sheridan runs offending-behaviour programmes at several prisons in the north of England. They promise to *Transform the way offenders think and reduce the risk of them reoffending after their release.* I know this because that's what it says on the business card she gave me at the start of our first session.

The interior of the consultation room has been changed around since my 'appointment' with Dr North, so that it appears less clinical. A small table that normally sits in the corner of the room with a peace lily on it has been moved to the centre with two plastic chairs either side of it, positioned so they face each other. Stacey sweeps her arm wide, like a gameshow host pointing out tonight's top prize and I nod appreciatively, flopping into the seat she indicates. The lily has gone, replaced by a box of tissues and a pen, and I try to locate it while she picks my file up from a stack on the desk. She follows my gaze as it darts around the room and I wonder if she thinks I'm contemplating making a run for it.

'How've you been since our last meeting?' She picks the pen up from the table and places it on the file on her lap.

I locate the lily. It's on top of a filing cabinet beneath the only window in the room. I nod my approval, which seems to please her. 'I'm very well, thank you,' I say.

'That's not what I asked you.' She smiles as though shaping her mouth into a curve will soften what she says next. 'Have there been any other... attempts to harm yourself, since we last met?'

'I'm sure if there had you'd know about it,' I say glibly.

Another smile. She opens my file and clicks the top of her ballpoint pen before starting to write. When she's done, she clicks the pen once more and drops it onto the open file. There's a glint in her eye and I drop my gaze to try to read what she's written:

Evades direct questions.

I baulk at how harsh it sounds, knowing how the severity of a professional's words can shape a stranger's view of me. Comments I don't want submitted to Dr North in case she deems me at risk. It's not the first time this has happened.

Refuses to co-operate.

The senior social worker's description of me when submitting the application for Hope and Clem's adoption.

Aggressive.

The reason an employer gave for sacking me when I wouldn't let him bully me.

I cross my right leg over my left to stop me from tapping my foot. Play nice, I remind myself. I also remind myself that I need her on my side.

'Have you spoken to your friend about the day you harmed yourself?'

Her question makes my breath catch. I look at her, alarmed and feeling horribly exposed. I knew our session would be tough but I expected her to coax me down paths I didn't want to take, not drag me by my hair.

'She must have had a terrible fright.'

I feel myself bristle. 'You mean Vonnie?' My voice is still and hard. 'We're pad-mates, not friends. Knowing when each other bleeds and the stench of each other's shit doesn't make us besties.'

I say it to annoy her but I end up feeling guilty, especially after what Vonnie said about being part of our own little family. I'm angry at Stacey for making me deny our friendship; I want to take my words back but I'm too damn stubborn. I press my lips together in protest.

When it's obvious I'm not going to say any more on the matter she tries a different tack.

'How've you been since our last meeting?'

I take a breath. 'I've been up and down,' I tell her honestly.

Her eyes bore into mine. *That's more like it*, they say.

'Only right now I'm about as low as it gets.' I realise what I've said when she leans forward eagerly, pen poised at the ready. My palms feel sweaty. I wipe them down the front of my leggings, aware that she's studying everything I do. I decide to level with her. 'You think I'm here because I want to keep my poxy job, but I'm here because my sister's dying and I need to get parole so that I can be with her.'

Stacey studies my face. 'That must be very difficult. How are you feeling?'

My shoulders drop in response. It's hard to explain how you feel to someone who hasn't been through the same experience. They listen to your problem in the abstract, and whilst sympathetic, they can't ever know your pain. I remember what Lola said when she refused to leave her cell on visiting day. That her body felt like thousands of atoms ready to explode. *That*, I want to say to Stacey. *That's* how I feel.

Stacey flicks through the first couple of pages of my file. 'I can't see anything in here about a new parole hearing. Has a date been set?'

I shake my head. 'My solicitor's put in an emergency application. I only learned about Hope's condition a couple of days ago,' I explain.

'You've been eligible to reapply for parole for several months. Is there a reason you chose not to?' She positions her head in its customary side tilt. The first time she did this, I thought she had a trapped nerve in her neck, but I learned during our session it's her listening stance, her invitation to me to share what's on my mind.

Careful.

'I'd decided not to bother.'

Her face registers surprise, prompting me to offer a garbled explanation. 'I couldn't face letting my family down again. It's hard for them, you know? Believing every time that this is the application that will be successful... until eventually they stop believing. I hated the thought of them losing faith in me.'

'No one wants to feel like they're letting people down,' she observes, as though I don't already know that, as though the women at Fairmile take drugs for the fun of it rather than to wipe out what's hurting them.

'Only now it really matters.' I tell her about Hope's condition, about how I need to be there for her and the girls.

Stacey considers what I've told her. 'Your sister's terminal illness is forcing you to step up. How does that make you feel?'

I let out a breath. 'Petrified.'

'Of what?'

I look away.

I'm frightened that somewhere along the way I've lost myself. That if I'm no longer the woman who walked in here sixteen years ago, who am I?

The weight of expectation.

I want to be happy but not too much that I'm punished for it.

'Take your time,' she says, glancing at her watch, which she's placed on the table between us.

'It's a lot to think about,' I say, resisting the urge to tilt my head in the opposite direction to hers.

'You realise your application for parole changes the remit of these sessions, don't you? It means I'm not only assessing your mental health; I need to determine that you're ready for release.'

'Aren't they one and the same?'

'Not really. It's one thing to be assessed as fit to operate in a controlled environment such as a prison. To be signed off as not posing a threat to members of the public is something else entirely.'

I look at her, confused. 'I've never gone through all this palaver before.'

'You mean for the applications that failed?'

I shrug, conceding her point. 'I'm hardly a threat to anyone. I never was.'

'That's not how it looks on your file.'

'If you're going to go off a bunch of reports then what's the point in me being here?' I push myself up out of the chair, ready to terminate our session when I catch her studying me with a half-smile. 'What's so funny?'

'Bolting at the first sign of trouble. Not a good look,' she answers.

I drop back into my seat and cradle my head in my hands. I

really need to do everything right for this application, yet here I am getting the basics wrong.

Stacey looks at me with something akin to sympathy. 'It's perfectly natural to be apprehensive, Mercy. The problem most long-term residents have when they're preparing to leave is admitting how daunted they feel. How can you convince a roomful of strangers you're ready even though you're not? How can you possibly be ready when you've been holed up in here for so long?'

I move my head to look at her.

'Does any of that sound familiar?'

My nod is slow. 'Tell me what I need to do, then. I can't be in here, not when my family needs me more than ever. Help me to get back to them, *please*.'

She leans forward in her chair. 'I want to help you, Mercy. From the moment you were first referred to me after your breakdown I wanted to help, but you kept shutting me out.'

My gaze flits to the peace lily but Stacey's silence draws me back.

'Starving a problem of oxygen doesn't kill it, it just makes it more desperate to survive. I'm willing to work with you on this so long as you're prepared to co-operate.' She looks at me sternly. 'I warn you now, it isn't going to be pretty.'

I take a breath. 'Let's do it.'

She leans back in her seat, satisfied. 'I've been looking through your records.'

I guess she doesn't mean my health record, which stays here in the medical block, but rather the court transcripts, witness statements and educational assessments that chart my time in the criminal justice system. I shift a little in my seat. If she's looking for a reason why I killed Gary Walsh, I'm not sure what I can add that will help her point to a particular moment in time and claim that was the proximate cause of all that followed. I don't think life is as linear as that. There are cracks and bumps and hairpin bends along the road that have to be navigated whether we see them coming or not.

'I understand you had a troubled childhood,' she states.

To call it troubled is to pick a word on a low shelf for convenience. I want to laugh out loud but with my history of wrist cutting it might convince her I'm crazy.

'It wasn't the greatest time, no.'

Social services knew about my siblings before they were born. Neighbours had reported their concerns about my care to the local authority when I was small, so by the time Clem and Hope arrived, kicking and screaming into the world, they were already on the child protection register.

'Do you have many memories of when you were young?'

Discarded roaches floating in my cereal bowl. Cremated toast.

'Not really.'

'Can you remember anything?' she pushes.

I look away once more.

My parents called me Mercy because they were born-again evangelists who thought giving their children virtuous names would demonstrate their devotion. Whether that devotion was intended for their god or to us kids is impossible to say. All I know is that me, Hope and Clem ended up in care the year I started high school.

I don't remember much of our time living as a family. I'm the eldest, so the others rely on me to fill in their memory gaps. Like the time when Hope and Clem shared an ice-cream cone and covered each other in raspberry sauce. How they hiccupped with laughter as Mum cleaned them up. How tenderly she wiped their faces while pretending to be cross.

That never happened, of course. Our mother, off her face on smack, was spark out on the sofa. The toddlers were on the floor by her feet, docile with hunger. They were good babies. Never cried. Knew crying would get them nowhere. When I heard the ice-cream van enter our street, I counted out loose coins left on the makeshift coffee table in our living room. Enough for a single cone. I held the coins safely in my hand as I let myself out of our terraced house, leaving the front door open so I could get back in again. Dad flew into a rage when he came downstairs to fetch a can of beer from the fridge and saw it open. Not because the twins could have wandered onto the road – that was never going to happen, they never budged from their position by Mum's feet, like sentries – but because the loan shark he was in debt to could have stomped in. It wasn't so much of a punch that he gave me, more a shove, but I dropped the ice cream and cracked my head on the stupid table. Satisfied he'd made his point, he wandered back upstairs.

Foreheads bleed such a lot, don't they? I was used to making a game out of things to save the twins from getting upset by what they saw. I got a spoon from the kitchen and scooped up as much ice cream as I could. Fed it to my siblings while joking that I was covered in sauce too. If you tell a story enough times, it becomes a form of truth.

There are no photographs from those early years. No days special enough to be captured for eternity. The memories Hope and Clem have were created by me, reframed so they grew up with happier versions of our pitiful reality.

Because our parents were out of it so often, I was forced to be the grown up, even though I had no real idea what that looked like. I'd study families at the park and get my cues from them. Small kids pushed on swings by parents that weren't comatose. By then the opportunity school offered was lost on me. There were bigger things I had to consider. Who would take care of the twins if their nappies needed changing or they were ill while I was out all day? I was the one who used to make up their bottles, balancing them on the bar of their buggy so they could feed themselves while I did my homework. After a while, it was easier not to bother going in.

Stacey's waiting for an answer.

'We went into care the day Mum OD'd.'

Of course, Hope and Clem don't remember it like that. They remember the lady with blonde hair taking them to a waiting car, that before she came for us we'd been playing a game. Who could put their outdoor clothes on the fastest? Who could fill a supermarket shopping bag with their favourite things and sit quietly on the sofa? Hope had put cream crackers and a jar of jam in her bag. Clem had packed the torch I'd given him when he started being afraid of the dark. My bag contained the twins' developmental health records and my previous school report. I added underwear for us all and a picture of our parents they'd had taken in a photo booth. None of us had toys to speak of. Anything that could easily be sold to fund my parents' next hit was gone. Our birthdays would be spent with them slumped on the sofa discussing the merits of a bag of brown or a wrap of white in the same way people deliberated between a Zinfandel or a Merlot, all the while eyeing the presents our grandparents had given us. We'd wake up the next morning to find our gifts gone. I used to tell the twins they'd been returned to the shop because they were faulty, and who needed 'stuff' to have a good time, right?

I remember Clem wriggling on the sofa. 'Need to pee-pee,' he'd said, over and over. I sent him into the garden to water the weeds. I could hardly let him use the bathroom, what with Mum lying face down in a pool of vomit, quite blue.

'I'd been the one who'd found her, the one who called the police – even at that age I could tell it was too late to ask the emergency call handler for anyone else. I didn't bother shouting for Dad as I knew he wasn't there – I'd heard him go out earlier.

Whether it was after he watched Mum inject her lethal dose, I'll never know. All I knew was that we were alone. That from this day forward our lives would be very different. I couldn't wait.'

I glance quickly at Stacey to see if she's shocked by my admission but her face is expressionless.

'I was sick of being treated like a social care exhibit.'

'What do you mean?'

'I lost count of the strangers with their sing-song voices traipsing through our home to check on my development. I wouldn't mind, but those appointments were booked several weeks in advance so on those days my clothes were clean and my hair had been brushed. If they'd peered a little closer, they'd have seen the insect bites beneath my hairline, the inflamed skin hidden by my dress where Mum had run me a bath but forgot to put cold water in.'

It's almost as if I'm remembering someone else's life, someone else's childhood. I was there but not there.

Stacey points to the file. 'There's no mention of any extended family. Were your grandparents involved much?'

Our grandparents were mythical creatures who'd visit on each of our birthdays then retreat, sad-faced, after a prolonged period of shouting. I shake my head. 'Mum's parents were preachers. I guess they felt short-changed, that for all their god-fearing ways they couldn't save her from herself. It was easier to distance themselves, I suppose, than deal with the fact their daughter was an addict.'

When they stopped coming to see us, I explained to Hope and Clem that they were too old to make the journey. Neither of them were over forty-five.

'What about your father's parents?'

'He grew up in care.'

She nods and writes this down. 'Did you like school?'

'I loved it, when I went. I did well in my lessons, but the

other kids made fun of me because my clothes were shabby and my shoes didn't fit.'

It's why I became so meticulous about my appearance once I started earning. How you present yourself matters. People believe what they see and I wanted to show them I was a confident woman, capable of doing anything I set my mind to.

'What was life like for you, when you went into care?'

I lift my chin to show her I'm not ashamed. 'It was better. We had regular meals, a structure, I didn't miss my parents one little bit.'

'Did you hope to find a new family?'

I shrug once more. 'I was farmed out to a couple of foster families but kept being sent back.' I see the pity in her eyes and look away to avoid it. 'It wasn't so bad,' I add quickly.

She rewards me with a smile. 'You were incredibly resilient, Mercy.'

My head rears up. 'Christ, I hate that word!' I bark, meeting her gaze head on. Telling someone they're resilient doesn't address the trauma they've endured or the scars they still carry. It just makes it harder for them to ask for help when they need it.

Stacey frowns. 'There's no need to hate it. It means you survived. Something to be thankful for, don't you think?'

I'm already shaking my head. 'What if you survive the trauma but it destroys a part of you that doesn't come back?'

There's something in her expression that makes me regret saying this out loud. 'I think we need to work on your positivity levels,' she comments.

There's a pause. I'm starting to revise my original impression of Stacey. She's more of a ball-breaker than I remember. No puppet to provide a distraction, just straight for the jugular.

'The last time we met you said you weren't ready to talk

about Gary Walsh's murder. Do you feel able to talk to me about it today?'

'Do I have to?' I want to co-operate but I'm not sure I'm ready to go that far, to delve that deeply.

She looks through my file as she formulates her answer. 'No. Not today if you don't want to. But I think it will help you present a more positive case to the parole board if you can demonstrate that you've re-examined your actions from the night he was killed, that the woman you are today would make different choices.'

'I told them that at my last hearing!' I say irritably.

She works her jaw as she skim-reads the content until she finds what she's looking for. 'I've been reading through the statement you gave at the time. I made a couple of notes to keep me on the right track,' she explains.

I nod cautiously, fearful of what she's found.

'In the transcript of your meeting with the parole board two years ago, you stated you weren't sorry that Gary was dead.'

I'm not. I smile tightly. If she's waiting for me to jump in and contradict her, she'll have a long wait.

Long before Gary died, I'd begun to regret the way I'd shape-shifted my siblings' memories. Shielding Hope and Clem from their past made their childhood seem bearable rather than shocking, bringing with it the trapdoor of being too trusting, unable to see people for what they were. As the eldest, the ordeal of our childhood stayed with me, like a shadow I could never outrun, no matter how hard I tried.

I knew Gary meant danger the moment I saw him. I could smell it on his skin. Hope, however, my sweet little sister who'd grown up surrounded by people she could trust, thought he was wonderful.

I look up at the ceiling, contemplating how much I can say, how much I need to hold back. Satisfied, I look Stacey dead in the eye. 'It goes without saying that I regret what I did. I thought the panel understood that. In relation to what I said, one of them asked me a direct question which I answered, pardon me for being honest.' I click my tongue against the roof of my mouth. 'Anyway, that's not the reason my application was turned down. They rejected it because Alice Maltby ended up in a coma...' The words trail off in my throat. My head's a jumble of things I'd like to say but can't. Trying to explain my past is like trying to push a heavy boulder uphill. I kick the table with my foot.

Stacey doesn't react but I can tell from her frown that she's processing what I've said. 'You're dealing with a lot of unresolved issues, Mercy, you're bound to be overwhelmed by it all. It's why I'm going to propose another appointment. That way you'll have time to reflect on today's discussion.'

Grilling, more like. I slump back in my chair, shoulders dipped.

'How about we meet this time next week?'

She clicks her pen open and enters the details of our next appointment into the shared diary with a flourish before adding it to her own. She clicks the pen closed and places it on the desk behind her, along with my file. I notice that when she slips her watch back on it hangs loose about her wrist, as though she's lost weight but hasn't had it adjusted as she doesn't trust it'll stay off. I wonder what that says about *her* positivity levels. She moves to the door and opens it. I stand quickly, causing the room to tilt. I meet her gaze and smile.

'I hope that was helpful?' she says, and I nod because she expects it.

CHAPTER THIRTEEN

It's times like this when it would be great to return to the solitude of a single cell. To burrow into my bunk and forget every excruciating minute of my session with Stacey.

Vonnie knows about my appointment and she'll have one eye fixed on me for the rest of the evening if I don't spill my guts, but I can't cope with more questions right now. I need time on my own to construct a version of events that I'm happy to share. I'm still smarting about what I said about Vonnie not being my friend. I feel like Judas. I wish I could have the conversation start over so I could say how I really feel.

If this session was supposed to make me feel better it's failed. Instead, I'm left reeling inside, like I've been made to sit through a film of my life where every disaster scene is played out in slow motion.

Here's the part where my parents neglect me. *Boom.*

Here's the part where I get bounced around foster care. *Boom.*

Here's the part where I tell the parole board I'm glad Gary Walsh is dead. *Double boom.*

Each scene examined in glorious Technicolor before Stacey

moves on to the next, like a talk show host interviewing a celebrity about an autobiography they've got coming out: *After the break we'll talk about the mother of five you put into a coma and take a close-up look at that nasty scar on your wrist.*

It's dinnertime association and the others are gathered round our table, eating. Tanya takes one look at me and instead of calling out her usual greeting, raises an eyebrow discreetly. That woman can read me like a book.

'Shove up,' Lola says to Debs, who shuffles along the bench to make room for me. I feel their eyes searching my face for a clue to my mood, but I have nothing to give them.

'Nah, think I'll get a bit of shut-eye,' I say without slowing down.

'You okay?' Tanya mouths and I give her a slow blink.

'I'll bring you a plate,' Vonnie calls after me.

'What she needs right now is space,' Tanya says with authority, her gaze following me to my door.

Once in my cell, I run through my checking ritual: *cutlery, mugs, mattress, table. Chairs, heating pipes, shelves. Torn photograph,* which now resides beside my pillow. I bypass the mirror and drop onto my bunk before using the remote control to switch on the TV. There's a property show on that Vonnie likes. People feign interest in buying a home in the sun so they can bag themselves a free holiday. I hop through the channels, settling on a film about American gangsters. I turn the volume up loud, and lift the pillow over my face. I wait for the shooting to start before I scream into it.

When I wake up the TV is off and Vonnie is leaning over me like an avenging urban angel. 'I brought you some curry pie. It's disgusting, but you've got to eat.' She points to a bundle on the table, wrapped up in foil.

'What time is it?' I ask, my eyes adjusting to the darkness.

'Gone midnight. You were spark out when I got back despite Al Pacino doing his worst.'

One of the chairs has been turned towards my bunk, Vonnie's tatty quilt draped over it. 'You slept there?'

'I wanted to keep an eye on you.'

My throat feels sore, like I've been swallowing stones. I push myself into a sitting position.

'Here,' she says, handing me a mug of cold camomile tea. 'I can re-boil the kettle if you like?'

I shake my head, finishing the drink in a couple of gulps.

She takes the mug from me and places it on the table. 'How about the pie?' she asks.

'Maybe later.' I smile stiffly. I find it hard to accept her kindness. 'I'm sorry, Von,' I say, barely able to look at her.

'It's only a pie. If you don't want it, I'll have it with my breakfast in the morning. I can eat what I like now I'm not worried about what Wayne thinks.'

I glance at the wall and catch my breath. My torn photo has been repaired and returned to its rightful place. Vonnie follows my gaze and laughs sheepishly. 'I persuaded one of the glue sniffers on Magda's wing to help out. You can barely see the join,' she says proudly.

Having another person do something for me is an alien concept. I didn't ask my teachers for help when I went to school hungry for fear of being disloyal to my parents. I didn't beg to be adopted along with Hope and Clem because I thought their childhood was more important than mine. I've never known what it's like to have my needs put first, let alone met. I find strength in being the giver, not the recipient. 'Von, I don't know what to say,' I mumble.

'Forget it.'

'No, I can't, and I'm so sorry for what I put you through...

when you found me that day. It must have been awful.' I look at her and feel a sadness I've never allowed myself.

Vonnie places a hand on her chest as it dawns on her what I'm talking about. 'Oh, Mercy, it was horrible! There was so much blood, and your face, it had gone all waxy.'

I can barely look her in the eye. 'What did you do?'

'I hit the buzzer and screamed at the screws for help, told them you properly needed it *now*, not in half an hour when one of them could be bothered to get off their lazy arse. I wrapped a towel around your wrist and held your arm over your head like you see them do on those TV dramas. I kept telling you that you'd be okay.'

She saved my life. Gave me the biggest gift anyone could, and I'd never thanked her.

I drop my head into my hands, too ashamed to look at her. 'I told that psychologist we weren't friends, Von. I'm so sorry!' I blurt. 'She was getting on my nerves, kept trying to get me to talk about things I didn't want to.' I hold out my wrist. 'Things like this.' I take a breath. 'She said how hard it must have been for you to find me like that but I didn't want to hear it, yet what you did for me that day was immense. I can never repay it, and I can never take away what you saw when you walked in on me like that, and for that I'm truly sorry.'

Vonnie moves my hands and lifts my chin so that I look at her. 'You told me once, when I first padded up with you, that other people's opinions of us are none of our business. I didn't understand what you meant at first, but I get it now. It's something I still need to work on but maybe you do too. Other people's opinions *don't* matter. I don't give a fuck what that psychologist does or doesn't know about our friendship, all I know is that you've had my back from the moment I arrived here. That day when I helped you, well, just for once, I had yours.'

Sometimes nothing more needs to be said. When I reach for the curry pie and split it with Von, we eat it in silence.

CHAPTER FOURTEEN

Tanya's animated at breakfast. She's holding court around the table but I'm unable to tune in. Vonnie and I sit either side of her, sluggish. It's been a long night. We stayed up until the early hours, until Vonnie could no longer keep her eyes open and I insisted she turn in. 'You don't need to worry about me,' I assured her. 'That awful moment was literally that. A moment in time.' I fixed her with a look so she knew that I meant it, and I did. If I truly regret anything in my life, it's the day I tried to end it.

I push the watery scrambled egg around my plate and take a slug of my coffee. 'Whoa, slow down, Tan, what's got you all bent out of shape?'

'I was telling the girls about this yesterday, Mercy–'

'A new supplier's flooding the prison with dodgy gear!' Lola informs me in a stage whisper.

'How do you know?' I address this question to Tanya, who's our official narcotics correspondent.

'I heard a couple of the screws talking. They spun the cells in block five last week and thought they'd hit the jackpot with the amount of brown they found. They did it again last night and found even more.'

'That never happens,' says Lola.

'Why's that?' asks Debs.

We all wait for Tanya to elaborate. 'Everyone knows some of the screws are in cahoots with the dealers. It stands to reason. Normally when these searches are carried out, they don't find anything because they've already tipped them off – the dealers move their stock until it's safe to bring it back.'

Which made it all the more galling when that heroin was found in my cell. It had been planted deliberately to take the attention away from the real culprit, but why not plant it behind the shower cubicles or the dining area or some other public place? Leaving it to be found in my cell – and therefore forcing me to take the blame for it – felt malicious.

'Now the searches are turning up gear it suggests someone new is bringing it in. Someone who isn't greasing the right palms yet,' Tanya concludes.

'Christ, who'd be daft enough to do that?' asks Lola.

I look at Vonnie sharply. *Wayne?*

She shakes her head a fraction but Lola catches it. 'What?' she demands.

Vonnie leans forward in her seat. 'Wayne told me recently that he was going to start dealing. Reckoned it'd be a one-off.'

'That's how everyone starts,' cautions Tanya.

'That's why I broke up with him. He isn't capable of running any sort of business on his own. He'd want me involved one way or another.'

'I bet he would,' Tanya chimes. 'All the better if you could have flogged it for him in 'ere.'

'You think that's what he was planning?' Vonnie's looking at me for confirmation that he was gormless, not manipulative.

From where I'm sitting, she'd have got her fingers burned either way.

'Water under the bridge, anyway, Von,' I tell her. 'He's part of your history now.'

Drugs in prison are a real problem, in fact the two go hand in hand. So many women come through those gates already addicts, like Tanya, committing crimes to feed their habit, their man's habit, or to line their pimp's pockets. Tanya is one of the lucky ones, despite the detox wing here not being large enough to accommodate proper rehabilitation, she's free from the pull of heroin. For so many other addicts the only option is to keep on using whatever they can get their hands on, which means drugs need to be smuggled in. On some days you can't walk ten yards without the smell of cannabis wafting out of someone's cell to greet you. In truth, it suits a lot of the officers for the women to carry on with their habit. It makes their job easier when everyone's medicated.

'According to the spice guzzlers in this block, this new stuff's potent,' Tanya informs us, serious-faced.

Vonnie's eyes widen. 'That's saying something, coming from them.'

'I know.'

'You get so high you'll need moon boots, I heard,' adds Lola, never one to be outdone. It's good to see her back on form. I hope the problems with her parents have worked themselves out.

Tanya frowns. 'The purer this gear is, the more dangerous it is. I'm going to speak to some of the other girls. Warn them not to go near it.'

I understand her alarm. The stress and boredom in prison, combined with peer pressure, is enough to make even non-users give in to temptation, never mind those trying to stay clean.

Even so. I give up on my scrambled egg and push my plate away. ‘Careful, Tan. You don’t want to go stepping on anyone’s toes. Especially when we don’t know who they belong to.’

Tanya’s having none of it. ‘We know some of the dealers, though! Magda and her crew have been supplying drugs round here for years, I could start by having a word with her.’

‘Like she’s going to listen to anything you’ve got to say? Just leave it!’ My tone is sharper than I intend. My parents’ addiction underpins every aspect of my childhood, and I suppose, everything that came after. It’s hard for me to be objective around drugs, which is what makes my friendship with Tanya all the more remarkable. I suppose it’s the fact she didn’t succumb to it. Once she saw how her family had been fractured because of her habit she fought it every step of the way and won, whereas my parents didn’t care enough about us to try. Tanya’s kids are adults now, but it’s not too late for her to build a relationship with them once she gets out. Drugs make addicts selfish but the Tanya I know is one of the most considerate people around.

‘I can’t ignore what’s going on, Mercy,’ says Tanya, defensive. ‘But I won’t go in all guns blazing, if that’s what you’re worried about.’

‘Who’s got visitors today?’ Vonnie asks, changing the subject. Now Wayne is out of the picture her parents have said they’ll come and see her, something she’d almost given up on.

‘I’m seeing my brief today if that counts,’ I tell her. ‘I’ve told Clem to hang fire for a while, put his energy into supporting Hope. Last thing he needs is to run round after me as well.’

‘How’s she doing?’ asks Tanya.

‘She has good days and bad days. The girls are trying to come to terms with it all but it’s a lot for anyone to take in.’

Tanya reaches across the table and grips my hand. ‘You’ll

soon be with them, doll, mark my words. I'm just glad you found out in time to kickstart the parole process again. And look, about that trip, I don't expect you to keep to it now you've got other things on your plate.'

'You're going no matter what!' I say sternly. 'I might not be able to tag along, though, we'll have to see how it goes.'

'I'll go if you can fit me in your suitcase!' says Vonnie, her arms are at right angles as she laughs. Already she's taking up more room, claiming her space in the world. Leaving Wayne was the making of her.

Lola nudges Debs. 'We'll come if you've got room for two more, won't we?' she offers. 'I could bring Danny!' Her face brightens at the prospect.

'I take it you're back on track with your parents?' I ask.

Suddenly she looks pensive. 'They're both coming in to see me today. I'm not sure if that's a good sign or not.'

'I'm sure it'll be fine,' I say, getting to my feet. 'My brief wants to start prepping for the panel hearing,' I tell them, trying to sound more confident than I feel.

Tanya gives me a thumbs-up. 'It'll be a formality this time, doll, just you wait and see.'

Liam is already seated in the legal visits room when I arrive. He stands to greet me when I walk in, ever the gentleman. He's put weight on since his last visit and it suits him, makes him look jolly. He asks for an update on Hope's condition and I'm grateful when he doesn't add any pitying platitudes.

'Ready to say good riddance to this place?' he asks. I notice that his scalp ripples when he smiles.

'Won't be a day too soon,' I say in reply.

He looks at me. 'There's something different about you,' he says, studying my face.

'Yeah, I asked my stylist to put in a couple of highlights,' I deadpan, touching my hair.

He shakes his head. 'I'm being serious. I've been worried about you. You look much better than I was expecting.'

I look away in case he notices the flush creeping up my neck. 'I was in a state the last time you saw me,' I remind him.

'I know, but even so…'

'I've got a good group of girls in here. They've spent the last few weeks holding me up, only I didn't realise that's what they were doing. Turns out we all need a helping hand at times, the hardest part is learning to accept it.'

'Is that why you're keen for me to see this Debbie?' Liam asks, making me wonder once more if he's telepathic.

I nod. 'Imagine only being able to see your kids at an appointed pre-booked slot. That's assuming her ex doesn't play dirty and forgets to turn up.'

He listens, solemn-faced, while I tell him what I know. 'It might not sound like much to you, Mercy, but posting those messages about him online was a serious breach of restrictions. The law takes this offence seriously. Evidence given in family court proceedings must be heard in private to protect the interests and confidentiality of the children. It can't be leaked into the public domain.'

'She realises that now.' I hope he has something more positive to say to Debs than that. Maybe my idea about him representing her wasn't such a good one after all. 'She knows she dug herself into a hole. What I want to know is, is there any way she can claw herself out of it?'

Liam considers my question. 'The best she can hope for is to appeal the conviction by apologising to the court and promising to remove the offending material from the internet.'

'Do you think you can help her with this?'

He sighs heavily. 'I don't know.'

'I know you can't say anything to me because of all that client confidentiality bollocks.'

He throws me a knowing look. 'She's not my client, Mercy. I'm just going to have a chat with her.'

'But you might consider it?'

He studies me as though looking for my 'off' switch. 'I've no idea. I'll need to find out about her financial situation.'

'I can help. Financially, I mean. Clem's made some shrewd investments for me while I've been inside. I'd be happy to help out if I can. She doesn't need to know about it. In fact, it'd be better if she didn't.'

He looks sceptical. 'Are you sure you can take on something like that?'

'I've managed paying your fees, haven't I? Though I'll be expecting a hefty discount for referring a friend.'

He shakes his head and sighs.

Is it me or do we resemble a bickering married couple? I wonder, pushing the thought to one side.

'Let's just see how it goes, agreed?' he says gravely. 'I'm not making any promises.'

'Cheers, Liam,' I say, keeping my smile in check.

'Now to the main point of business.' He opens his briefcase, pulls out a manila file and places it on the desk between us. He opens it and glances at a letter, the contents of which he knows off by heart.

'We have a date,' he tells me, pleased with himself. 'The hearing's in two weeks' time. Do you feel ready?'

Ready to convince a panel of strangers that I'm a different person when I'm not? I sit back in my seat and give the prospect some thought.

'I've been seeing that psychologist again.'

'Is everything okay?'

I'm touched by his concern and nod to reassure him. 'Yeah, apparently the doc won't sign off my medical report until I've completed an assessment.'

'Is it helping?'

I pull a face. 'Not really. It's churning things up I'd rather forget.'

'But if it means you're more prepared for the parole hearing, then it's a good thing, isn't it?'

I shrug. 'I hope so. Look, Liam, this will be my third rodeo. Isn't it a sign of madness to keep doing the same thing over and over and expect a different result?'

'Think of it as third time lucky.' He beams at me.

'I was hoping for something more encouraging than leaving it to chance,' I tell him scornfully.

I lean forward and rest my elbows on the table. 'If Gary Walsh was alive today, Hope would be dead, her twin girls nothing more than a due date on a calendar that never arrived. I'm not sure how Clem would have coped with that. Me either, for that matter. Hope and Clem's welfare, their happiness, has always been my responsibility, even when it wasn't, after the Caplans adopted them. Everything I did, I did with their security in mind.'

'That much was evident from the first time we met. The fact that you refused to have them give evidence–'

'No point, was there?' I cut in. 'Since I was pleading guilty.'

'Contrary to my advice, you pleaded guilty to murder rather than manslaughter. The judge had no choice but to hand down a life sentence.'

'He was lenient with the tariff though.'

Liam leans back in his chair and makes a barking sound that I've come to recognise as his laugh. 'You know, Mercy, in all my years in this godforsaken job, not one of my lifers has ever said that to me.'

'Then there's a first time for everything,' I tell him, enjoying the moment.

There's tension in our block. I feel the electricity of it as I move along the corridor, see the excitement on several women's faces as they huddle in their groups. I look for someone I trust enough to tell me what's happened. A mousy woman in dungarees catches my eye.

'What's going on?' I ask.

'Surprised you don't know. That mate of yours had a run-in with Magda. She started it by the look of it, although Magda had the last word, you know how it goes.'

I don't like the sound of that one little bit. I need to check that Tanya's okay. 'Where are they now?' I ask her quickly.

'Back in their cells. The screws came and broke it up. Told everyone to back off or we'd be put on lockdown.' No one wants to miss out on their precious association time. Tanya doesn't have a pad-mate so seeks out company whenever she can, says it stops the demons messing with her head. I set off to her cell to find out what the run-in was about, though I've a damn good idea.

I knock on Tanya's door briefly before pushing it open. 'Tan–' I call out, her name catching in my throat when she turns to face me. There's a cut on her cheekbone, the kind you get if you've been punched by someone wearing a knuckleduster.

'What the hell?'

'It's okay, you should see the other woman,' she says, but we both know that's not true. Magda won't let anyone get the better of her.

'Christ, Tan, what happened?'

'I had a word with Magda.'

'I can see that much.'

'I asked her if she had any idea who was bringing that new gear in.' She shrugs.

'And?'

'She punched me.'

'Just like that?'

She throws me a look and I realise that that's exactly what Magda would do. 'She told me to stay out of her lane, whatever that means.'

'You know what it means, Tan. I told you not to go meddling.'

'She's not as innocent as she's making out.'

'None of us are.'

I pick up a flannel that's drying on the heating pipe and rinse it under the cold-water tap. I wring it out then fold it before placing it on her cheek. 'That should help with the swelling.' I glance at the back of her hands as she holds the towel in place. No knuckle damage that would have shown she put up a fight. 'You must be getting old, girl. You're definitely losing your touch.'

Tanya eyes me. 'I'm not that daft. Magda fights dirty. If I'd touched a single hair on her head all her cronies would have piled on.'

'Promise me you're going to leave well alone now.'

Tanya winces when I playfully press the towel down on her cheek. 'Guess my bones *are* getting older. My body can't take the knocks like they used to. Don't want to hobble out of here an invalid.'

'Especially when you've got two weeks in the sun to look forward to... Now, I need you to hold on tight to that while I go back to my cell.' I place her hand over the flannel as I back away.

'Association time isn't over yet.'

'No, but there's something I need to do first.'

Magda's cell is recognisable by the number of minions she has keeping guard outside it. Inconsequential women on the outside but in here, on Magda's coat-tails, they're women to be reckoned with. As I approach the cell door one of them tries to block my entrance. I shove her away. Two more women step forward. I hold my ground.

'Let her in,' Magda's thick Eastern European accent orders from within her pit. The women fall away at her bidding.

'Like what you've done to the place,' I say, scanning her cell as I step inside. The interior is immaculate. Besides looking mean and intimidating, her minions do her cleaning and laundry. If there's a Tripadvisor rating for prison cells, this would be a full five stars.

Magda is in her sixties, heavy built with long grey hair that she wears up in a bun. Pink cheeked with a double chin, she looks like a doting grandma rather than a con with gangland connections spanning the north of England. Serving a ten stretch for money laundering on a massive scale, she now runs a lucrative jail-based trade in non-prescription pharmaceuticals and telecommunications, or drugs and fanny phones to her regulars.

She's seated at a small table playing cards with Lena, a woman she sleeps with on and off. The woman's head is shaved and sits on her shoulders as though it sprouted there without a neck to support it. She has two sleeves of tattoos, each sporting the name of prisons she's served time in: Bronzefield, Downview, Holloway, and York, amongst others. I wonder if she's given thought to where Fairmile will go.

'Leave us,' Magda says, dismissing her. We wait while Lena gathers up the cards then pockets them, murmuring something in self-taught Ukrainian that has them both smirking.

'No prizes for guessing why you're here,' Magda says, kicking the leg of the vacated seat opposite her. An invitation for me to sit.

I take my time.

'I thought you and me had a deal,' I say to her.

CHAPTER FIFTEEN

Magda fixes me with a look. 'I agreed not to sell your friend any of my merchandise. I never said anything about not punching her face in.' Her Eastern European accent falls away when she doesn't have an audience. Her speech is a hybrid of Mancunian and Liverpudlian, a result of growing up on several notorious estates during her formative years.

I throw my arms wide. 'What the hell, Magda? What did Tanya even do to you?'

'She came over here shouting her mouth off. I wasn't having that.' Her eyes narrow into mean little slits. 'Anyway, what are you going to do about it?'

'So we're back in the playground now?' I ask her.

'You'll be in the infirmary if you don't watch your mouth.'

'Is that how we're playing it?' I push myself up and lean over the table so our faces are inches apart. 'You owe me,' I remind her. 'And don't you forget it.'

Alice Maltby's face looms between us.

'How many times have I got to say it? I didn't know that mad bitch was going to go off her head,' says Magda, defensively. 'She was the one who came to me, remember, banging on the cell door, begging for something to make her forget what she'd done. I was only too happy to oblige.' She shrugs. *Caveat emptor*.

'Happy to oblige? She came away with a crack smoker's starter kit: a makeshift pipe and enough rocks to make her think the Martians had landed.'

In the lead up to *the incident*, Alice Maltby had been seen lurking outside Magda's cell on a regular basis. 'The only reason I didn't tell the governor who supplied those drugs to her was I knew there'd be no point. If she hadn't bought them from you, she'd have bought them from someone else.' I lost my chance of parole because of what *I* did to Maltby, not Magda.

'There you go, then.'

'Not quite. We struck a deal. In return for my silence, you promised me you wouldn't overload a first timer like that again. That from then on, you'd start new punters off on small doses, nothing more.'

'So?'

Dealers in prison have the same moral compass as dealers on the outside. Find a new punter you can turn into an addict and you've got a customer for life. Unless they overdose. The deal I'd struck with Magda was an ethical compromise. I couldn't stop the supply of – or the demand for – drugs in here, but I could at least persuade her to make sure the amounts doled out were safe. This new supplier that Tanya has heard about threatens to derail that equilibrium.

'I'm a great believer in keeping my enemies close, Magda. Only there's a rumour going round there's a new supplier muscling their way in. Selling gear that's off the scale.'

Magda shrugs.

'I'm surprised. I thought you'd have put the kybosh on it before it got started. You must be slipping in your old age.'

'It's a free market economy.'

I snort out a laugh. 'That's bollocks and you know it. During your time here you've stamped on every bit of competition that reared its ugly head, so don't give me any crap about live and let live. That approach isn't in your wheelhouse.'

Magda looks thoughtful for a minute. She gets up to check the minions waiting outside aren't so close to her door they can hear what's being discussed behind it. She drops back into her seat. 'I swear I don't know who's bringing this stuff in, Mercy. And, you're right, whoever's selling it has got a brass neck on them, doing it under my nose.'

I look at her, incredulous. 'You really haven't got a clue, have you? What about the con who's shifting the gear once it's brought in?'

She shakes her head. 'I truly don't know. If I did, don't you think I'd have done something about it?'

I don't doubt it for a minute.

'Look, it's bad enough that someone's undercutting me right under my nose, never mind that no one's willing to squeal on them. First thing I did when I heard about it was speak to the screw that brings my stuff in, but they claimed they had no idea who it was. I wasn't impressed by their answer, I won't lie to you. I expected the couple of grand a month they shake out of me to include intel. They reckoned breaking the law and being on a dealer's payroll isn't a topic of discussion in the staffroom.'

'They could have a point,' I concede. I give her a sly look. 'I don't suppose you'd tell me who this puppet of yours is? Whoever it is, they strung me up good and proper with that block of smack.' What I wouldn't give to settle that score.

It's as though Magda can read my mind. 'Sorry, Mercy,' she says, sounding anything but. 'I've got to protect my livelihood. It's tough for me as well, you know.' Ignoring the look I throw at her, she ploughs on regardless. 'It's hard commanding respect when someone out there is undermining me. I've been doing my best to downplay it. Your mate stomping over here shouting the odds didn't help matters. What could I do? Admit in front of half the block that someone's running rings round me or slap her to shut her up?'

'I can see your dilemma.'

My sarcasm is lost on her. 'There you go, then. She left me no choice.'

Magda may be part of the problem, but within these walls she's also part of the solution. I shake my head, like a disappointed teacher. 'I'm trusting you to make sure what happened to Maltby never happens again. You need to dig a little deeper. I want you to find out who's behind this stuff coming in before someone overdoses.'

'And then what?'

I haven't got an answer for that yet. I push myself to my feet. 'Let's find out who it is first. Then we can put our heads together.'

A grin stretches across her face as she looks me up and down. 'I like the sound of that.'

'In your dreams,' I tell her. Besides, despite her flirting, she and Lena are the real deal.

I pause in the doorway. 'And I can tell Tanya you don't bear her any grudges?'

The sound of a vibrating phone fills the air, causing a smutty grin to spread across Magda's face.

'Whatever,' she says, shoving her hand into her jogging bottoms to retrieve it.

The alarm bell peels out, signalling the end of association as I head back to my cell. The landing is crowded as inmates gather in last-minute huddles before being locked up for the night.

'Thought you didn't mix in dubious circles,' snipes a gravelly voice behind me.

I slow my pace so that Officer Frame draws level. 'It wasn't a social call,' I tell her.

'I figured as much, given I dragged your skanky mate out of there earlier, kicking and screaming the odds. So, was that you throwing a warning flare over Magda's bows? *Go near her again and I'll pull your hair out.*' She coughs up a laugh. 'You tough girls are so *mean*.'

We're out of view of the security cameras thanks to the inmates jostling around us. I reward Frame with a full beam stare before shoulder slamming her into the wall. 'Only when riled,' I hiss into her ear. 'And this is for damaging my property,' I add, jabbing her in the ribs. 'I really wouldn't advise you to do it again.'

Grimacing, she reaches for her radio then thinks better of it. 'I'll take that. But if I were you, I'd keep a lookout over that shoulder of yours,' she hisses back.

CHAPTER SIXTEEN

'Hey, Mercy! Over here!' Debs is looking brighter than I've seen her for days. She's sitting at our table, tucking into her lunch along with Tanya. 'I've just had a call from Mr Douglas.'

It takes me a few seconds to register who she's talking about when I realise she means Liam. I can't remember the last time I called my solicitor Mister anything. I look at her beaming face and can see that whatever he had to say has cheered her up no end. 'He's agreed to represent me. And not only that, Mercy, he's waived his fee. Can you believe that?'

'Top man,' I say, meaning it.

I walk over to the serving hatch and collect my lunch. It's Friday so it's battered fish and chips that look like they've been through the fryer several times.

Vonnie and Lola arrive at our table carrying their food trays. They've come straight from the visitor centre. Vonnie is animated, suggesting her visit went well. 'My dad says I can move back in with them when I leave here. At least that's one less thing to worry about. All I need now is to find a job...'

Suddenly hungry, I tuck into my lunch as I listen to everyone's suggestions of how Vonnie can earn a living that doesn't involve shoving packs of meat down the front of her hoody. It's only as I scrape my plate clean that I realise Lola isn't joining in.

I turn away from the others so that I can speak to her discreetly. 'Your parents' visit didn't go so well, then?'

'Something like that.' She's been pushing a lump of batter around her plate with a fork. She gives up, dropping the fork onto her plate.

'You okay?' I ask.

'Not hungry,' she mutters, getting to her feet.

Tanya glances up as Lola leaves the table, a worried expression on her face. 'Something's bothering that girl but she won't talk to me about it. Has she spoken to any of you?'

Debs and Vonnie shake their heads.

'I'll go and see if she's all right.' I get to my feet, chiding myself for not keeping an eye on her. I've been preoccupied with Hope, haven't paid as much attention to Lola as I would have liked.

Tanya places a hand on my arm. 'Let Vonnie go. She's closest in age, Lola might be willing to open up to her.' I nod in agreement before returning to my seat. Tanya turns to Vonnie. 'Off you pop, doll. Go and see what's up with her.'

Vonnie looks up, surprised, but does as she's told.

I wait until Vonnie has left the table. 'Hark at you, barking orders.' I turn towards Tanya in time to catch a look pass between her and Debs. 'What's going on?' It's my turn to bark.

'Go on, then, ask her,' Tanya says, widening her eyes.

I look at Debs expectantly.

'It was something you mentioned the other day,' she says, reddening. 'About that woman attacking you.'

'She means Alice Maltby,' Tanya says pointedly, as though there's a line of women who've taken lumps out of me during my time here.

'I asked Tanya what happened but she said I needed to ask you – I know it's got nothing to do with me,' Debs adds quickly, saving me the trouble.

I regard her. 'Why do you want to know?'

'Because you said that was the reason you lost out on parole. It doesn't seem fair.'

I look at her and realise we've inhabited two different worlds if she believes in the concept of fairness. The look Tanya throws me says she's thinking the same thing. 'I told her it was your story to tell, Mercy, not mine. I'm going to leave you to it, mind. No one wants an audience.'

I watch Tanya as she makes her way towards our wing.

'You don't have to tell me anything,' Debs reminds me.

'I know.' It'd do no harm to get the details right in my head, I reason. Especially since Stacey Sheridan's hell-bent on dissecting every aspect of my life.

I take a deep breath. Blow it out. Decide to fill Debs in as best I can.

'The governor thought moving Alice in with me would help her integration into the prison. In case you haven't worked it out yet, Governor Cassidy is a piece of work. When it suits her, she claims I'm a good influence, and on this occasion she claimed it so loudly even I believed it.' I smile wryly. 'Mistake number one. Plus, there was the not insignificant incentive of getting parole on the back of it if I did as she asked. So in theory it was a win–win, or at least that's how I was sold it.'

'What was Alice's opinion on this?'

I widen my eyes at her. 'You see, that's a brilliant question!' One that I hadn't had the temerity to ask at the time. If I had, and the answer had been forthcoming, then all that came after might not have been so shocking.

Debs angles her head, waiting.

'Alice was apparently fine with sharing a cell with me, in fact it had been her idea.'

'How was that possible?'

I shrug. 'Killing her children had put her in the public eye. Whether the governor liked it or not, Alice Maltby was high profile. Every decision made about her would be scrutinised. That was a lot of pressure for the staff. When her lawyer arranged a meeting with the prison management team to discuss safety arrangements during her sentence, they were caught with their trousers down, as no special arrangements had been put in place. Cue headless chickens. After all, Alice was deemed one hell of a trophy for violent inmates. Then she pipes up that yours truly had been nice to her during her induction. So nice, in fact, that she was confident she'd feel much safer if we shared a cell.'

'No good turn goes unpunished,' remarks Debs.

'Got it in one.'

'So there I was, rueing the day I'd ever said hi to her, while trying to keep up my end of the bargain.'

'Did Alice tell you padding up together had been her suggestion?'

'Oh yeah, she was really proud about it. Couldn't resist flaunting that she had the governor's ear. Reckoned Cassidy would do anything to keep her happy. She'd drip feed it into every conversation, like she was waiting for some sort of reaction, a challenge even, so she could demonstrate all over again how much sway she had.'

'She wasn't interested in endearing herself to you, then?'

I shake my head. 'No, she wasn't.'

'What was she like with everyone else?'

I think about this. 'It was a while before she had any direct contact with other prisoners. The women on the block were livid she was here but were powerless to do anything – other than set upon her in the shower cubicles. For that reason, for the first couple of weeks she was let out of our cell to take showers when everyone else was locked up. She ate in the cell too. The POs would drop off cereal boxes and sandwiches in the morning, and a hot meal later on. After a while she started venturing out and would come and sit with me and Tan. Our presence was enough for the others to leave her alone. As long as we were with her, she was fine. Everyone hated her though. I mean, after what she did, how could you not?'

Debs nods in agreement.

'The atmosphere changed during Alice Maltby's time here. Each prison block has its own eco-system and tempers on ours flared more quickly, fights got nastier. It took a few stilted weeks for me to work out how to live around her. We occupied the same space but I made sure to keep her out of my head. Even so, she wouldn't stop pestering me about my life. "C'mon, stop being coy, not like you don't know why I'm here," she'd taunt.

'Something about her was off. The way she spoke to me... it was like she already knew the answers to the questions she was asking, you know?'

Debs' nod is slower this time.

I try to explain. 'She kept asking about the man I killed.'

Debs places her hand over her mouth. We're in uncharted territory. I've never discussed the circumstances surrounding Gary Walsh's death with her and she knows better than to ask.

I close my eyes, recalling how Alice had bombarded me with questions:

'You killed the owner of that bar, didn't you?' she'd asked out of the blue one day.

'Well if you know so much about it, why are you asking?' I'd answered.

She'd just grinned.

Sometimes when she spoke to me she stared off into the

distance, but behind that glazed expression, a lot was going on. I thought of what she'd done to her children and tried not to second guess her.

'The following evening, lights out, we were in our bunks when she'd piped up, "I used to go in there drinking".'

I knew how calculating she was. How she didn't make a move without working out the consequences. She was playing me but sometimes it was impossible not to take the bait.

'Sorry, Alice, did you say something?' I didn't want to make it easy for her.

'I used to go in that bar. The one owned by the fella you killed.'

Call it pride, but she finally caught me on her hook. 'Gary didn't own the bar, I did,' I snapped. I pictured her eyes, gleaming in the darkness.

'He used to own it though, back in the day.'

'A long time ago, yeah.'

There'd been a pause. 'Rumour had it he ran up gambling debts. Got in over his head, which is why he had to sell.'

I considered my answer. 'That sounds about right.'

I sensed her satisfaction. 'You caused quite a stir when you rocked up and bought him out. A dolly bird like you.'

She really was intent on pushing my buttons. 'I was no dolly bird, love. I was a fully experienced bar manager.' I'd worked in the licensed trade since I was old enough to drink. Had worked my way up the ladder in several pub chains across Manchester, putting money aside for an opportunity just like this one. Something niggled away at me. I'd bought the bar nineteen years ago. Either she'd done her research on me, or she knew me back then. I certainly didn't remember her.

'Then you went and kept him on,' she said.

'That's me, love. I'm all heart.'

'Even though he was a scumbag.'

'You're preaching to the choir there.'

She went quiet for a couple of minutes and I thought, or rather hoped, she'd fallen asleep.

'Know where I can get any gear?' she'd asked, out of the blue.

'What the hell...' I hadn't been expecting that. 'I don't do drugs, Alice,' I'd replied patiently. 'Now if you don't mind, I need my beauty sleep.' I'd thought that would put an end to this odd conversation.

'Sure you've not got anything to take the edge off?'

'You're starting to do my head in, Alice. Go to sleep.'

She made a sound like a witch's cackle. 'I know about that heroin.' She sounded smug. 'So stop acting like you don't know where to go if you want to score.'

I hissed out a line of expletives. Only a couple of weeks in and someone had been gossiping with her, all too happy to dish the dirt on me, no matter whether it was true or not. I felt betrayed. 'For your information someone planted that stuff in here!' I said sharply. 'A word to the wise. Don't believe everything you hear inside.'

And that's when she said it. The calculated comment she damn well knew would grind my gears.

'I've got no idea what you're on about. I don't know about anything that happened in here. I'm talking about your bar. The one you bought from Gary. About the heroin stashed there the day you killed him.'

When I open my eyes, Debs is still looking at me, her hand returned to her side as she waits for me to carry on. I decide to give her the edited highlights:

'I reckoned Alice was trying to goad me into a reaction. I thought she recognised me from news reports at the time and decided she'd have a bit of fun at my expense. Unbeknown to me, she'd never wanted to serve her time in prison. She'd already put in a request to transfer to a psychiatric hospital. Of course, I didn't find that out until later, when the... *incident* got into the papers.'

Child Killer Rushed To Hospital After Attack By Cellmate

'If I'd known that, I'd have seen her game playing for what it was and certainly wouldn't have responded the way I did.' I pause. 'She started using. Said she needed something to take away the pain. That's what I didn't understand, see. The pain that tormented her was self-inflicted, no one forced her to kill her kids. I kept encouraging her to stay clean, I mean, I felt duty bound to make sure she was okay given the deal I'd made with the governor, but after a while I could see I was fighting a lost cause so I left her to it. I couldn't babysit her twenty-four seven regardless of what Governor Cassidy thought. She'd started taking crack, which really messed with her head. Then one evening, when she was high as a kite she held a home-made knife to my throat and threatened to slice my head off. Everything after that's a bit of a blur, as you can imagine. There's not much more I can tell you. One minute Governor Cassidy is standing outside my cell trying to de-escalate the situation, next minute Alice is fighting for her life. By the time the POs stormed in we both needed urgent medical attention.'

Debs nods her head vigorously, in sympathy. The alarm bell peels out, signalling the end of association. She gets to her feet. 'Do you think that's why she held you hostage? To prove to the authorities that she was still a danger to others?'

It was my turn to nod. 'I've no doubt about it. It certainly fast-tracked her transfer request. I just wish she hadn't been hell-bent on bringing me down in the process.'

I look away as I say this, so Debs can't see that I haven't told her everything.

I click the kettle on when Vonnie comes in, her expression telling me she's in need of it.

'What did Lola have to say?' I ask her, throwing an herbal teabag in her mug, then mine.

She flops into a chair and frowns. When I finish making the drinks and push hers across the table she accepts it gratefully. 'She said her parents want her to stay away. They reckon Danny's settled; they don't see any point in changing things round now just because it suits her...' Vonnie frowns.

'What?' I prompt.

'Nothing. She clammed up. Said she didn't want to get into it.'

I consider this. 'Did you see her with her parents in the visitor centre?'

Vonnie nods.

I roll my eyes impatiently. 'C'mon, Von! How did they seem? Did it get all confrontational?'

Vonnie twists her head from one side to the other as she casts her mind back. 'Not really. To be honest, it all looked very civilised. I mean, there were no raised voices or anything. Danny got a bit restless so Lola's dad took him over to the play area. I suppose, thinking about it, Lola didn't look too happy about that. Mind you, I wouldn't go near those toys if you paid me.'

'Lola didn't go with him, then?'

'No, she just sat and ate the chocolate bar her mum had bought from the kiosk. Danny's a cute kid, Mercy, but you've got to ask if maybe her folks are right. It must be hard work bringing up a child on your own, and Lola can barely take responsibility for herself, let alone anyone else.'

I take a sip of my drink and shrug, deciding it's probably

better not to get involved. In truth, I need time to organise my own thoughts and the images swirling around my head, put them in some semblance of order before my next appointment with Stacey Sheridan. The conversation with Debs has made me uneasy, bringing up awful memories that I'd thought were behind me. I blame Dr North. She was the one with a bee in her bonnet that Alice Maltby's attack was unresolved, and Stacey's insistence that we explore this during tomorrow's session is starting to weigh me down.

There were a lot of things I got wrong about Alice Maltby, yet my initial impression of her turned out to be spot on. Watching her approach the welcome desk on her first day in Fairmile I'd thought she was unremarkable, the kind of woman you didn't really notice. Which is what gave her the opportunity, it turned out, to do what she did.

CHAPTER SEVENTEEN

There's a commotion on the wing. Officers' boots echo on the landing as they respond to a call.

'Better not hold us up, I'm starving,' mutters Vonnie, running a brush through her hair as she examines her complexion in the mirror.

I pull my blanket back over my shoulders and close my eyes. 'You're always starving,' I remind her. It doesn't matter that the food we're given is disgusting; mealtimes in here are something to do, a precious activity to mark our time through the day, although part of me thinks Vonnie actually enjoys them. She moves to the cell door and puts her ear against it.

'Hear that, Mercy?' she asks.

'What?' I'm not inquisitive like Vonnie, five more minutes in Never Never Land suits me just fine.

'That's the point I'm making. The screws have stopped running. That means they must be tending to someone close by.'

My eyes snap open. I push myself into a sitting position and cock my head to listen. A young woman's yelling for sleeping pills. Her shrill voice sounds alarmingly familiar.

'Is that Lola?' Vonnie asks.

My answer falls away at the sound of grating metal. Someone is unlocking our door.

Officer Murdoch stands in the doorway with a worried frown. 'I need you to come and calm your friend down. She's been hitting her call button claiming to be ill. Now she's demanding sleeping pills. The doc's not on site today so she'll not get any meds either way.'

'Plenty out there who'll give her something to take the edge off,' I finish for him. He waits outside while I throw a sweatshirt and leggings on over the T-shirt and shorts I slept in before joining him on the landing.

Officers waiting outside Lola's cell, ready to drag her to the seg, throw a disappointed look in my direction. 'You lot can stand down,' barks Murdoch. 'I'll radio if you're needed.' He turns to me. 'If they'd gone in, she'd have ended up on report and she isn't a bad kid. Reckon you can straighten her out?'

'I'll do my best.'

He unlocks Lola's door and I step inside.

Like Tanya, Lola doesn't share a cell. I used to think having space to yourself was a good thing; I guess it depends on whether you like your own company.

Lola's pacing the floor. Two paces, turn. Two paces, turn. Two paces, turn. Not a lot of space to use up the adrenaline that's pumping through her.

'I JUST NEED SOMETHING TO HELP ME SLEEP. HOW HARD CAN THAT BE?' she yells at the door.

I put my finger to my lips. 'For Christ's sake, Lola, keep it down. Never mind seg, they'll have you on the psych ward and you don't want to end up there, believe me.'

This seems to do the trick as her ranting stops. She eyes me warily. 'Why are you here?'

'Murdoch knows we're friends. Besides, I'm a peer support worker, remember? Do I need to go back and get my vest?'

We both laugh.

'That's better,' I say, sensing the crisis that was brewing inside her has started to subside. 'Seriously, though, Lola, what's going on?'

She leans against the wall and closes her eyes. 'Why does anything have to be going on? Why do people always ask me that?'

'What do you mean? Who else has asked you that?'

She opens her eyes; her gaze fixed on the wall opposite. 'Teachers, during my last year in school when my grades started to slip. Friends, when I stopped wanting to hang out with them. Do I need to go on?'

I follow her gaze to a cluster of new photos beside her bunk. Baby photos of Danny at playschool and nursery; his little face staring down at her from the confined walls. 'I used to keep them under my mattress,' she admits.

A thought forms in my mind but I push it away. I mean, this isn't the 1960s when pregnant schoolgirls were hidden from view, sent away to stay with sympathetic aunts if they were lucky or homes for wayward girls, if they weren't. Surely that isn't what happened here? I couch my next question carefully. 'Did these teachers and friends know about Danny?'

Lola shakes her head. 'I already told you. My parents said they'd bring him up as their own.'

'Yes, but you'll have needed support during your pregnancy. I'm sure your midwife and GP were fine but it's not the same as having friends rally round, or the support of a sympathetic adult.'

Lola visibly pales. 'Mum gave me all the help I needed. She's a nurse.' She stumbles over her words and while she answers me, I've been doing the maths. Danny is four years old.

'You had him during the pandemic, didn't you?' I study her closely. 'While schools were closed during lockdown?'

She nods. I know from what Hope said that during that time pupils were given online lesson plans to keep up with their education, however that lack of face-to-face teaching was bound to have been detrimental to some.

I consider what Lola's told me but no matter how hard I try to fit the pieces together, there are too many gaps to make sense of it. She's holding something back, I can feel it, I just don't know what.

I angle my head so that I'm studying her profile. She's breathing into her chest, rapid intakes that will make her light-headed. 'Next time you exhale, pretend you're blowing out through a straw,' I tell her. She does this a couple of times and her breathing returns to normal. She rewards me with a smile.

'You said your mum's a nurse, Lola. Did you give birth to Danny at home?'

A wave of emotion flashes across her face until eventually she nods.

'Nobody knows he's yours, do they?'

She looks away.

'During the pandemic we used to joke in here that the public finally got a taste of what it's like to lose your freedom.' Although being confined to your home with your loved ones seemed like paradise to me. 'Mind you,' I add, watching her reaction, 'you must have found a way to slip out undetected, given you ended up in the family way.' I start to laugh.

'Stop it!' Lola shrieks. 'You haven't got a clue!'

'Then tell me.'

She stares at me, eyes wide like a frightened rabbit. 'I promised I'd never tell,' she says meekly.

'And how's that working out for you?'

Lola stays silent.

'Lola love, just because someone doles out misery doesn't mean you have to take it from them.'

'I know.' She sniffs. 'Oh, Mercy, I love Danny with all my heart but Mum won't let him go.'

'She's got no claim on him, Lola, trust me. Why don't I get my lawyer to speak to you, put your mind at rest. He could send them a letter spelling out your rights.'

'No, that's the last thing I want.'

I look at her, confused. 'Why not?'

'Mum says the moment other people start poking their nose in Danny'll be taken into care.'

'She's trying to scare you into doing nothing, that's all!'

'No, she's a nurse, remember, she knows about these things.'

'What things?'

I watch as her chin drops onto her chest. The fight has gone out of her. 'I didn't end up in the family way because of some boy, Mercy. I was raped. Only the person who raped me was my dad.'

We stand for a moment in silence. Me staring at Lola open-mouthed; Lola staring at something beyond my vision. In all the scenarios I'd imagined that might explain her distress, this wasn't one of them. Careful, I remind myself. How I react now will likely determine whether she tells anyone in the future.

'God, I'm so sorry, Lola.'

She moves to her bunk and drops down onto it, hugging her knees. I opt for the plastic chair beside her table, then listen as the rest of the story tumbles out of her.

'It's the fear of Danny going into care that stops me from reporting him,' she says simply. 'When I realised I was pregnant, I went to my mum and told her what had been happening. That every time she worked the night shift at the local hospital, Dad came into my bedroom and didn't leave until he was red-faced and drenched in sweat. She didn't bat an eyelid. We were well into the pandemic by the time I started to show and, like you said, home schooling was the new normal. I gave birth on the kitchen floor. Danny came out, red-faced and irritable, the image of his granddad.

'"We'll say no more about it," Mum said, scooping him into her arms, already claiming him as her own. The following week, I watched her slip a box of condoms into the bathroom cabinet. That was the first night I drank myself into oblivion.'

'No wonder your drinking got out of hand.'

Lola's police record is long but with little variation. Vandalism, property damage, causing affray. Each misdemeanour carried out while drunk.

My stomach heaves at what she's told me. I can only imagine what Lola's is doing. Some people have the capacity to cause pain like it's their God given right. I wonder if her parents are aware of the harm they've done, the irreparable damage they've inflicted. Trauma doesn't exist in isolation; the traits of it travel down generations like eye colour or a birthmark. Right now, Lola's paying for whatever caused her father to be the way he is. Without medical checks it's impossible to know the impact Danny's parentage will have on him.

I try to think of something I can say to her that won't come across as an empty platitude. 'You don't need to deal with this on your own anymore, Lola. We'll figure something out.'

She starts to cry and I hand her toilet tissue from the roll beside her loo to wipe beneath her eyes. 'Give your nose a good blow when you're done.' She does as she's told. When she's finished, she examines the contents of it: streaks of snot and black mascara.

'Lola, do me a favour. The woman you're going to be in a few years needs you to be strong. Do you think you can do that?'

I wait for her to nod.

I jerk my thumb towards her cell door. 'Don't give this lot

any reason to delay your release. There are some fights you can't win and going up against the system is one of them. You got that?'

Another nod.

'Then let's get some breakfast.' I bang on the cell door for Officer Murdoch to let us out.

CHAPTER EIGHTEEN

I look up at the clock above the reception desk in the medical wing. Five minutes until my appointment with Stacey Sheridan. Having spent both morning and lunchtime associations checking on Lola, I'm exhausted. She's reluctant to tell the others who Danny's father is, though I've persuaded her to reconsider. She needs a lot of support right now, more possibly than I'm able to give. I know the others will want to help any way they can.

Left with nothing to distract myself, I start to anticipate Stacey's questions, analysing my life in the lead up to Gary's death, played out in glaring technicolor.

The day of his murder, I'd found heroin stashed in the bar. In the cellar, to be precise, behind barrels where he hadn't expected me to look. Which I wouldn't have if we hadn't been due an environmental health inspection, and a landlady pal of mine hadn't been given an enforcement order because an officer found rat urine in her cellar. As a result, I'd ordered a thorough scouring of the premises, and on the basis that I never asked my staff to do anything I wasn't prepared to do myself, I'd slapped on the Marigolds and headed down the cellar steps with a mop and bucket.

When I found the brown plastic-wrapped blocks stacked neatly in a pile, I knew exactly what they were. I'd seen enough of it during my childhood, albeit heavily laced with other substances to make it go further, in tiny wraps and snap bags on the coffee table at home. I felt like I'd fallen through a trapdoor taking me back to the life I'd left behind, to a world I'd worked so hard to escape.

I had few qualifications to speak of when I left school, but I was willing to work hard. Hope and Clem were settled with the Caplans, which meant I could focus on doing something with my life, the only problem was I didn't know what. Armed with my leaving care grant from the council, I moved into a bedsit cheap enough to rent but close enough to the city centre that I could be sure of casual work. Kitchen hand, pot washer, waitress, you name it, I turned my hand to it. The hours were grim and the pay and conditions poor but it was a start, the first step on my career ladder. I had no idea where the ladder was going to take me but I knew what I wanted from it. Forget flash cars and splashing the cash, I wanted security. A door that I could lock and leave the outside world behind, a place to call my own. It didn't sound like much, but it's a lot when you've never had it.

Working in the licensed trade suited me. The long hours distracted me from missing Hope and Clem; the hard work kept me fit. Plus, the advantage of working unsociable shifts meant I had less time to spend the money I earned and more money to put away. Over time, my savings and my confidence grew.

I'd met Billy in the first restaurant I'd worked in but I didn't let that put me off, besides, by the time we went our separate ways I'd discovered a love for working front of house. I enjoyed the banter with the customers, remembering their names and thinking of ways to make their night out special. I'd listen to their problems, offering advice where I could. I worked hard to make everyone's day better.

I was made bar manager just before my 24th birthday and was earning good money, which meant I could put some aside for the twins. They were due to start college the following year and I had dreams of buying a place big enough for them to live with me so we could experience some time as a family before they branched out into the world. In wild moments, I dared to hope that one day we'd run a business together, build something solid for our future, but that seemed a long way off. It was more realistic to take small steps. It was pure fluke that I came across the Dog and Duck when I did. It was on a rare night off, meeting a friend for a drink before going to the cinema. I'd passed the bar dozens of times over the years but hadn't ventured in. It looked battle worn from the outside, a bit too spit and sawdust for my taste, but it meant we didn't have far to walk and it had started to rain. The interior was a pleasant surprise. Dated, as I'd suspected from the exterior, but loads of room. Plenty of high tables and chairs clustered around and a fireplace that, although unlit, looked as though it would make a stunning feature. The guy behind the bar was too loud for my liking but he seemed to charm the punters. What I thought had been a pre-cinema crowd stayed – as we did, in the end – enjoying the atmosphere. The barman turned out to be the owner. We struck up a conversation when we ordered a second round of drinks. He informed us his name was Gary Walsh and he'd just put the bar and the property above it up for sale. It was last orders by the time we rolled out of there, with Gary's phone number saved in my mobile and a note in my calendar to call my bank in the morning.

It was no walk in the park by any means. Before the bank let me take on the mortgage I'd needed a guarantor, and you could have blown me away when the Caplans stepped up. I'll never know how much pressure the twins put them under to do this, or perhaps they saw it as a way of making amends for splitting up our little family, for all the years that had been lost between us. Whatever the reason, I was on cloud nine. I kept Gary on behind the bar because although he'd been a poor manager – hence the debts I discovered once I got a closer look at the books – I didn't want to lose our regulars while I set about finding new customers.

The bar didn't serve food so the first thing I did was install a kitchen. The area out front was easily divided to create a space for dining and we were close enough to a block of offices for expense account lunches and payday blowouts.

Fast forward two years and things were looking up. Business was booming. Word had spread about the chef I'd hired and tables were booked several weeks in advance. I'd renovated the living space upstairs and the twins came to stay during college term time, moving in properly – with the Caplans' blessing – when they'd completed their courses. Clem had studied hospitality while Hope had completed a sales and marketing course. Both came to work full time in the business. We were together as a family at last, living the dream I hadn't dared was possible.

The only fly in the ointment – and for fly read giant disgusting cockroach – was Gary.

He was one of those men who didn't know how to have a relationship with women that wasn't sexual. Work boundaries confounded him so he blatantly ignored them. If you were nice to him, he saw that as an open invitation to take things further. I think I bamboozled him. How could I work in such close proximity to him and not find him attractive? He knew I could read him, though, and when he tried to read me, he saw a woman he couldn't control. So he set his sights in a different direction and made a play for my sister.

Stacey's smile is already in place as she opens the consultation room door. 'Come on in, Mercy,' she says, like I'm an old friend who's come calling rather than a patient she needs to determine is of sound mind. We sit in the same seats as before.

'How have you been since last week?' she asks, my file already in position on her lap, along with her clicky pen.

I decide to level with her. 'It's not been without its challenges.'

Her face is a picture of concern. 'I'm sorry to hear that. In what way?' She crosses one leg over the other, rebalancing my file accordingly.

I blow out a breath. 'Doesn't matter now,' I say, deciding the incident with Frame and my subsequent retaliation are water under the bridge. 'I did speak with Vonnie, though.' I study her for a reaction.

'Your cellmate?' she enquires.

I shake my head. 'No, she's my friend. A good one, actually. She saved my life.'

Stacey is listening but she doesn't respond. She's waiting. I look around the room as though the words I want to say are painted on the walls. 'You…' I shake my head. How hard is it to say *You were right?*

'Take your time,' she says serenely and I don't blame her for milking it.

'I asked Vonnie if she wanted to talk about that evening, like you said, and it turns out she did. She helped me see that night through her eyes. The state I was in, how she felt when she found me, and afterwards. It felt good being able to acknowledge what happened, and to reassure her I didn't feel that way anymore.'

'I'm sure she was pleased to hear that.'

I nod, waiting for her to write some of this down. A comment on my positive attitude wouldn't go amiss for the parole board, but her hands remain on top of the closed file, as does her pen.

'Do you feel ready to talk about the events leading up to Gary's murder?' She tilts her head and waits.

'Yes,' I say, grim-faced, since I know I don't have any choice. And so the conversation I've been dreading to have with her, begins.

Stacey listens without interrupting as I tell her about the early days setting up the bar. Overseeing the menus with the chef, working out staff rotas and getting to know the regulars better. Some days I would accompany Hope when she visited the office blocks nearby, handing out leaflets advertising Happy Hour, Two for One meal deals and set-price business lunches. Other days I'd work front of house with Clem, who was a natural with the customers. I was so proud of them. Both so capable and confident, a world away from how they'd been as babies, too scared to cry for milk.

'And how was your relationship with Gary during this time?' Stacey prompts.

'It was purely professional,' I say quickly with a shudder. 'He may have thought he was God's gift to womankind but I saw through him. He reminded me too much of Billy for me to make that mistake again. Besides, you don't shit where you eat.'

That statement was proven to be true when he started up with my sister.

'I'd noticed a bit of a flirtation between him and Hope and I prayed it would go away if I ignored it. She was a slip of a girl and he circled her like a shark closing in on its prey. I tried putting her straight about him, but no woman in love wants to be told she's got lousy judgement, and she was certainly smitten.

It started to cause friction between us and I wasn't having that. I could hardly look out for her if she moved into his flat, so I swallowed down my dislike of him and put on a smile when he took her out after work, even though I wanted to punch his lights out.'

To my dismay Stacey clicks her pen and writes something down.

'That's not a euphemism for murder by the way,' I add quickly. I smile but it's lost on her. She sees me squinting at the page open on her lap and moves it slightly so I can't make out what she's written. Spoilsport.

'What didn't you like about him?' Her eyes lock on to mine as she tries to read me.

I look at her aghast. 'Where do I start? A gambler paying off a string of debts, he was hardly eligible bachelor material, was he?'

Little did any of us know back then that gambling was the least of his vices.

Stacey encourages me to continue with a nod.

'Overnight he went from employee to boyfriend of the boss's sister, then unfortunately, on to husband, which he thought elevated him to the level of boss again. It didn't help that along with him I'd kept on several of the original bar and cleaning staff. Most of them, to be fair, had made the transition to calling me boss easily enough. It was Gary who'd had the problem, trying to pressure them to do his bidding over mine. I put him straight though.' I smile but the gesture's empty.

'How was Hope's relationship with him at this point?'

I shake my head in despair at the memory. 'I'd told her she was making a big mistake the day before she married him. I knew he wasn't right for her. This might sound funny but it crossed my mind once or twice that he only married her to get back at me.'

'Because you rejected him?'

'Not in the way you mean. Though I did think me wanting his bar but not him was a dent to his fragile ego. By now he was knocking Hope about.' I pause as my sister's injuries flash in front of me: black eye, split lip, broken tooth – those were the only wounds she'd let me see. The worst ones she kept hidden, so it was a long time before I learned the extent of it.

Stacey gets up and pours some water from a plastic bottle into a paper cup, which she hands to me. It's only as I reach for it that I notice my hand's shaking. I take a sip, then another, and gather my thoughts.

'She tried hiding the bruises from me at first but we lived under the same roof and I could hear what was going on. Clem was beside himself but there's no muscle on him. Gary would have laughed in his face if he'd tried to intervene. The only person he'd listen to – who had leverage over him – was me. I took him to one side one day and had a quiet word. I knew enough from working in the bar to know what men who hit women are like. You say anything in front of their partner to warn them off and she's the one who pays the price the moment they're on their own. I made it clear that Hope hadn't been disloyal to him but I wasn't deaf, I could hear what he was doing to her. I told him that he wasn't vital to the business anymore. He had to start treating her with respect or he'd be out on his ear.'

'How did he take it?'

I huff out a sigh. 'He toed the line, or rather that's how he made it look. What really happened was he started to hit her when I was at the cash-and-carry, or had taken a rare day off and gone out for the day. He hit her where it wouldn't show and made her keep quiet, telling her there was more where that came from if I ever found out.'

It was also when he started bringing the drugs in. Although I didn't know that then.

I take another sip of water, gulping it till it's gone. When I look down the empty cup is crushed in my hand.

'Hope lost all her confidence. She couldn't understand what she was doing that made him so angry all the time. Why do women do that? Why do they let men make them feel responsible for their mood?' I level my question at Stacey but she doesn't answer.

'He even hit her while she was pregnant.' I hang my head. 'I wished I'd known.' *I'd have killed him sooner.* The words, unspoken, hang in the air.

'When did you find out that he was still hurting her?'

'When do you think?' I laugh, but it tastes bitter on my tongue.

'Can you tell me what happened?'

I blink slowly. Remembering that night is like falling into a black hole. Ironic, really, given what transpired. One minute my life was normal, predictable, some might even say dull, but when you've lived with chaos, uneventful is what you crave. I had my business, my independence, and most important of all, I was reunited with Clem and Hope. I was living my best life. Next minute I was in freefall, slipping further and further away from everything I held dear.

I take a breath. 'It was after closing time. I was clearing up in the bar with Clem. The rest of the staff had gone home. Hope was in the back room putting her feet up. She was in her last trimester, and carrying the weight of those babies around all day was starting to take its toll.'

Hope suited being pregnant, and I could already see she was going to make a great mum. We looked at baby books together and chatted about names – things that Gary was never interested in doing. Her excitement had rubbed off on me. Billy had taken away my chance of being a mother but I was about to become an aunt, and I vowed I was going to be the best one ever.

'Gary had been changing a barrel in the cellar.' He'd been down there for some time, although I had a good idea what was taking him so long. I keep this to myself.

'It was Clem who heard him first. Rather than shouting, he was hissing out a series of swearwords at Hope, obviously not wanting to draw our attention to his rage. Clem was looking at me, ready to take my lead. My hackles were already up; Hope didn't need any aggro at this stage of her pregnancy. I waited to see if he calmed down. Remember, I had no idea at this point that he'd continued to beat her, despite my previous warning. Hope started whimpering, which spurred me into action. I told Clem to finish clearing up while I went to find them.'

I pause. Stacey offers me more water but I shake my head. I need a moment. I'd played by the rules all my life. Never broken the law, always paid my taxes. I'm about the re-live the split second it took to step off the precipice.

'Where were they?' Stacey prompts.

'They were standing in the hallway facing each other. Hope's hair was tousled, I assumed because she'd been dozing. Later, she told me he'd stormed into the back room and dragged her into the hallway by her hair. The cellar door was open behind them. It was typical of Gary not to follow procedure. We drilled into every member of staff that if they went down to the cellar they must always close the door behind them. The steps are steep and it's a concrete floor, lethal if someone unwittingly enters and takes a tumble.' It's like I'm there, back in the hallway with them. 'Gary's voice had risen. He didn't see me. I doubt he could see anything at that point other than red mist. He started calling Hope filthy names and as I moved towards them, I saw him jab her in the stomach.' I feel the intense heat of rage just recalling it.

'Hope was cowering in front of him and in that moment, I saw her future mapped out. The beatings would become more brutal. Those babies, if they survived, would learn to fear their father before they'd even been born. He put his hands around her throat. I couldn't believe what was happening, what was unfurling in front of my eyes. It felt like we'd come full circle despite all my efforts, that everything I'd done to make sure Hope and Clem had a good life counted for nothing. Hope had traded the good life me and the Caplans had provided for her for an abusive marriage, and now her life was in danger. I yelled at Gary to stop but instead of doing as I asked, he started laughing and as he did so his hands started squeezing tighter around her neck. His family later claimed he did that to scare me, to stop me from coming any closer, but I had no time to work out his intention. I mean, they weren't there, how could they know what he intended to do? I *was* there in that moment, watching Hope's eyes bulge and her face turn purple. I had to act fast. Make a decision, knowing there'd be no chance to make another. I took a run at him. He put out a hand to stop me getting close and with both of mine I grabbed at the one that remained around Hope's neck and pulled back his thumb until I heard a crack. He pulled his hand away, swearing, and then I shoved him away from her. He'd been drinking during his shift, he wasn't as steady on his feet as a man of his age should have been, the push I gave him sent him staggering backwards. If the cellar door had been closed, he'd have slammed against it, no harm done, but it wasn't. He seemed to teeter at the top of the steps then fall backwards.' I remember the crunching sound as his head bounced off each step. I drop my head onto my chest.

'Are you happy to go on?' Stacey asks and I realise she doesn't get it. The traumatic part of this scenario was when I thought he was strangling Hope, not when he fell. The sound of his head bouncing off the concrete brought nothing but relief.

'The rest of it's a blur,' I tell her. Hope hurrying into the back room for her phone to call emergency services, me going down into the cellar to check if he was dead. Clem peering at us from the top of the stairs.

'I remember the first police officer on the scene taking my statement... then being taken outside to the waiting police car.'

Stacey's been writing as I've been talking. She stops now and peers at me.

'You look done in. Shall we leave it there?'

I picture her at home, the grime of this place wiped away, curled up on her sofa sipping a glass of something white and crisp. *That* is leaving it. For me, long-suppressed memories have been uprooted and scattered like debris after a hurricane. Now they've been exposed, I'm in no hurry to put them back.

'I'm ready to talk about Alice Maltby if you want.'

Her brow rises a fraction but that's her only outward display of surprise.

'There's one condition,' I say, waiting for her to remind me that's not how it works.

'And what's that?' she says instead, catching *me* by surprise.

'I want you to tell me what's written in my file about the incident.' I know that she's read it; she admitted as much during our last session.

'What difference will that make?' she asks.

I feel the weight of her gaze and return it. 'It'll determine whether I finally admit the truth.'

CHAPTER NINETEEN

Stacey is as good as her word. She flips through my file and removes a sheet of paper from a clear plastic wallet. 'It's a photocopy of the incident report,' she says, handing it to me.

I hadn't expected her to agree so readily, so her co-operation catches me off guard. I smile my thanks as I take it from her, using the opportunity of breaking eye contact to gather my thoughts. I consider how the content of this report will alter my recount of the incident with Alice Maltby. It feels a bit like a poker game: before I declare my hand, I need to know what cards my opponent is holding.

Maltby wasn't a narcissistic killer as the medical experts quoted in the press during her trial first thought. She was a psychopath. She showed no emotion or empathy and had the ability to hurt you yet not feel anything whilst doing it. She also knew something about the day Gary died that no one else did.

I carefully read through the content of the report.

Fairmile Prison Incident Report

Date: 01/08/2022

Prisoner 258380 Reid, Mercy Block no: 4 Cell no: C17

Prisoner 470602 Maltby, Alice Block no: 4 Cell no: C17

Officer Frame, attending a 'cell bell' call from C17, found on arrival that a barricade had been placed behind the door. On looking through the hatch, Prisoner Maltby was seen holding a bladed instrument to Prisoner Reid's throat. Prisoner Reid's face was bloody and bruised, her movement was slow as though she had suffered significant injuries. Maltby appeared unharmed at this stage.

Officer Frame followed protocol and radioed the incident into the control room. It was noted that Reid remained calm at this point. Maltby was shouting and swearing and had the appearance of someone under the influence of an illegal substance.

Officers responding to the call cleared the landing and the block was put into lockdown measures: prisoners returned to their cells for their own safety. Officer Frame tried to establish why Maltby had taken Reid hostage. Maltby stated she would only speak to the governor.

Governor Cassidy attended the incident along with an officer trained in negotiation. Maltby demanded drugs and to be transferred to a psychiatric hospital immediately. If her demand wasn't met, she stated she was going to kill Reid. Governor Cassidy informed her that a transfer would take time to organise, but she could be moved to the segregation unit while she waited if she didn't want to remain on the block. She was informed that drugs were not negotiable, however she would be seen by the prison doctor as soon as one was available.

When Maltby rejected this offer, Governor Cassidy declared the situation a Category A incident, and following guidance from Gold Command, requested backup from ORRU.

So far so good, I think as I read through the report line by line. Nothing contentious. The choice words Officer Frame spewed through the hatch at us both didn't make it into the report, but you can hardly blame her for giving a better account of herself. Most people embellish the facts in situations like this, make their contribution more heroic, certainly a lot less antagonistic. I remember being informed that the ORRU (Operational Response and Resilience Unit) had been scrambled. These are specially trained officers called in to serious incidents behind bars, the Prison Service's SAS, if you like. They're experts in scenarios such as hostage situations, removing people from cells, and sieges. In fact, pretty much the situation I'd found myself in. I think we were told they were coming in the hope that Maltby would give herself up. It ended up having the opposite effect. Hearing the cavalry was on its way made her all the more entrenched.

Aware that Stacey is studying me for a reaction, I read on.

An hour into the siege, Prisoner Reid's breathing appeared laboured (a broken rib had punctured her lung) although she made the following threat: 'If you lot don't get this bitch off me, I'll take matters into my own hands.'

Prisoner Maltby is alleged to have whispered something in Reid's ear. It was noted at this point that Reid began to show signs of distress.

There was a struggle and before the ORRU reached the cell both women fell onto the floor.

The disturbance was classified as 'local surrender', meaning that although the ORRU was notified they did not intervene.

When local officers gained access to the cell they found Maltby lying on the floor unconscious.

Both women were taken to Manchester Royal Infirmary.

Prisoner Reid admitted assaulting Prisoner Maltby in an attempt to escape. When asked why she hadn't waited for the response team to enter the cell she declined to comment.

Following hospitalisation due to a significant brain injury Maltby was transferred to Ashworth psychiatric hospital.

After an internal inquiry, the senior management team agreed that Reid's response had been excessive, however, given the circumstances leading up to the incident, the governor recommended that no further action be taken against her.

I snort with derision at that last statement, tossing the report onto the table with contempt. Stacey retrieves it and returns it to its rightful place in the plastic wallet.

'What it doesn't say in there is that although the governor deemed no action needed to be taken against me, she saw fit to inform the parole board of Alice's injury, annihilating any chance I had of release.'

'You sound incensed.'

I look at her, exasperated. 'Wouldn't you be? Especially the way the press reported it. You could tell they'd been fed a statement from some faceless official. *Move along, please, nothing to see here.*'

Stacey gives me a minute to compose myself before fixing me with that smile. 'So, I've fulfilled my part of the bargain, Mercy. You've read the report.' She leans back in her chair. 'What really happened?'

I run my hands over my face. 'Alice had become addicted to crack. The problem was she couldn't afford it, so she resorted to funding it any way she could. She stole things, sold them on. Remember, everything in prison has a currency. Sugar, soap, vapes, you name it. There was always some sort of ruck going off because of her thieving. Someone accusing her or catching her in the act, fights, a night in the seg, the women started getting wise to her. Fewer opportunities to steal meant fewer opportunities for her to get off her face. She stopped taking care of herself. Her behaviour on the wing had made her into a pariah, and frankly there wasn't much more I could do for her. Which is when she decided to dabble in other things.'

'Like what?'

'Weapons. Like I said, everything in prison has a currency. She would spend her days making weapons out of whatever she could lay her hands on and sell them on to inmates with scores to settle. She'd make shanks, welded together from plastic and razor blades. Garrottes, made from torn clothing and shivs from pens, toothbrushes, and toilet brushes with the handles shaved into points. The day it all kicked off she must have managed to get her hands on enough cash to score, because when I returned to our cell at the end of association, she was on her bunk already out of it.'

Alice sat up when I entered, slurred a greeting, the skin under her eyes a bluish purple. I pretended not to notice that her gaze followed me around the cell.

'You never bothered asking me, did you?' she demanded.

'Go to sleep, Alice. I'm not in the mood for your games.'

She sat up straighter. 'Aren't you intrigued how I know about Gary's heroin?'

I blinked slowly. I really didn't want to go there again.

I'm aware Stacey's waiting. 'She said something that made me realise she knew Gary.'

Stacey nods for me to continue.

'She'd been dropping hints for some time. Making snide comments here and there, but I'd mostly ignored them.'

'What about?'

'About my bar. She knew that I'd bought it from Gary, that I'd kept him on as an employee. Then out of the blue one night she told me she knew about the heroin.'

'What heroin?'

I explain about the stash that I'd found in the cellar. 'The moment I found it I went ballistic. To think that as well as knocking Hope about he was dealing drugs in the bar I'd worked so hard to turn into a success. I knew he had gambling debts; I just didn't think he'd stoop that low to pay them off.'

'Did you confront him?'

'I tried.'

There was no phone signal in the basement. I'd thrown off my Marigolds and marched upstairs to call him. 'I found his number in my contact list and hit dial. I was livid. "The bastard, bringing smack into my fucking bar, I'm going to kill him," I muttered over and over while I waited desperately for him to pick up. As far as I was concerned, he was finished. His phone rang out and went to voicemail. Not getting to speak to him took the wind out of my sails but also gave me time to think about how I should deal with this. Bringing drugs onto the premises put my business at risk, and then there was Hope, and the babies we were eagerly awaiting. I wondered if there was a way I could deal with it without making the situation worse.

'I had to get rid of the drugs. I couldn't afford to have them on the premises for a moment longer. What if a member of staff found them? What if the environmental health officer had found them instead of me? We'd be finished, and as landlady I'd be the one up for prosecution.'

Stacey gives me her full attention. 'So what did you do?'

'I shifted the heroin out of the cellar to give him a fright. My intention was to show him that if I could find it, anyone could. I wanted him to take it back to where he'd got it so everything could return to normal.'

Stacey's leaning forward in her chair. 'What happened?'

'He turned up late for his shift. He'd switched his phone off, obviously because he didn't want to take my calls. I was furious.

I mean, how did he know I wasn't calling him about Hope or the babies?' I shudder to think of his callousness.

Stacey's about to ask another question but I'm already ahead of her, butting in with the answer before she has a chance to ask it. 'The reason I didn't text Gary or leave him a voicemail was because I didn't want to get caught up in it all if he got himself arrested. I didn't want anyone jumping to the wrong conclusion, assuming I'd been aware of his dealing, or worse still, was in on it with him. So he must have seen half a dozen missed calls from me and decided to switch off his phone.

'He always had a bit of an attitude but there was definitely a swagger about him that night. I reckoned he was enjoying getting one over on me, already mentally spending the money he was going to make on the back of the stash he thought was still hidden in the cellar. I could imagine him gloating that he didn't need his poxy job. Bastard.'

Stacey is shaking her head. 'Actually, that wasn't what I was going to ask you, Mercy,' she says carefully. 'You were telling me about Alice Maltby. About what happened the night she attacked you. I was wondering how Gary's death was relevant?'

'I'm just getting to that,' I tell her.

CHAPTER TWENTY

Date: 01/08/2022

Block no: 4 Cell no: C17

Alice's pupils are dilated. Her breath coming in rapid little gasps. 'You've no idea who I am, have you?' She shifts position so that she's sitting up, her legs dangling over the edge of her bunk. I wonder if the earlier sluggishness was an act, as she's hyper vigilant now, her penetrating gaze boring into me, watching every movement I make. She's spoiling for a fight; she's waiting for me to oblige her and start one.

'Go on, admit it,' she pushes.

She's right, I don't have a clue. I know her as Alice Maltby, the child killer. An aberration of nature that I happen to be sharing a cell with. She's starting to get agitated; I need to think of something to appease her.

'You said you used to drink in my bar, Alice. I'm sorry for not recognising you, I've been somewhat preoccupied.' I indicate the four walls hemming us in.

Alice shrugs. 'I went there a lot when Gary was in charge, wasn't so keen on it when you took over.'

I tip my head. 'Each to their own.'

'I was there the day you killed him. I know what it was really about.'

Now I know she's lying. 'You can't have been,' I say confidently. 'Things didn't kick off with Gary until after closing time.'

She starts to laugh. 'I don't mean when you did the deed, you daft cunt, obviously I wasn't there then. I meant when you threatened to kill him.'

I look at her blankly as I try to fathom what she's talking about. What threat? I didn't see Gary until he rocked up late for his shift and the bar was so busy by then, there was no time to take him to one side about what I'd found in the cellar, let alone make threats. I was still furious with him about the heroin, I just didn't get the opportunity to tell him. 'We were run off our feet that night. I didn't say anything...'

'It was during the afternoon,' Alice informs me, a malicious smile forming on her lips. 'There was hardly anyone in.'

It's not hard to think back to that day. It's only ever been a blink away, no matter how much I've tried to expunge it from my memory. Yes, Alice is right, the bar was quiet that afternoon, so quiet in fact the staff member on shift was able to serve punters while working her way through a crossword. I didn't mind as other days you could be run off your feet. That's why I took the opportunity to clean the cellar when I did. Gary wasn't working until later, I daresay if he had been he'd have offered to run down the cellar with the mop and bucket himself if he'd known what I had in mind.

When I'd stormed up the cellar steps after finding those drugs, I'd been hell-bent on speaking to him. Correction, having it out with him. Yes, I was seriously hacked off and wanted him to know about it, I certainly wasn't paying any attention to who was in the bar when I called him.

'You were standing by the optics using your phone,' she says. 'The barmaid was on the other side of the bar clearing away glasses. I was where I normally stood when I drank in there. At the end of the counter near the fruit machines.'

That didn't surprise me. I'd wanted those things gone the moment I took over but Gary had persuaded me to keep them. 'If you gentrify the place too much it'll lose its appeal.'

Alice looks pleased with herself. I look at her smug smile and vow that the first thing I do after my release is rip out those machines, with my bare hands if necessary.

'You said you were going to kill him for bringing smack into your bar. I heard you, clear as day.'

'What?' I remember muttering something vile while I waited for him to answer my call. It had been said in the heat of the moment, to no one but myself. A roll of nausea works its way from my stomach to my throat. 'Obviously I didn't mean it,' I tell her.

'He ended up dead, didn't he?'

She fixes me with a stare as her drug-addled gaze locks on to me and I force myself not to look away.

I try to make her understand. 'His death was nothing to do with dealing drugs and everything to do with my sister. I walked in on him throttling the life out of her. He'd been abusing her for months. I had to do something!'

'Save it!' she screeches and I remember that I'm reasoning with someone who snuffed out her kids. 'Gary was a scumbag; I don't give a fuck about him.'

'So what's your problem, then?' I demand, readying to square up to her if she jumps down from her bunk.

'I didn't have a problem back then. You were sent down anyway, so I never thought any more about it. Then I saw you in the induction block when I was brought here and I reckoned you'd come in handy. I saw you looking at me and I thought you recognised me too.'

'I was just being nice,' I say truthfully.

This seems to annoy her. 'I never wanted to be sent here, you know! I wanted to go to Rampton or Broadmoor but the politicians had to have their pound of flesh, didn't they? Kept chipping away until they got what they wanted. Me sentenced to life with no possibility of release.' She glowers at me. 'I know what happens to women who hurt their kids in places like this. I know I can never let my guard down. When I saw you, I thought my luck had changed. I remember thinking, we're both lifers from the same neck of the woods, she'll look out for me. When the governor approved my request to pad up with you, the prospect of being here didn't seem so bad.'

The cell is acrid with stale breath and body odour. Alice isn't a tidy woman. She leaves her belongings scattered on the floor and thinks nothing of using my mug if hers is dirty. I reach for it now and find her crack pipe in it.

I swallow but my mouth is dry.

Alice, unaware of the shift in atmosphere, carries on with her rant.

'Then I hear on the grapevine you've got parole coming up. That didn't make sense to me. I mean, everyone knew you'd nobbled your sister's old man so how come you were getting off so lightly? I asked my lawyer how you could be up for parole when you were sentenced to life, like me, and he explained about the tariffs. That yours was set at twelve years whereas mine is set at forty. He told me how it was calculated and it got me thinking. The judge took into account that you were saving your sister's life, which is why you got such a discount, whereas, if it had been a dispute over drugs, say, and you killed Gary out of spite after mulling it over all afternoon, he wouldn't have been anywhere near as lenient. I wonder how that little nugget of information would go down if the truth came out? Reckon you could kiss goodbye to that tariff and any prospect of parole!'

Sweat pools under my arms and in the crease beneath my breasts. The thought of the future I'd been too fearful to hope for, that I'd started to believe in, being snatched away is too much. I flatten my voice. 'That's not how it happened, Alice.' I tip her smoking paraphernalia out of my mug and crush it underfoot. I wish it was her, the dark thought crawls out, unbidden.

'You stupid bitch!' She jumps down from her bunk and slams me into the wall. Her elbow smashes into my nose and I look on as blood spurts down the front of my top. I stagger backwards, dizzy from her attack, stars flickering at the edge of my vision. I duck to avoid her clenched fist but I'm too slow, she has the strength of ten women thanks to her drug rush. Blows rain down on both sides of my face, my ribs. I hear a sickening crack. My breath when it comes is short and ragged. I hit the call button and shout for help. What happens next is a blur. Alice picks up a chair and I brace myself thinking she's going to hit me with it when she turns it upside down and removes a home-made knife that's taped underneath it. I look at her in disbelief. 'Alice, what are you doing?' I ask, which is stupid as I can see what she's doing. She holds the knife towards me as she drags the table and chair behind the cell door to barricade us in. She starts dragging my mattress from my bunk but she can't do it one handed.

'GET OFF MY STUFF!' I yell.

She turns to me and places the knife to my neck. Just a flex of her wrist and that sharp blade will sever an artery.

'You do it, then,' she instructs, her voice cold as ice. 'Step out of line and I'll top you, got that?'

I grunt a yes and do as I'm told; the tension in the cell has gone up several gears. It's no longer a battle of wills; it's a matter of survival.

I drag the mattress behind the door, all the while aware of the sharp blade millimetres from my skin.

'I could slice your head off, if I wanted,' she boasts.

I feel the adrenaline coming off her in waves and I don't doubt it. Once the mattress is in place, she pushes me into the centre of the cell so the PO that responds can see what they're dealing with. Her actions baffle me. She'll go on report for assaulting me but being caught with a blade will result in a severe loss of privileges, possibly an increase in her sentence, though the fear of having two extra years added to a forty stretch is negligible.

My heart sinks as Officer Frame's voice screeches through the hatch. 'What the fuck?' she shouts before reaching for her radio.

'Are you injured?' Frame is calling through the hatch but it hurts too much to speak. I stare at her mouth through the hole in the door and hope she can see my injuries are more than just a bloody nose. Inmates have been known to stage assaults to get time in the infirmary, I hope she sees beyond that and knows this is the real deal.

I listen as she puts an emergency call through to control. I've watched incidents like this play out over the years, but with the passive interest of a spectator. Now I'm caught up in the middle of it, I'm praying for a rapid response.

Alice presses the blade into my neck. 'Fuck off, screw, I want the organ grinder, not the monkey. Get me the governor!'

The sound of radio static penetrates the cell along with the sound of steel toe-capped boots. Reinforcements are here.

'That's enough, Maltby.' Frame's voice has gone up an octave. She's not sure how this will pan out, which makes two of us.

'I want the governor!' Alice repeats her demand.

I try to reason with her. 'Alice, you're not thinking straight because of the drugs. It's not too late to pack this in.' My voice sounds strange and my jaw doesn't move the way it's supposed to. I wonder if she can understand what I'm saying. My side hurts like a bastard too. Is Alice really holding me hostage or is this some awful nightmare that I've imagined?

'I need to sit down, Alice.' I slump against her; her left arm encircles me in a vice-like grip, like we're two hens out on the lash.

'Get me the governor or I'll cut her!' she demands, ignoring my plea.

Alice moves the blade to my chin. I gasp as something sharp slices into it.

'She's on her way, Maltby,' Frame informs her. 'No need to do anything rash.'

'Is Mercy okay?' I hear Tanya call out my name but I daren't respond, Alice's knife is tracing a line down my chin. I try not to move.

'Back off!' yells a PO.

Officers are assembling on the other side of the door; their heavy boots and jangling keys give them away. The alarm bell signals that inmates must return to their cells. 'Lockdown now!' several POs yell. The landing echoes with the sound of doors clanging shut and keys turning.

Amid the chaos an authoritative voice addresses Alice through the hatch. 'Alice, before we have any sort of discussion, I need to know that Mercy is okay.'

Governor Cassidy.

Alice relaxes her pressure on the knife. Blood drips from my chin, merging with the blood that oozed from my nose minutes earlier.

I feel the governor's gaze as it settles on me. 'How are you bearing up, Mercy?' she asks.

'Could be better,' I tell her.

She addresses her next comment to Alice. 'She needs to be checked by a doctor. Let her go now and we'll deal with this at local level. No need to take extra measures.'

'She's going nowhere. It's me that needs moving. I want out of this shithole and off to Rampton, or Broadmoor, or anywhere where I won't have to look over my shoulder for the rest of my life.'

'Transfers take time to arrange–'

'So you'd better get cracking, then.'

The governor stands her ground; easy to do when you don't have skin in the game. 'These things can't happen overnight, but what we can do is put you into the seg if you like, not as a punishment, just so that you're away from the other residents. Is that what you want?'

Alice considers this. 'When will I get my transfer?'

'I don't know. There are procedures to go through–'

'Not helpful!'

I'm with Alice on this.

'I'm sure we can apply a little pressure, push things through a little faster,' Governor Cassidy says.

'Does this help?' Alice returns the blade to my chin, draws a second line parallel to the first, this time with more force. I try to pull away but can't shake from her grip. Struggling would make the wound bigger. She examines her handiwork, nodding in satisfaction. I think she's done, then out of nowhere her face contorts. 'SACK THAT, I'VE CHANGED MY MIND!' she yells. 'Why should I make it easy for you? Get me out of this shithole NOW or I'll kill her.'

'Mercy, do you want to take a break?'

Stacey's concerned voice pierces through the haze. She peers at me as though assessing whether we should carry on. 'I'm okay,' I say, absent-mindedly tracing the scar on my chin with my little finger. It's part of me now, like a skin tag or a mole. The nurse who stitched me up said that if I hadn't been in custody I'd have been referred to plastics, would have had nothing more than a silvery line to mark where Alice chibbed me. Instead the skin is puckered, as though the thread holding it in place had been pulled too tight.

'I was terrified when Alice turned on me,' I say honestly. 'I mean, beating me up was bad enough but when she pulled that knife on me... Well, that took it to another level. Even so, up until then I was stupid enough to think she was using me as a bargaining tool to get transferred out. Even though she'd got her transfer – the governor had pretty much agreed to it in principle – she'd seen fit to move the goalposts.'

Get me out of this shithole NOW or I'll kill her.

'Then it dawned on me. Nothing they agreed to would appease her. She was hell-bent on destroying me, punishing me for getting what she thought was a better deal from the judge who sentenced me.'

'What happened?' asks Stacey.

In the blink of an eye, I'm back there again. Locked up with a madwoman threatening to kill me if she didn't get what she wanted.

The click, click, of the governor's heels can be heard as she hurries from the landing.

I'm starting to tire and can't see any progress. Alice is as agitated as she was when she jumped onto me from her bunk.

She wants a transfer out – and it sounds like the governor's getting it sanctioned. So what's going to happen next? Are they going to leave me here with her until the transfer is rubber-stamped? The pain in my jaw is getting worse and so's my breathing. I'm genuinely in fear for my life. 'If you lot don't get this bitch off me, I'll take matters into my own hands!' Anger distorts my voice, makes it sound as though it belongs to someone else.

'You tell 'em!' says Alice, pleased with herself. A smile plays on her lips. 'You'd better be careful though, start getting handy and you'll not get parole.'

'It'd be self-defence, Alice,' I mutter.

'That old chestnut,' she sneers. 'By the time I've finished no one will believe that.'

With the knife still at my throat she moves her head so that it's inches away from mine. Her voice is barely a whisper when she says, 'Just because I've got what I want doesn't mean you're off the hook. Sometimes a win's only a win when the other person loses. Forget parole, darlin'. The only way you're leaving this cell is feet first. THAT'S when I'll tell everyone you killed Gary because of his drug dealing. I can just see that dozy brother and sister of yours weeping at your graveside, nothing but your broken halo to cling on to. Won't that be just fucking dandy?'

I've heard enough. Maltby's words ring in my ears and it feels like everything I care about is spinning away from me. I move my head back and before she realises what's is happening, I slam it into hers with such force she careers into the metal rail of the top bunk, collapsing like a ton of bricks. I run my hand along my throat, checking it for damage. I feel dizzy. The force of the impact has made me see stars. I blink them away before falling to my knees.

That's when the officers barge through the door.

The consultation room comes back into focus. I feel Stacey's eyes on me. 'One headbutt and she was out for the count,' I joke to lighten the mood.

Alice was out of it for longer than that, it turned out. Unconscious for six hours. A head CT scan revealed a bleed to the brain following damage to her temporal lobe. When her head had ricocheted from mine to the metal frame of the bunk it had caused her brain to swell. A subdural haematoma, the surgeon informed the governor. Following emergency surgery to relieve the pressure on her brain she was put into an induced coma to aid recovery. After a period of occupational therapy at the psychiatric hospital she was transferred to, doctors treating her were pleased to report that most of her cognitive function had returned. Apart from her memory.

'No recollection of what she'd done to her children.' My words were heavy with disappointment.

'And no memory of a certain threat she made to you,' Stacey adds sagely.

I lock eyes with her. 'I know how it looks.'

'And how is that?'

'That I assaulted her to stop her from revealing the threat she heard me mutter. And yes, maybe part of me did want to silence her. I had a lot to lose. But I was scared for my life and I had no idea when anyone was going to burst through that cell door. When she lowered her head to mine to taunt me, I saw an opportunity to stun her and grab the knife from her hands. I wasn't to know her head would slam into the bed frame. The doctors said it was the impact of that which caused her serious injury. A fluke, they called it.'

Stacey considers something. 'What happened to the heroin you found?'

'Not long after I'd been remanded, I called home and spoke to Hope. She was crying. Two men had called round saying Gary had been looking after something for them, and as his wife she now had twenty-four hours to find it. I told her about the stash Gary had hidden in the cellar, explaining that I'd moved it to my sports bag in the boot of my car just to get it off the premises. I told her she needed to take it to them and never mention it to anyone.'

Stacey regards me. 'What about your injuries, are you recovered from them?'

I point to where my ribs had been broken. 'It took about eight weeks for my punctured lung to heal.' I place an index finger on both cheekbones. I needed surgery to realign my fractured jaw but it's no longer symmetrical. 'My smile is lopsided now.' Her gaze moves to the jagged line on my chin. 'No lasting damage,' I say.

'And what about your more recent scars?'

I tug defensively at my sleeve before making a decision. Slowly I roll it up and hold my wrist out to her. The criss-cross of scars are no longer pink. I trace my fingers over them, taking my time. 'Losing parole like that, after Alice, felt like a slap in the face. I didn't ever want to put myself through it again, but if I didn't, what was I left with?' I drop my arm to my side without covering it. 'I'd never really looked at my scars until after my conversation with Vonnie,' I admit. 'Not properly looked. I was too ashamed. But they're part of me now. A reminder that the greatest cure for the horror of today, is tomorrow.'

'I'm glad to hear that.'

'You know, for so long I've felt ambivalent about getting my release. I mean, what was I going back to? The bar's ticked along without me, in fact it's done better than that, Hope and Clem have made it into something special by all accounts. The stamp I put on it all those years ago will barely be recognisable...' I trail off, remembering the day I was driven through Fairmile's gates with Tanya like it was yesterday. I've come this far for a reason.

'How do you feel about parole now?'

I need to be there for Hope, for her girls, to help them through the biggest challenge they've ever faced. 'I want it more than anything,' I tell her.

She nods as she writes this down.

'What happens now?' I ask.

Her eyes meet mine and we stare at each other, like finalists in a blinking contest.

'I'll inform Dr North that our sessions are now concluded. I'll then prepare my report for the parole board.'

'Am I allowed to ask what you're going to write in it?'

The corner of Stacey's mouth flickers. 'I shall inform the panel that you genuinely want to progress with your life and have displayed evidence of improved self-control and better emotional management. I'm satisfied you have the skills to manage your risk of future violence. This was extensively tested during the time you were held captive by Alice Maltby and I will state that in my opinion you were treated harshly following that incident.'

I feel butterflies taking flight in my stomach, but I need to be sure. 'For God's sake,' I say to her, 'in English, please!'

Stacey allows herself a smile. 'I'm supporting your application for release, Mercy, and I'll do all I can to make sure you get it.' She studies my reaction and it's only when she pushes the box of tissues towards me that I realise I'm crying.

CHAPTER TWENTY-ONE

TANYA

The sound of a key turning in the lock startles Tanya awake. Groggily, she watches the door swing open, groaning inwardly at the bulky body appearing behind it.

'Get up, you lazy tart.' Her visitor strides into the room, closing the door behind them.

Blinking, Tanya rakes her hair back from her face before pushing herself into a sitting position. She often has forty winks at this time of day, plenty of the girls do. The afternoon lull between lunch and dinnertime association, when everyone is confined to their cells, is a drag. Best thing to do is sleep through it. No good comes of being bored in prison.

She eyes her unwanted visitor with suspicion, sees sweat rings under the arms of a normally immaculate shirt.

'You must have thought you hit the jackpot when you came here.'

'What are you talking about?' Tanya's voice is thick from sleep. She moves her tongue around her mouth to moisten it. She's parched, but she'll wait until she's alone before she makes herself a drink.

'Bed, heating, three meals a day. Surprised you didn't get

repetitive strain injury back in the day, the number of hand jobs it would have taken to pay for that on the outside.'

'That's all in my past.' Tanya speaks quietly. She tries to read her visitor, tries to think of a reason they're standing in her space, a reason that required them to close the door. She thinks through possible scenarios, not liking any of them one little bit.

'Are you sure about that? How do you know you won't go back to turning tricks when you get out? I mean, what other skills do you have?'

'I know how to treat people with respect,' Tanya says defiantly.

'That isn't going to pay the bills though, is it?'

Tanya looks away.

Her visitor follows her line of vision and scoffs. A magazine cut-out of a woman with perfect teeth is stuck to the wall with Blu-Tack. Beside it a dog-eared Polaroid of three freckled kids staring wide-eyed at the camera. 'Do you think they still remember you? Then again, they must do, given the number of times they've knocked back your visiting orders.'

Tanya chews the inside of her cheek, refusing to get into it. 'Can I help you with anything, officer?' She can afford to be genial. She's learned this morning that her parole has been approved, only ten more days and she'll be a free woman. Soon Fairmile and its screws will be nothing more than a memory.

Her gaze shifts to a picture she'd ripped from the travel section of a magazine and added to her wall. A sandy beach overlooking the crystal waters of the Aegean Sea. She's never been abroad before, never walked on sand, never felt the ocean between her toes. Every night since Mercy told her about the trip she's arranged for her she's had the same dream. In it, she wears a white cotton dress as she walks barefoot along the shore, the heat of the sun warming her face. Tanya doesn't know what it's like to be carefree but being on that beach must come close.

She has no time for religion, too many bad things happen to good people for her to believe in a god that gives a damn, but if there's a heaven, a place where the soul can be at rest, this beach must be it.

She feels her visitor's gaze on her and looks away guiltily. She's given them an in and they both know it. She looks on as a fat finger jabs at the magazine cutting. 'You really think she's going to come good on a promise she made to a dirty skank like you? She said it for the attention, that's all. So everyone thinks she's the great I am.'

Tanya tuts as she gets to her feet. 'Go and bark at the traffic or whatever else it was you were doing before you came in here.' She swats the fat fingers away and peers at the picture as though it's a portal into another world.

This angers her visitor. 'I'm doing you a favour. Telling it like it is before you find out the hard way and make yourself look an even bigger loser than you look already.'

Tanya narrows her eyes. 'What's it to you anyway?'

'The pair of you get on my wick. Ever since you both arrived you've lorded it over everyone, as though being on a long stretch gives you status.'

Tanya shakes her head. 'It's never been like that. We don't talk about our pasts to anyone else, we never have. We have a rule, if someone doesn't want to talk about what brought them here, they don't have to.'

'Oh, you have a *rule*, do you? See what I mean? Who put you in charge? Last time I looked I was the one who held the keys.'

'Shame you can't hold your tongue,' Tanya mutters.

'What did you say?'

'You heard. Now if you haven't got anything on me, you'd better do one.'

'Funny you should say that.' Her visitor's voice drips with ice.

Tanya looks on as a snap bag of heroin is dangled in front of her. 'Why have you got that?'

'Oh, let me see. Because I just found it in your cell.'

'You and I both know I haven't seen it before.'

Her visitor smiles. 'Do we? Are you sure about that?'

Tanya feels the slow drip of unease. Her gaze flickers from her visitor's mean face to the clear bag of brown powder she holds between her fingers. 'What are you going to do with it?'

'Hmmm, let me see. Maybe I want to see if your past really is behind you.'

'I don't have to prove myself to you.'

'Whatever. A fiver says it'll be coursing its way through your skanky veins before I leave.'

'In your dreams.'

A knock on the door interrupts them. Tanya looks on as her visitor opens it.

'You!' she gasps, watching as this unexpected caller fills the doorway.

'Get in before someone sees you!' her visitor berates the newcomer, but it's obvious from their tone they're thick as thieves.

It's all slotting into place. 'You're the one bringing in the new gear, aren't you?' Tanya states, not needing an answer. She jabs a finger towards the newcomer. 'And you're the one flogging it.' She rolls her eyes. 'I've seen it all now.'

'I don't think you have.'

Before she has a chance to resist she's being gripped by the arms, the flannel airing on her sink is rammed into her mouth, preventing her from screaming. She feels a sharp pain in her back as she's shoved onto her bunk. She struggles but it's pointless, her spindly arms and legs are powerless against her attacker's deadweight. She tries to shout but the towel stifles it. She looks on, terrified as her new visitor pulls drug-taking paraphernalia from their pocket and makes up a lethal cocktail before passing it to the bent PO.

'All you had to do was keep your nose out, but you couldn't do that, could you?'

Tanya stares at the loaded syringe as it inches towards her. 'Going round the block warning the women off the supply we were bringing in. A bit pot calling kettle, if you ask me! I mean, what gives you the right to mouth off like that given your history? I'm all for live and let live but you've made that fucking impossible now. Shame, so close to your release too. Never mind, it's not unusual for lifers to lose their bottle when it's time to leave prison. They realise they won't be able to hack it on the outside, decide it's not worth the effort trying.'

Tanya feels the needle push into the crease of her elbow, looks on as the deadly mix shoots under her skin. The hit is instant. Strong enough to kill and Tanya knows it. She feels it move through her veins like a fire coursing through her body. She seeks out the photo of her children, hopes that one day they will find it in their hearts to forgive her. Her eyes flicker closed and when she opens them again, she is on her beach, walking towards the ocean. The long white dress she wears clings to her calves as the water laps around her ankles. *This really is heaven*, is the last thing she thinks.

CHAPTER TWENTY-TWO

It's like a weight has been lifted. For the last two years, Alice Maltby's wild claim that Gary had been a victim of spiteful revenge has sat so heavily on my shoulders I'd begun to doubt myself. *Had* I intended to kill him that night? *Had* I responded to Hope's cries with murder already planted in my mind? Was I really a cold-blooded killer?

If you've never been in this position the difference may not seem like much, but let me tell you, it is huge. It means I no longer need to fear my anger. I can get wound up if something doesn't go my way and not worry that someone will die as a result of it. Besides, Gary's death was caused in part by his failure to follow workplace procedure. The fact that he couldn't keep his fists off Hope means I don't mourn him and never will, though I'll be careful how I phrase that during my parole hearing.

It's dinnertime association. The women clustered in groups along the landing look different to me and I know that already I'm distancing myself. Like an employee who has handed in their notice, the ground beneath me has shifted, I'm here but not here. I see a path, a way forward, a future beyond these walls.

As I look at the women around me with fresh eyes, I see that more of them are spaced out than normal. Tanya is right, this new supplier is certainly causing problems. A woman who'd gone through her induction session a month ago shuffles past me. Emaciated, scrawny, her cheeks are hollowed out. I make a mental note to speak with Magda again, see if we can't smoke out the person behind this.

I head to the dining area to share the news that Stacey has signed me off but Tanya isn't there and I want her to hear it first. I can picture her reaction, her toothless grin as she performs her happy dance. A smile plays on my lips at the thought of it. I can barely contain myself. Maybe I'll get to go to Turkey with Tanya after all, with Hope and the girls even, if Hope stays well enough. Wouldn't that be something? Vonnie looks up as I approach the table and asks how my session went but I'm cagey and she doesn't push. I jerk my thumb in the direction I've just come from. 'What's going on? It's like zombie apocalypse out there.'

Debs shakes her head. 'Buy one joint, get one free by the look of it.'

'Tan'll do her nut when she sees them. She said this would happen,' says Vonnie.

'Where is she?' I ask.

'Probably still dozing.' Lola gets up from the table. 'I'll go and give her a knock.'

I feel a shiver of unease on my shoulders, as though someone has just walked over my grave. 'No need,' I tell her quickly. 'I'll go.'

Something feels wrong. Tanya naps regularly in the afternoon, she makes no secret of it. It's not uncommon for recovering addicts to sleep a lot, it's a form of distraction, a way of getting through the day, takes their mind off the habit they ruined their life for. Even so, there's no way she'd sleep through association time. The grating of metal as the doors are unlocked elicits a Pavlovian response in most prisoners. Confined to our cells for the best part of a day, we become conditioned to recognise what the turning of the key means. That freedom, if only for a little while, is imminent.

There's a shift in the air. My earlier unease becomes an electric current that travels the length of my spine. Something is wrong but I don't know what. Call it a sixth sense, but when you've lived on a prison wing as long as I have you can feel the underground current, know instinctively when something is amiss.

I can't see the danger or smell it, but I know it's there.

Tanya was up in arms about the supply of drugs flooding the block, she made no secret of it. What if I'd misunderstood her fear? What if it was about more than her protecting the newbies coming onto the wing? What if she was worried that the temptation of cheap gear would be too much for her? That she'd revert to her old ways.

I push my way through the women gathered on the landing.

'Oi, watch it!' someone yelps as I elbow past.

'You seen Tanya?' I ask.

I'm greeted with a blank expression. I move on quickly.

'Anyone seen Tanya?' I call out to another group. The women shake their heads in reply.

I start to run. Running isn't allowed on the landing but something is amiss, I can feel it. As Tanya's cell comes into view, I know immediately that something is wrong. Every other cell door on the landing is wide open as women move freely between them. Something sharp twists in my gut.

Tanya's door is closed.

My chest thuds as I sprint the last few metres to her cell. I stop outside her door, too scared to go in. 'Tan!' I call out, hoping I'm worrying over nothing, that she'll come to the door groggy and call me a daft cow for freaking out.

She doesn't answer.

I push the door open and step inside.

Behind her barred window dark clouds cast the cell in an ominous gloom. I stand in the doorway for a moment as my eyes adjust to the dim interior. I wrinkle my nose. The air smells of vomit and something more cloying.

Tanya is huddled on the bed with her knees drawn in. 'Tan?' I say. My voice is high-pitched. She doesn't answer. A wave of nausea works its way from my stomach to my throat.

I turn on the light in the hope it will disturb her but she doesn't move. In an instant I'm beside her, shaking her by the shoulder, shouting her name. 'Tan! Tan!' What I wouldn't give right now to hear *May the Lord have Mercy on your soul*, followed by her gravelly laugh.

I peer at her closely. She's been sick. The vomit has pooled round her face, started to sink into the crumpled bedding beneath her. Her flannel is beside her and I use it to clear the debris from her mouth. Her face is blotchy, her skin cold as marble and when I roll her towards me, I see the needle of an empty syringe embedded in her arm. The truth of it hits me like a blow to the chest.

Tanya is dead.

The world becomes a kaleidoscope of moving images that turn and crash into each other. I hit the cell alarm button and yell for help, then run out onto the landing, searching up and down the wing for an officer close by to come and confirm what I already know, but there's no one there. Women making their way along the landing turn to stare at me, a look of incomprehension on their faces as I wave my arms around like I'm crazy. I *am* crazy.

'WE NEED HELP! NOW! PLEASE! HELP! SOMEONE HELP HER NOW!'

I run back into Tanya's cell and she's still lying there not moving and *think, think, think*, what can I do for her? What does she need? She is cold and dead but soon everything will be happening to her, rather than for her, I've seen it before. An officer will come in and check her pulse then perform CPR while they await orders from control. More officers will put the landing into lockdown. Paramedics will arrive and go through their prison death procedure, followed by the police to determine there are no suspicious circumstances – but Tanya will still be dead. All I can do in these final few minutes is keep her company. I climb onto her bunk, wrap my arms around her so that she isn't alone. I push my nose into the back of her neck and breathe in what's left of her, before she's reduced to nothing.

CHAPTER TWENTY-THREE

It's the next morning before they let us out onto the landing. Vonnie accompanies me as I make my way uncertainly towards Tanya's cell. My head is heavy, like I've woken from a terrible dream that still has me in its grasp. Was it a nightmare? Did I imagine it? Please, let it be so.

My head dips as Tanya's cell comes into view. A PO stands by the open door like a sentry. The interior has been stripped and deep cleaned, every trace of her gone. An inmate on cleaning duty puts a new mattress on her bunk. Beyond her cell, women gather on the landing. Some are crying, others, who didn't know her, look on, caught up in the excitement of it. They watch us approach, pointing and nodding in our direction. Do they think I can't see the shifty looks they're giving me? I try to swallow but the boulder in my throat won't budge.

'Let's go,' Vonnie whispers.

I turn away. My hands shake as I rake them through my hair, willing myself not to ball them into fists. I want to kick and punch and scream the place down. There's no place for anger, I remind myself. Anger gets you nowhere.

Why would Tanya do this?

Vonnie's voice. More insistent. 'Let's go find the others.'

The dining hall is quiet, the gawpers reluctant to leave the scene of sorrow for watery scrambled eggs and toast. Vonnie leads me to our table. The others stand and cluck around me while she fetches coffee. I watch as she steeps our mugs with sugar then brings them to the table.

'Fuck's sake!' cries Lola, summing up how we feel.

I sip at my coffee, staring at the spot where Tanya should be sitting.

I should have picked up the signs.

I should have seen she was struggling.

I should have taken her fears more seriously.

The others are silent. Sometimes words just don't cut it.

I slump back in my seat, dazed. When I left my appointment with Stacey yesterday, I'd started to believe that the world was full of possibilities. Today, the future I imagined has gone.

I stumble to my feet, pushing away Vonnie's hand when she tries to restrain me.

'Where are you going?' Debs calls after me, but I don't stop to explain.

I'm heading to Magda's cell, and this time I want answers.

Magda's minions must be off paying their respects as there isn't the usual wall of muscle to contend with. A lone henchwoman straightens herself as I approach. She looks mean and intimidating but when she blocks my path, I shove her out of the way with such force she doesn't have it in her to come back at me.

Magda hears the commotion and is at her cell door. What she sees on my face has her backing away.

'I'm sorry about Tanya!' she splutters, searching my face. Her gaze drops to my hands to see if I'm carrying a weapon.

I hold them out to her, empty. She watches as I ball them into fists.

'I swear to God, I could kill you,' I growl as I move towards her. I stop, remembering the last time I made a threat like that and hope the woman outside doesn't make the mistake of misunderstanding the context the way Alice Maltby did.

'I promise you the drugs weren't mine!' Magda says quickly. Her arms are in front of her, defensive. 'I told you I'd let things go with Tanya and I meant it. I didn't give her the gear, Mercy.'

Something in her expression makes me think she's telling the truth. I feel the fight drain out of me. I drop into a chair and shake my head. I don't know what to believe anymore.

'I never thought she'd cave in like that,' I mutter. 'I believed her when she said she was off it for good. She got hooked on pregabalin that a locum prescribed while she's been in here. She told me that because of that, a single dose of heroin could kill her. Reckoned it was one hell of an incentive to stay clean.'

Magda considers my words. 'That's what she told me when she came here shouting the odds.' She looks sheepish. 'She told me she was speaking up for the women who didn't know the risks. She knew she could never touch the stuff again because just one dose would be a death sentence for her.'

I look at her askance. 'So why did she do it, then?' I put my head in my hands. Perhaps you never really know someone. Perhaps Tanya was selfish like my mother after all. And yet.

Something flits across Magda's face. She drops down into the other chair, fixes me with a look. 'Mercy, I think we've got this all wrong. I don't think Tanya did this.'

CHAPTER TWENTY-FOUR

The others look at me agog. We're huddled around the table in the dining hall, voices low for fear of someone overhearing us. I've told them Magda and I don't believe Tanya wanted to kill herself, and that because of her other medication, a quick hit while no one was looking was never on the cards for her. 'Magda reckons someone killed her,' I tell the others. 'And I've got to admit, I do too.'

'Are you sure about this?' asks Debs. She doesn't know Tanya like the rest of us, has no reason to disbelieve the short statement that the governor released to the press. That Tanya's overdose was just another sad statistic of life in the criminal justice system, worded a certain way so the public won't blink when they skim over the headline. For most people, the concept of criminality is in the abstract, the individuals operating within it, sub-human. If you can't relate to the situation, it doesn't matter, right?

'Course she's sure!' snaps Lola.

'Who would do that to Tanya, though?' Vonnie asks, and on this I'm less confident.

I lower my voice further. 'We can't be certain, but it makes sense that it's the person who's been bringing the new supply of drugs in, given the shitstorm she whipped up mouthing off to Magda the other day.' I hold my hand up to stop the potential objections before they come. 'Magda is adamant *she's* got nothing to do with it and, well, I believe her.'

'So what do we do?' asks Debs. 'Do we tell one of the POs?'

We smile at her kindly. 'No one listens to cons,' Lola explains. 'That's just the way it is.'

'I was wondering,' I say, turning my head to Vonnie, 'if Wayne would be able to shed some light on who the supplier is? If he's as tight with his dealer as he made out to you, maybe he could get him to put his ear to the ground.'

It's risky, I know. Wayne could misconstrue Vonnie's request for help as a mating call, one that he'll be all too happy to respond to with fervour. If she doesn't keep her wits about her, she'll be back to square one.

'It's okay,' she says as though reading my mind. 'Anything for Tan. I'll go and give him a call now.'

I place my hand on her arm as she gets up. 'We keep this to ourselves,' I say, looking around the table. 'Whoever did this to Tanya could come after us if they find out we're sticking our beaks in.'

'Agreed,' they say in unison.

Vonnie returns from her call to Wayne looking glum. 'He thought I was ringing to get back with him. I considered stringing him along, but it didn't seem fair, so I told him I wanted a no-strings attached favour.'

'Did he agree?'

She looks at me, disappointed. 'No. This is Wayne, remember, there has to be something in it for him.'

I sit down on my bunk. 'Tell me what you said to him.'

'I told him what happened to Tan. He said he was sorry, that she seemed a game old bird.'

'He's a piece of work,' I splutter. 'She was the same age as me!'

Von looks at me wide-eyed.

'That's what drugs do to you.' I shrug, thinking how Tan's life would have started to change, once she'd had the dental surgery and some sun on her skin.

'Anyway, he said there was no way he could help. Him and Ronnie, his dealer, are busy building up their patch, they don't have time to go round acting like Feds.'

I can see where she went wrong. Asking someone without a moral compass to do something altruistic is a non-starter.

'I think we need to reframe this proposition to him,' I say.

'What do you mean?'

'Magda's tight-lipped about who the member of staff is she has on her payroll. But she let slip a while back that they earn a couple of grand a month off the money she makes.'

'Whoa, nice little earner for someone.'

'Exactly. So what's to say the staff member bringing in the new supply isn't on a similar deal?'

'And?'

'Well, if you tell that to Wayne, broken into words of one syllable, he might be able to grasp how lucrative it is. You know, if there's enough profit left over out of what these dealers make to pay out that kind of money... It might motivate him to find out who this person is so it leaves a way in for him and his mate once they've been removed.'

Vonnie blanches. 'When you say, removed, Mercy...'

'I mean reported to the authorities, Von, I'm hardly going to act like a mob boss now I'm up for parole.'

Her face brightens. 'Your shrink's agreed to sign you off?' she asks eagerly.

I'm ashamed that she finds out like this. She deserves to witness my joy, not just my sadness. 'I'm all but touching distance from it,' I say cautiously. I see the look that flashes across her face and can tell that she's hurt. 'I was evasive yesterday because I wanted Tan to be the first to know. And then, well, after everything that's happened...' My words trail off.

'I get it. Tan was your best mate. I've never had one,' she admits. 'Wayne always claimed my friends got in the way of our relationship, not that we did anything together other than shoplift and get the bus to his dealer.'

I regard Vonnie. 'I don't think I've ever had a "best" friend either. I think different friends can be important to you at different times in your life for all manner of reasons. That makes each one of them special.'

Vonnie's shoulders lift. 'Let me make another call and see if I can't get that daft lump to change his mind.'

I sit, not moving, long after Vonnie has left to use the phone, her footsteps echoing along the corridor. I drop my head into my hands and close my eyes. I snap them open again when all I can see is the image of Tanya lying on her bunk. Something inside me starts to shift and tear. I can't shake off the feeling that I could have done something more, offered to help her find who was responsible for the new drugs coming in. Instead, all I offered were a few words of caution – which deep down I knew she'd ignore.

The room starts to tilt as my breathing goes into overdrive. I run to the toilet and throw up. I wipe my mouth with the back of my hand, splash cold water on my face. Guilt pulsates through me like an electric current. 'I'm sorry, Tan,' I say into the void.

I'm the guardian of her memory now. She never got her happy ending, but I vow she will get justice.

Von bursts into our cell with a jubilant look on her face. 'Wayne's agreed to help! He's going to get his dealer to speak to the local faces he's in cahoots with. No one's got looser lips than a con on a winning streak. Says he'll get onto it straight away.'

'You sure he knows he'll get nothing in return? From you, I mean.'

She throws me a look. 'That ship has sailed, but you were right, he sees this as a business opportunity.' She looks worried. 'You don't really want him running his business from here, do you? It feels wrong, after Tanya.'

I shake my head. 'If things go according to plan, then the shutters will come down so fast on this wing once we've outed the supply chain that there'll be no chance for anyone to step into their shoes.'

'Let's hope so,' says Von.

'How long does Wayne reckon they need to get round all his dealer's contacts?' I ask her.

'Forty-eight hours. He says I'm to ring him the day after tomorrow.'

I nod towards the ceiling. This is for you, Tanya.

CHAPTER TWENTY-FIVE

Liam sits waiting for me in the legal visits room. It's the first time I've been out of my cell since I went to see Magda two days ago.

Three days since Tanya's murder.

Vonnie's been bringing me food despite me telling her I've no appetite. 'What would you do if it was the other way around?' she asks me, and I pull a face.

'I'd tell you it's a free country and if you want to starve then knock yourself out.' She caught me grinning when I said that, though I refused to admit it.

The wing has returned to normal, the rent-a-crowd mourners who formed a vigil outside Tanya's cell the morning after her death haven't returned. I'm not ready to deal with people like that yet, people for whom Tanya's passing was nothing more than a ripple of excitement in an otherwise tedious day.

Liam gets to his feet. He's wearing a pristine shirt beneath his suit jacket and a worried frown. The lines in his forehead are deep. His eyes rake over me as though he's looking for answers to a question he hasn't asked.

'Don't give up,' he says.

When I rang to tell him about Tanya, he got it straight away. Maybe you have to work with lifers to see us as people, to view us as more than the crime we've committed. Tanya had paid the price for killing the man who beat her while pimping her out, yet I can imagine her epitaph; her achievements listed in proportion to their scale, like ingredients in a ready meal.

Killer. Junkie. Whore. Mother. RIP.

To me she was just *Friend.*

My gaze locks on to Liam's face. To the compassion in it. 'I'll try not to,' I answer.

And so to business. My parole hearing, he's pleased to inform me, has been arranged for two days' time. 'You'll be ready, won't you?' His gaze returns to my overworn clothes and unkempt hair and I offer him a weak smile.

Hope would normally have brought something in for me to wear but I don't want her coming here. She insists she feels well most of the time, but that's not the same as *being* well. 'Don't worry, I've got it all under control,' I lie.

Liam visibly relaxes. 'Dr North has confirmed she supports the psychologist's recommendation for release, so all you've got to do is turn up and wow the panel.'

'Don't you mean *knock 'em dead.*' I twist my mouth into a grin to let him know that I'm joking.

He looks at me awkwardly. 'Have you thought about your answer? For when the panel asks if you regret what you did?'

I feel his gaze on me as I consider my response. 'I'll never regret saving my sister's life,' I say stubbornly.

He tenses up. 'That's the part where you may come unstuck, then.'

I shrug. 'I can't help it if my answers don't fit perfectly into their neat little squares.'

Liam removes his jacket as though he's resigned himself to

being here for a while. I'm struck by how toned he is for someone who spends all his time poring over case law. He catches me looking, moves his head imperceptibly. I guess being ogled by women serving long custodial sentences must be a hazard of the job. I wonder what Tanya will say when I tell her I've been perving over my lawyer. Then it hits me like a fist that she's gone.

'It's okay,' he tells me, seeing my stricken face, and I hope his telepathy can't reach all my private thoughts. 'We'll keep at it until you get it right.'

He looks on, perplexed, when I start to laugh.

Debs and Lola *happen* to swing by my cell during association time. The giveaway it's pre-arranged are the mugs that they're carrying. 'Make yourselves a drink if you want one,' I tell them. I've hunkered down in my bunk. When Vonnie went out to get our lunch I didn't realise she'd send in reinforcements.

They put their mugs by the kettle but sit down without bothering to switch it on. Debs speaks first. 'Liam says your hearing's this week.'

Snitch. 'That's a breach of client confidentiality, that is,' I reply.

'He said you'd say that.'

I was going to ask if she'd seen him without his jacket on but for some reason, I want to keep my pervy thought to myself.

'I've got a date for my appeal,' Debs tells me, referring to the application Liam submitted to overturn the sentence meted out to her in the family court. 'It's the week after next.'

'That's great, Debs, I'm pleased for you. I told you Liam's a good 'un.'

She pauses, or waits, because I can tell that there's more. 'I can lend you the blouse I wore to court when I was sent down,' she offers hesitantly. 'For when you attend your parole hearing.'

'Lucky shirt, is it?' I snipe. I catch the look on her face and shake my head wildly. 'I'm sorry! I know you mean well.' I run my fingers along my scalp and tug at my hair. 'It's all happening so fast I haven't given much thought to what I'm going to wear, to tell you the truth.'

'Liam said as much.'

So I hadn't fooled him, then.

'Vonnie says she'll do your make-up.'

I roll my eyes. 'It's a legal hearing, not the *Strictly* final.'

'She knows. She just wants to help, like I do.'

I sense Lola's gaze on me. 'How've you been?' I look quickly at Debs before turning my attention back to her.

'It's okay, I've told her about my dad. Vonnie knows too.'

Debs widens her eyes at me to convey her revulsion at Lola's situation but she doesn't say anything, from now on it's about helping Lola feel better about her life, not worse.

'My parents are sticking to their guns about not letting me see Danny, so things aren't great. It was a lot easier when he was a baby. Now he's bigger he's starting to be aware of the tension between us. My drinking hasn't helped.'

She's right. There's nothing I can say to sugar-coat that. 'Forget everything that's gone before, Lola, it's what you do now that matters. You've been dry for how long?'

'The two weeks I've been back in this shithole,' she mutters.

'And before that?'

'Six months.'

'There you go, then. You fell off the wagon briefly, that's all.'

'I suppose so.'

'Seriously, Lola, every day you're turning a corner, don't lose sight of that.'

'Not much of a prospect though, am I? Every time I broach

the subject of having Danny come and live with me, Mum says the same thing: "You'd actually prise him away from the only stable home he's known?"'

'His father's a paedophile,' I remind her.

'Yeah, and you know what her stock reply to that is? "Fine, let them take him into care. I'm not kicking my husband out because you couldn't keep your knickers on for him." I wanted to spew the first time she said that to me.'

'Some people,' I mutter, shaking my head.

'I can't ignore everything Mum says though. What if she's right and I'm destined to keep falling off the wagon? I couldn't sleep last night worrying about it. My mind was racing. The problem is I still think about my next drink, even in here. I can't help it, especially when I get stressed about Danny, which is all the time, and when I have a drink, I think I'm invincible; the brakes never go on, then afterwards I hate myself.' Lola pauses for breath.

I sit up on my bunk and pat the space beside me. Lola plonks herself by my side. 'Tell your mum you're determined to stay sober and will continue with AA meetings when you get out. Remind her that Danny's your son and you have rights. Stick to your guns and don't get embroiled in a slanging match.'

'But if I upset her, I don't get to see Danny.'

'She's already preventing you from seeing him. You need to show her that she doesn't have the upper hand anymore. Two weeks and you're out of here. Reduce the contact you have with her. Let her stew about what you've got planned.'

She looks alarmed. 'What have I got planned?'

I put on a show of looking more confident than I feel. 'That's a minor detail. One we can work on over the next few weeks.'

Debs studies me. 'You realise, don't you, if we all play our cards right, we'll all be on the outside soon. Won't that be brilliant?'

Not all of us, I want to say, but I don't want to burst her bubble. My thoughts segue to Tanya, and Turkey, and the future stolen from her.

'Imagine,' I say, trying my hardest to do just that.

Dinnertime association

'You got a minute, Mercy?'

Magda appearing in my doorway is a sobering sight. Running her empire takes up all her time; she doesn't drop in on anyone.

'This is a turn up for the books. Glad you made it past security.' I look pointedly at Vonnie who's eating a Pot Noodle while she flicks through a magazine. She doesn't bother glancing up.

'Seems I've got a bit of a problem,' Magda says. She looks at the chair opposite me and I nod. She lowers herself into it. 'Any news your end?' She picks at her fingernails while she waits for my answer.

'Vonnie's waiting for an update,' I reply. 'How about you?'

She moves her head slowly from side to side. 'I've been met with a brick wall everywhere I turn,' she admits. She looks distracted. 'I'm wondering if I'm losing my grip. I'm getting on a bit now.'

'You've got a good few years of knee-capping and extortion ahead of you. I wouldn't go throwing the towel in any time soon,' I say good-naturedly. 'Unless you'd prefer to make an honest living,' I add quickly.

'Some old dogs aren't meant to learn new tricks. They're just meant to perform the old ones better.'

I throw her a look. 'A bit cryptic, Magda. Care to elaborate?'

'Be more choosy about who I consort with,' she explains. She looks done in and I have to remind myself that even bullies have off days.

She heaves out a breath. 'I was on the landing earlier. There was a woman wearing a bracelet the exact same as Lena's.'

'If you shop in mid-range stores…' I joke.

Magda's face doesn't flicker. 'I made it for her in the craft workshop.'

My eyebrows shoot into my hairline and I work hard to pull them back. There are weekly craft classes in the education centre where those bored enough can learn collage, quilling, origami, and making things out of recycled items, or as I prefer to call it, tat. I keep my eyebrows in place as I hear her confession: that when she's not renting out dodgy telecoms and dealing pharma, she's sitting in a circle making friendship bracelets. I guess we've all got to blow off steam.

'You get to bring in your own materials, once they've been vetted,' she explains. 'I made the bracelet out of leather from an old bag that belonged to my mam. I stitched Lena's initials inside it.'

Vonnie's stopped reading and is following our conversation. We lock eyes for a second, blink, then look away.

'Lovely,' I say, unsure what else Magda wants to hear.

Her face goes slack. 'You'd think so, wouldn't you? Lena loved it when I gave it to her. She's never taken it off.'

'So this woman's stolen it, then?'

Magda scratches her head. 'That was my first thought,' she admits. 'So you can imagine my reaction.'

I picture the offender laid out in the medical room.

Magda can tell from the alarm on my face what I'm thinking. 'She managed to tell me that she found it… before things got too physical,' she adds quickly.

Maybe not laid out, then.

She opens the palm of her hand to show me a tri-colour plaited bracelet; it's the kind of thing worn by students and surfers. The edges are frayed where I presume it slipped off Lena's wrist.

Something heavy settles in my stomach. I feel I already know the answer but I have to ask the question anyway.

'Where did she find it?'

Magda shoves it into the pocket of her dungarees and swallows. 'Tanya's cell. Said she found it down the side of her bunk, where the mattress butts up against the wall. She was part of the cleaning team who cleared it out.'

It's common knowledge that cleaners get first pickings when a cell gets turned over. It's why the waiting list for that particular job is so long.

'How the hell did it get there?' asks Vonnie, forgetting that she's not supposed to be listening.

'That's not the question that needs asking, is it?' I turn to Magda and can see we're on the same page. 'Why the hell didn't Lena tell you she'd lost it?'

I turn back to Vonnie. 'Time to make that call to Wayne, Von. See if he can corroborate that Lena's gone rogue.'

'Hark at you with your *cor-rob-o-rate*,' Vonnie jokes as she climbs down from her bunk. She's trying to lighten the mood but it's too late for that. I force out a laugh but Magda doesn't even try. She's hurting, raging, too busy planning her next move.

I don't bother telling her that there's bound to be a simple explanation. One that doesn't involve Lena dealing drugs behind her back and murdering my friend.

We await Vonnie's return in silence.

'Wayne's dealer certainly pulled out all the stops,' Vonnie says when she returns half an hour later. 'He knows a couple of small-time faces who've been supplying Forest Bank Prison and Strangeways. He paid one of them a visit on the pretext of sounding them out to join forces to supply Fairmile. His mate warned him off, told him Magda's set up was a one-woman enterprise. That if he valued his nads, he'd keep the hell away.' She looks at Magda as she says this.

'See, your rep's still intact,' I tell her, nodding at Von to continue.

'Wayne told him that can't be right. That he'd heard someone else was dipping their toe in the water. Making a killing by the sound of it too. I'm sure he didn't mean it like that,' Vonnie says quickly. I flap my hands, encouraging her to get on with it. 'The guy he was speaking to said it was news to him but he'd ask around. He was coming round to Wayne's line of thinking, that if Magda's not got the monopoly anymore, it leaves the way for others to take a punt.'

Magda and I wait. 'He got back to Wayne this morning. Said, and I'm using his words, not mine,' Vonnie adds carefully, '"Hey, mate, you'll never believe it. The person shafting Magda is none other than her butch girlfriend, Lena. Reckon she's got a big pair of balls on her." No offence, like,' Vonnie says quickly.

'Where's the supply coming from?' Magda asks sharply.

'Lena's got a cousin just finished a ten stretch for armed robbery. Decided to branch out into narcotics instead. Went on a reconnaissance trip to Morocco, came back thinking he's Pablo Escobar, by all accounts. Makes sense they're keeping it in the family, I suppose.'

I nod in agreement. 'How's she getting it in here then?' I turn to Magda. 'You sure she's not using your mule?'

Magda shakes her head. 'I'm not sure about much at the moment, but I'm pretty certain of that.'

'It has to be another screw,' says Vonnie. 'Lena'd need a shedload of visitors to smuggle in the amounts Tanya was talking about. It's not feasible.'

'Agreed,' says Magda, still trying to get her head around it. 'To think that my Lena would do something like this.'

She's talking about the betrayal, which must be devastating, especially if it threatens her livelihood. I fix her with a look. 'What about Tanya though? Lena's bracelet was found between Tanya's mattress and wall. It could have come off in a struggle. Do you think Lena would force a recovering addict to take drugs?' A thought occurs to me. 'Or even inject them into her, if she put up a fight?' I stare at her.

'Yes,' she says dismissively, as though that isn't really the point.

My breath catches as I process this. Lena murdered Tanya.

My eyes bore into Magda's forehead. Behind it lies a brain shaped differently to mine. We're angry at the same person for very different reasons. We can still make this work. Your enemy is my enemy, and all that.

'I know you're pretty cut up about this...' I begin, cursing my choice of words. Lena will pay for betraying Magda, and when I think what she did to Tanya, there's a part of me feels she deserves what's coming to her. However, what I want is justice. I need to harness Magda's anger and put it to our advantage. I eye her steadily. '...but before you do anything rash, we need her to lead us to this prison officer. The one she's in cahoots with. You understand that, don't you?'

Her eyes have taken on a glazed look, as though the red mist has already descended.

'Magda, please...' I push.

'Okay,' she says eventually. 'Tell me what you want to do.'

CHAPTER TWENTY-SIX

'Are you completely insane?' Vonnie is beside herself.

She'd listened, incredulous, as I'd laid out my plan to Magda. A plan that I'd concocted on the hoof, with all the meticulous detail of notes scribbled on the back of a cigarette packet. They'd both stared at me when I'd finished.

'So you're basically going to trail Lena until she makes contact with this bent screw of hers?'

'I don't see any other way. We can't take this to the governor yet, we don't have any proof.'

'We could give her the information that Wayne found out for us.'

'Information isn't evidence, Von.'

Vonnie frowns. She can see my point but she isn't happy. 'Lena could kill you too,' she says quietly.

Magda hasn't contradicted her, which is concerning, I admit.

It's for this reason that I'm standing in our cell holding a phone Magda has spirited out of her orifice, attempting to keep up as she talks me through its functionality. A career in Carphone Warehouse beckons if she ever goes legit. The main function I'm interested in is the record button, and how to make a recording without drawing attention to myself. She runs through the procedure with a couple of bells and whistles thrown in and after a couple of failed attempts, I'm good to go.

I'm wearing my *Here to Help* yellow vest, which seems counterintuitive since I don't want to draw attention to myself or have anyone stop me for advice, but it gives me a freedom of movement not available to other prisoners.

'Seriously, Mercy, have you thought this through?' Vonnie persists.

'Probably better that I don't,' I answer truthfully. If I thought about it too much, I'd run for the hills. Assuming I could get past the prison gate, that is.

As I step out onto the wing, I slow my walk to match the shuffle of those around me. I nod as I pass a group of women on the landing, they nod back. If they wonder why I'm meandering like them rather than walking briskly to the induction block as I normally do, they don't show it. A newbie approaches me and asks how she can sign up for education classes. I tell her, all the while scanning the horizon for Lena. I lean over the landing rail. The safety mesh that separates the landing from the floor below – installed to thwart suicide attempts and missile throwing – creates a mosaic pattern of the women standing in line to order their canteen.

'Looking for someone?' Officer Murdoch calls out to me. I remember his kindness the day I learned of Hope's condition. As far as Murdoch's concerned, there's no *them* and *us*.

I shake my head. 'Just making sure the women I inducted last week are settling in.'

He studies me. 'I'm sorry about your mate.'

I nod, unable to trust my voice.

He shoves bony hands into his trouser pockets and lets out a sigh. 'How are we supposed to stop it happening when you're all locked up out of sight for so long.' It isn't really a question, more a show of frustration. 'There just aren't e-fucking-nough of us to go round.'

'There wouldn't be any drug deaths if the drugs couldn't get in in the first place,' I say, eyeing him.

He doesn't blink. He's not been here long enough to strike up allegiances. 'You're preaching to the converted there.'

I try my luck with him. 'Any idea who's bringing it in?'

He turns his close-to-retirement face to me. 'No, and I don't want to know. Where there's drugs there's violence. They don't pay me enough to play detective.' He regards me shrewdly. 'I believe you've got a parole hearing coming up.'

It isn't a question but I nod anyway.

'A word to the wise, then. Focus on the next phase of your life and keep your head down. There's many a person come unstuck because they involved themselves in the business of others.'

I watch him amble away, my hand skimming over the illegal phone in my pocket as I resume my search for Tanya's killer.

And then I see her.

Walking purposefully through the social area on the ground floor, Lena takes a left towards the shower block. I move quickly along the landing, hurrying down the stairs and through the communal area, keeping her in view. She isn't carrying a towel or washbag so unless she intends to dry herself using one of the hand dryers, my guess is she isn't going for a shower. It occurs to me that I'm also not carrying a towel or washbag, a part of my cunning plan that I hadn't properly thought through.

She swings round as she nears the entrance, and I wonder if she can sense she's being followed. I drop down to the floor, start fiddling with the laces on my trainers. Lena's face looks shifty as she scans the women milling around but thankfully, I don't attract her attention. When she turns and steps quickly into the shower block, I follow her in. She bypasses the toilets that flank the entrance to the changing area, heading towards the showers tucked around the corner. I slip into the toilet cubicle closest to the showers, closing the door quietly before sliding the lock into place.

The toilet has been blocked with skid-marked loo roll and the once white porcelain is now the colour of smokers' teeth. I close the lid and sit down, lifting my feet onto the lid in case whoever's meeting Lena checks under the gap in each door for anyone loitering. Since the smoking ban, women come in here for an illicit cigarette, though going by the grubby knickers and discarded Femidoms on top of the sanitary bin beside me that's not the only thing they get up to.

I realise as I sit here that I know nothing about Lena's past. All I know is that she's a bully and is responsible in some way for Tanya's death. I wish I'd realised this sooner. I could have added *Bring something to defend myself* to my plan.

The partition walls are greasy as though many hands, knees and other body parts have slapped against them over the years. The graffiti is predictable, *Tracey loves Kim*, a drawing of someone's labia, and several inmates have been outed as 'slags'.

I sit in silence, my ears alert to everything going on around me: water running through the cistern next door, a tap dripping into one of the washbasins out front, and the sound of Lena pacing the floor. Footsteps echoing on the hard tiles signal the arrival of the person she's meeting. The jangling keys indicate it's a PO.

Instead of a greeting there are sounds of a scuffle and a body being slammed against the wall repeatedly. 'Fucking bitch!' Lena yells. *Thump. Kick.* She's punching soft tissue; a blow to the face would be hard for them both to explain away. I use the opportunity of the racket she's making to slide the lock open on the cubicle door so I can open it a fraction. I peep through the gap. I see Lena but not the person she's laying into. I slip Magda's phone out of my pocket and hit *record*. Place it on the toilet seat. I turn back to the gap in the door. If I crane my head around it, I'll have them both in my line of vision. I give it a try.

Lena is laying into Officer Frame.

I don't know how it's possible to be disappointed in someone that hates you and you hate back, yet that's how I feel. When someone is obnoxious for as long as you've known them, when they've denigrated you and your friends for being inferior, for being worthless, for being a general waste of skin, there's some part of you that believes the truth of it, that there must be some flaw inside you that this other person can see. And even though you hate the way that makes you feel, you believe this person is better than you, that even though they treat you like crap you deserve it. As far as I know Frame is cruel, not bent, and yet here she is, getting several shades kicked out of her for a reason I hope Lena is about to make very clear.

The slamming stops as abruptly as it begins, followed by heavy breathing. Frame breaks the silence. 'Feel better now you've got that out of your system? *Ooof*.'

Lena answers with her fist.

'You have one fucking job!' snarls Lena. 'All you have to do is bring in the gear. How difficult can it be?'

'That's where you're wrong, sweet cheeks,' spits Frame, brushing herself down. 'I do more than bring the gear in. I've been working on our strategy. Thanks to me, Magda doesn't see us as a credible threat.'

'You reckon?'

'I was the one who set it up so that we'd find smack both times I spun the cells, the governor's under the impression she's dealing with amateurs. At the same time, turning the cells over regularly puts pressure on your bird to rein it in. Everyone knows she's the biggest dealer in Fairmile. Any crackdown will have a huge impact on her business. Gives us plenty of opportunity to muscle in and take over her share.'

'Yeah, I remember that was our *intention*.' Lena's voice drips with ice. 'Remind me where killing a junkie came into the fucking equation.'

'She was shouting her mouth off about the gear that was coming in.'

'Nobody was listening! How has killing her made any difference?'

'It hasn't, I suppose.' Frame shrugs. 'Though I did get a kick out of it.' The smile she gives Lena is pure evil. 'Watching her face when I stuck the needle in…'

Her reply makes my chest thud so loudly I have to hold my breath to compensate. Lena's stone-like features flinch ever so slightly. 'I've met cold-blooded murderers with more heart than you.'

Frame puffs out her cheeks. 'Pleasure's all mine,' she says, tipping her head.

Lena regards her with distaste. 'Back to business,' she drawls. 'My brother's got another batch for you to bring in. He'll drop it over to your place tonight.'

Frame nods.

'How soon can you bring it in?'

Frame considers this. 'The day after tomorrow. Deano should be on the gate so it won't be any problem. As long as I keep bunging him a couple of hundred quid here and there, he's happy.'

This seems to satisfy Lena. 'No fuck-ups this time. No more cell spinning.'

'I'll see what I can do,' mutters Frame defiantly.

Lena's face darkens. 'You really don't want to get on the wrong side of me, you know. I can put you in the ground without breaking into a sweat. And unlike you, I don't need a syringe full of smack to do it.'

The casual way they talk about killing Tanya sends me reeling. I close the door and slide the bolt across but I step back too quickly, knocking the mobile phone onto the floor. It lands with a clatter.

'What the fuck was that?' demands Lena.

I grab the phone off the floor.

'Who's there?' demands Frame. I hear her footsteps stomp across the tiles. She's heading towards the toilet cubicles. She stops outside mine. 'Get the fuck out!' she yells.

I freeze. If she finds me, if she finds me with a phone, a phone that's recorded her and Lena discussing killing Tanya and smuggling drugs into the prison, I'm dead.

I clamp my hand over my mouth to stop my heavy breathing.

'You heard me!' Frame says.

Resigned, I'm about to unlock the door when I hear a familiar voice.

'Wind your neck in, Frame. I've been sent to find you,' barks Officer Murdoch.

'You shouldn't be in here,' Frame insists.

Male officers are only supposed to come into the shower room in an emergency, like a fight or code-red – when someone's cut their wrists or is a swinger. What *is* he doing here? Am I still about to be rumbled?

'Hall manager wants to see you; said it was important.' The next time he speaks his voice is low. 'You seem to have trouble remembering I'm the senior officer on this wing, Frame. Next time you have a memory lapse like that I'll have you put on report.'

Frame mutters something to save face before doing as she's told.

'You'd better get going too,' he says to Lena. 'Association time's nearly over.'

'Right you are,' she says suggestively. 'Unless you'd like me to stay and keep you company?'

'If it's all the same to you I'll pass,' says Murdoch.

'You know you want to,' Lena calls to him in a mock sing-song voice but, like Frame, she does as he says.

The room falls silent.

There's a knock on the cubicle door. 'You can come out now.'

I pocket Magda's phone before I unlock the door and step out. 'Talk about good timing,' I say sheepishly.

'We don't have long,' he says. 'Frame's about to knock on the hall manager's door and find out he doesn't want to see her. I'm not sure she'll see the funny side.' His face grows serious. 'What the hell are you playing at?'

I don't know whether he can be trusted so I try to deflect him with a question. 'Why did you follow me?'

He gives my question some thought. 'In truth?' He shakes his head. 'I don't know. Something didn't feel right. You do the job as long as I have and you get a sense for things. When I asked you who you were looking for and you gave me that cock and bull story about checking on new inmates, I knew you were up to something. You lose your friend to an overdose and you start asking me how I think the drugs are coming in. All the while your eyes are darting around the place like there's someone you really need to see. When I saw you take off down the stairs at a rate of knots, I figured you must have found them.' He gives me a look. 'Only Lena isn't someone you normally consort with, yet you were going after her like a dog chasing a rabbit, both hightailing it here. It got my antennae twitching. Made me think I'd better check what was going on. Then I see Officer Frame making a beeline for the same place and I reckoned whatever the two of you were up to, if she caught you, you'd be for the high jump. Thought I'd step in and defuse the situation, only to find you're nowhere to be seen and it's Lena and Frame who are in cahoots.'

I blow out a breath. 'Jesus, Murdoch, I could kiss you.'

He steps back in alarm. 'I've already been propositioned today, thank you very much.'

'I'm pretty certain you just saved my life.'

'What are you talking about?' He eyes me curiously.

'I need to speak to the governor, it's urgent. Will you help me?'

'You can't just see the governor at the drop of a hat, you know. There's a process to follow, starting with there needs to be a damn good reason.'

'How does murder sound?'

His eyes bulge. 'What?'

I consider playing Lena and Frame's conversation to him but am worried he'll take one look at Magda's phone and confiscate it before putting me on a disciplinary.

I change tack.

'Why didn't you let on I was here? Why did you lie to Frame about the hall manager wanting to see her?'

He takes his time before answering, as though he's replaying the scene in his head. 'Something felt off. I heard Frame yell "Who's there?" as though a noise had disturbed them.'

I nod eagerly. 'It was me. I dropped my– I banged the cubicle door,' I say quickly.

Officer Murdoch nods. 'I walked in while she was shouting and I was happy to let her think it was me that had been lurking about. She's bad-tempered so much of the time I'm used to it, but when I saw her standing there I could see she wasn't angry, she was scared. I wondered what she and Lena had been talking about that would get her so rattled. Lena was spooked too. And since you were missing from this little meeting it got me thinking you didn't want either of them to know you were here.' He fixes me with a look. 'You look pretty rattled yourself, now I'm thinking about it. So, everyone's rattled and now you want to see the governor. Give me one good reason and I'll take you there myself.'

I pull Magda's phone from my pocket.

'Just listen,' I plead when he opens his mouth to object.

CHAPTER TWENTY-SEVEN

Officer Murdoch shows no emotion as he listens to the recording, but his eyes briefly meet mine when we get to the part where Frame admits to getting a kick out of killing Tanya. 'You need to get that copied,' he says, holding his palm out to me as if to say he doesn't want to know how I get that done. 'Then we go to the governor.'

'Aren't you shocked?' I ask him.

His shoulders visibly deflate. 'I blew the whistle on a colleague for dealing at my old place. They ended up with a conviction and I got a transfer.'

'No good turn goes unpunished,' I tell him, remembering Deb's words to me when I'd recounted my set-to with Alice Maltby.

'Which is why you need a copy of that recording. That way if something, somewhere down the line doesn't go your way, you've got leverage.'

I can see his logic but we're running out of time. 'I don't know how long that's going to take and we're due to be locked up any minute. You heard them, Frame's bringing a new batch of drugs in the day after tomorrow.'

'*Get that copy*,' insists Murdoch. 'You think I'd be here if I'd been smart enough to protect my own interests? Go on, get a move on. I'll come and get you when Frame's shift's over. We'll go to the governor then.'

The henchwoman guarding Magda's cell is the one I'd had a run-in with. She doesn't try to bar my way when I tap on Magda's door and step inside. Lena is sitting in the same seat as before. She regards me with such contempt I have to reassure myself that's the way she is and she has no idea I was listening to her and Frame in the shower block.

'Leave us,' Magda instructs and for once I'm grateful she's a woman of few words. She closes the cell door behind her once Lena has gone. 'I can't bear to be in the same room as her anymore,' she hisses. 'I hope you coming here means you've got something.'

I play the recording for her. She grimaces when Frame refers to her so dismissively but when Lena speaks her face turns to granite.

'I need you to make a copy of it before I go to the governor, so I've got backup if something goes wrong.' Like the governor trying to shaft me is essentially what Murdoch is warning me about.

Magda seems undaunted. 'Leave it with me,' she says. 'I'll get it done this evening.'

'No, Magda. If it's all the same to you, I'll wait.' I'm not sure I can trust her either. She's in love with a woman who helped murder my friend. I'm not sure even she knows where her loyalties lie.

Her mouth stretches into a grin. 'You'd better look away then,' she instructs me as she fiddles with her under-carriage.

Governor Cassidy regards me like I'm something repugnant. Which, given the convicts who've been through Fairmile's doors over the years, is a bit rich.

I'm standing across the desk from her in her office, Officer Murdoch is by my side. At his request there are no other officers in the room.

She listens grim-faced, while I play the recording, wincing visibly at times as though she has indigestion. When the recording finishes, she gets up to look out of her window, though I don't think she sees anything other than the shitstorm that's fast approaching.

'Okaaay...' she says slowly, before returning to her seat.

Now she's leaning back in her chair with a face that says she wished she'd pulled a sickie this morning; nothing more taxing than a box set and a bottle of Cab Sav ahead of her. Instead, she's here, having to deal with the grenade that's landed in her lap and she doesn't like it one little bit. She shifts her gaze to the corner of her office as she ponders the contents of the recording.

As I'd hoped, its existence has wiped away all the obvious questions that follow when you make a serious allegation. *Are you sure that's what they said? Are you sure that's what they did? Are you sure it was them*? *Could you be mistaken? Mental?* The nifty little file on this phone has done away with all of that. All I had to do was hit the play button and *bam!* our upwardly mobile governor is practically horizontal.

'Do I need to remind you that the use of unauthorised mobile phones is strictly prohibited?' she demands.

I stare at her wide-eyed. Okay, she's angry and she's swinging low. I've had all afternoon to process what she's obviously still wrestling with.

'I wanted to bring you credible evidence of who's been smuggling the drugs in. I couldn't see any other way.'

She stares at me, stoney-faced. 'Very well. I'm prepared to overlook this if you tell me where you got the phone.'

'Or what?' I challenge. Officer Murdoch was right. Deny, minimise, blame. The stock response when a whistleblower comes knocking. 'Surely that's not the issue here?'

'Indiscipline must be rooted out at every level.'

'I had a feeling that might be your response,' I tell her, careful to leave Murdoch out of it. He's been bitten once; he's under no obligation to get bitten again. 'So before I approached Officer Murdoch here, I had a copy of the recording made. For insurance purposes.' I offer her a smile but we both know it's fake.

'Not wise to be issuing threats this side of your parole hearing.'

'Works both ways.' I mimic her tone.

The governor's attention returns to the mobile, which I'd placed in the middle of her desk. She points, without touching it, like she knows where it's usually kept. 'It's not admissible in court, even if I did do something with it.' She says this to Officer Murdoch.

I bite down on my cheek. She's looking for help but doesn't want it from me.

Murdoch regards her. 'You heard the tape, Gov. Frame's bringing in heroin the day after tomorrow. You've got a chance to catch her red-handed.'

She perks up at the prospect of coming out of this smelling of roses. 'Yes, of course. I'll speak to gold command, get everything in position.' Only then does her attention return to me.

'You realise this is a highly sensitive situation?'

'You realise one of your officers killed my friend?' My shoulders are raised, bracing for battle. 'Tanya never baulked at serving her sentence. Accepted every day of it as the price to be paid to be free from her pimp. She deserves justice too.'

The governor sags as though the fight's gone out of her. 'On this we're agreed,' she says eventually. 'If we're going to put Frame and Lena away, you must tell no one about what you've brought to me today. You're also going to have to trust me. Do you think you can do that?'

I nod, because frankly there's no other option. If you're going to go down an alley blindfolded, you've got to believe you won't trip up.

CHAPTER TWENTY-EIGHT

PAROLE HEARING

My panel consists of three members who take it in turn to introduce themselves: an ex-judge, a magistrate, and a psychiatrist. There's a joke in there somewhere but Liam's warned me to behave. No minorities are represented on this panel. Only me, on the wrong side of it, reinforcing the stereotype.

The ex-judge has a double-barrelled name and a piercing stare. The magistrate is bald with an impressive ginger beard, and the psychiatrist has dark shadows beneath both eyes. I've already forgotten their names.

Justice Double-Barrel explains the procedure and I nod to show I'm keeping up with him. I smile at each of them in turn while pressing the palms of my hands against my thighs. Something about the psychiatrist's blouse catches my attention. Two similar sized stains have appeared on the front of it. She needs to express milk by the look of it, and soon. Debs has lent me a jacket as well as the shirt she wore to court and I tug on the lapel while widening my eyes to get the psychiatrist's attention. She acknowledges me with a slow blink before turning to pull on a suit jacket slung over the back of her chair.

I've done it for the sisterhood, but if it helps demonstrate high-functioning empathy, I'll take it. Liam gives me the side-eye and I wonder if my thoughts have appeared in a bubble on top of my head.

'As you know, Miss Reid, from your *previous* parole hearings...' The judge sounds judgy but I suppose it's an occupational hazard. '...that the purpose of today is to determine whether you pose a risk of serious harm to the public. I must inform you that the decision made by this panel is a majority one.' Which roughly translated means I need to convince the other two that I'm not public enemy number one as there's not a hope in hell of winning *him* over.

'If you are deemed eligible for parole, you will be released on licence, serving the remainder of your sentence in the community under the watchful eye of the probation service.'

I bet he's a riot at parties.

He summarises my case for the benefit of those who haven't read the file.

'Mercy Reid pled guilty to the murder of Gary Walsh on 23/07/2009. In her statement she claimed the victim was acting violently towards her sister, Hope, in a manner that caused her alarm. In coming to Hope's defence, she pushed the victim away, intending only to separate them, however, Mr Walsh fell down several steps into the cellar, as the door leading to it had been left open.'

He reads out the remarks made by the judge when I was sentenced: 'You have pled guilty to murder. In the circumstances, the sentence I pass down must be one of life imprisonment. The issue for me is the minimum term you must serve before you are first considered for release. I have taken into account the circumstances surrounding Mr Walsh's murder, and order that you serve a minimum of twelve years. Whether you will be released or not at that stage, at any later stage, or indeed at all, will be a matter for the parole board to consider.'

There's a curl to his lip as he reads this out but I try to see past it.

'We will begin by examining your behaviour whilst at Fairmile, along with reports submitted by the prison doctor and your psychologist.'

I consider my chequered history on the wing and wonder which side the scales will tip. I hope like mad it's on the side that gets me released.

Witnesses are called to give evidence in support of my application.

My offender manager speaks first. He runs through the courses I've attended since my sentencing, along with the programmes I've participated in to address the cause of my offending. I've done a *lot*. If Fairmile was a scout troop, my sweater would be covered in badges. He struggles when it comes to the 'journey' I've been on as he's only been in position six months. My previous OM went on maternity leave and never came back, not that I blame her. The panel nod at him and thank him for his time. He's failed to mention that I'm a peer support worker, that I help the newbies settle in and keep their spirits up. I glance at Liam in alarm. He shrugs. He writes something on the pad in front of him and turns it so I can read it. *Tell them when it's your turn.* I add it to the hundred and one things I'm already trying to remember.

Stacey Sheridan speaks next. It's hard to keep up with the psychologist's medical jargon but the dossier in front of each of them contains a hard copy of her report, which she'd sent out in advance. Her purpose now is to drive the main points home; if they've questions, they'll ask them when she pauses for breath. I look on as my life is summed up in a smorgasbord of adjectives: Abused, Neglected, Overprotective, with a smattering of

Generalised Anxiety Disorder thrown in. If there's a dating app for the damaged, then I'm an attractive proposition. The psychiatrist asks her a question; Stacey slam dunks it without breaking a sweat. I feel like she's on a personal crusade and I wonder if there's anything in her past that resonates with mine, or maybe she's just good at her job. If her evidence is a musical composition, she's building to the finale one beat at a time.

She holds up a finger as though she's just remembered something. 'What's more, in my professional opinion, the decision not to release Mercy at the last panel hearing was seriously flawed.' She nods as she says this, as though driving her point home. I want to bump fists with her and gyrate but Liam, already ahead of me, places a hand on my arm. *Damn that man.*

Judge Double-Barrel suggests we adjourn for lunch. The psychiatrist is the first to her feet. I look at the size of the bag she slips over her shoulder and hope she's remembered to pack her breast pump.

'How do you think it's going?' I ask Liam once we're alone.

'These things are always hard to call–'

'This is me, remember? Sixteen years of being told when to eat and sleep. I'm not a rookie who needs breaking into the harsh reality of justice slowly.'

He considers his answer. 'It couldn't have gone any better,' he says eventually.

'So what's with the frown?'

'When the hearing resumes it'll be your turn to make your case.' He searches my face to check I understand the enormity of it. What'll be required of me to get the outcome I desperately want. I feel the fear of opportunity and push it away.

'It's yours to lose, Mercy. Your freedom, your future, all of it. It's down to you now.'

When the panel reconvenes it's the magistrate's turn to speak. Maybe they've had a half-time talk and he's been found wanting.

Liam side-eyes me once more.

'Mercy, this is your opportunity to address the panel.' The magistrate's smile is kind. The wedding band on his left hand is shiny but he's too old for this to be his first marriage. He's experienced failure and come back from it. I shape my smile to mirror his.

'Can you tell us what you plan to do once you're released?' he asks.

This I can do. I sit up in my seat and lean forward, as though I'm speaking into an imaginary microphone. 'I've got a bar, well, it's more of a gastropub now, thanks to my siblings who've been running it in my absence. I set it up years ago, long before everything that happened... *happened*, you know... My brother's name's been above the door since my conviction. I suppose I'm lucky it hasn't gone to his head. When – if – I'm released I'll help him run it.' They've been informed of Hope's condition. The magistrate smiles sympathetically as I describe the Dog and Duck to them in all its glory, along with the live-in accommodation above.

'I hope it's okay for me to say this...' I add cautiously. Liam looks up sharply but it's my turn to give him the side-eye. *Trust me*, I hope it conveys.

'It's just that, well... this is all a bit weird, isn't it?' I spread my hands wide to show that I mean *this*. Sitting in front of strangers pleading for my freedom.

'I can't help thinking, you know, of the women who've sat in this same chair over the years telling you what they're going to do when they leave prison, the way regular folk tell their hairdresser about where they're going on holiday. But unlike most holidays, the reality is never as good as the dream. When women leave here, they need a job, a home, without it it's hardly surprising they go back to their old ways. All I've ever wanted was stability. I never had it as a child so I worked damned hard to achieve it when I became an adult, for me and my siblings. *We were secure.* And yet I still managed to end up in jail.'

A vein I've never noticed before starts to throb in Liam's temple.

'Unlike those other women, who were poor or addicted or, God forbid, poor *and* addicted, I thought I was set up for life. So you see, I'm not sure what I can say to you that will reassure you the life I'm returning to will keep me on the straight and narrow. I never thought, back then, that I'd see myself here, but here I am.'

There's a silence, which Liam tries to fill with coughing. This isn't the answer we practised. Stacey stifles a smile as she pours him a glass of water.

Judge Double-Barrel looks up from the notes he's been taking. I've a feeling he thinks I hate men. I wonder, given my experience of them, if he's right.

'If you could go back in time, to the night of Mr Walsh's murder, what would you do differently?'

I scratch my head. I try to appease Liam by replying with one of the responses I learned by rote during our rehearsal.

'I'd call the police the moment I saw the danger Hope was in.'

Double-Barrel nods and writes down my answer.

Liam blows out a breath.

'And Gary would be the one serving time, for *her* murder.'

Liam draws it back in again.

Double-Barrel stares at me. I meet his stare head on. 'Sixteen years is a long time to reflect on the action I took that night. At the time I only had a matter of seconds.'

A hare's breath.

A blink of an eye.

Hesitate and Hope's dead.

'Gary was bigger than me and bent out of shape with rage. When he fell, he went down like a ton of bricks. I ran down the steps after him to check his pulse. It would have been a miracle for him to survive that fall.'

A miracle that would have been wasted.

I turn to Liam. 'I'm sorry,' I say, owing him that much. 'I just can't see a scenario that would have offered a better prospect than the one I took.' I wonder if this is the moment to mention my peer support work but decide against it. My freedom won't be approved or denied based on my little yellow vest.

'What about now?' the psychiatrist intervenes. 'What if you were to face a similar situation again?'

I smile at her, grateful. Of this I am certain. 'Hope and I are older now. Wiser. We know that men like Gary don't change because you want them to. They don't change at all. It's the reason why she's never had another relationship. Same reason I'm in no hurry to go looking for one either. This experience has altered us. The one thing I want my nieces to learn from this is if someone like Gary comes along, they should both run a mile.'

She nods at my answer and I hope I've said enough, because that's all I've got.

CHAPTER TWENTY-NINE

There's something odd about this morning. The vibration that warns something big is about to go down is rife, the air thick with excitement. Vonnie and I venture out of our cell with caution. I hope it's something to do with Officer Frame. She's bringing the next shipment of drugs from Lena's brother into prison today. With any luck she'll be caught in the act. Governor Cassidy was tight-lipped in my presence about what action she was going to take, but Officer Murdoch has passed snippets on to me as and when he can.

The day after we'd taken the recording to her, he'd sidled up to me on the landing as I leaned against the rail, observing the women below. He told me Cassidy had called in reinforcements that same evening. Anti-corruption officers alongside homicide detectives from Greater Manchester Police had sat around the boardroom table while she played them the recording I'd made. Murdoch had been the only other PO in the meeting. 'Frame's been put under surveillance. Officers are parked outside her home ready to film Lena's brother dropping off his next batch. Once they're certain she's in possession of the drugs the next part of the sting will take place.' Murdoch looked pleased.

'Why don't they just arrest her for Tanya's murder and be done with it?' I'd asked. That, after all, was the most serious charge.

'Even if the recording you took was admissible in court, a clever defence lawyer could twist the meaning of her words and put all the blame on Lena. After all, she's a convicted killer.' He turned his head to look at me, registered my surprise. 'She killed a business rival with her bare hands. A half-decent lawyer could claim that Frame made the confession under duress.' Murdoch sees my disappointment. 'It's your recording that's put all this in motion. She'll get what's coming to her. They both will. Be patient.'

So, for the past twenty-four hours, patience has been my middle name. I've gone about my peer support work as usual, shared meals with Lola, Debs and Vonnie and tried to act normal.

Vonnie gets released in two days' time. She's nervous. 'I went from living with my parents to living with Wayne, then back again. I've never really stood on my own two feet, have I?' she admits. 'I'm starting to wonder if it will ever happen.'

'You'll work something out,' says Debs.

'When I get out at the end of the month I'll come and find you. We can have a party!' Lola shrills.

'No parties, remember?' I look at Lola sternly. She lowers her head. 'A coffee and a cake then!' she says, brightening.

All this change. Vonnie leaving so soon after what happened to Tanya. The thought of remaining here without them if I don't get parole... I push that prospect out of my mind. I need to get parole. I need to be there for Hope. I need this opportunity to start living again.

Today is the day the sting on Frame is to take place. Even though no one else knows this, the atmosphere on the wing is electric. The women can tell something significant is happening, they just don't know what.

'Any idea what's going on?' asks Lola. She can feel it too.

I shake my head. I'd decided not to tell her and Debs what was happening. The knowledge could put them in danger and that's the last thing I want. Lena is ruthless and Frame has the key to our cells. I shudder. The days she's on shift we are literally sitting ducks. Apart from me, the only people on the wing who know about the recorded confession are Vonnie and Magda, and Officer Murdoch of course. The longer it stays that way, the better.

We clear away our breakfast things and make our way upstairs to our landing. I glimpse Murdoch marching towards my cell so I pull away from the others – telling them I'll catch them up – then hurry towards him. Male officers aren't allowed into our cells unaccompanied, so we stand by the landing rail once more, looking at everything around us but each other.

'We've got her, Mercy!' he announces without preamble.

'Tell me!' I say, eager to hear all about it.

He becomes animated as he talks me through the morning's events:

'It all happened first thing. The governor replaced Deano, the officer who Frame's been in cahoots with on the gate, putting a new guy in his place. He wasn't happy but there was nothing he could do to warn her as the car park CCTV had already picked her up parking in the staff section, so it was fait accompli. You should have seen her face when she stepped into the foyer and he wasn't there to wave her through. To make matters worse, the governor had made sure the drugs dog was waiting. She didn't stand a chance.' He sounds pleased. What I wouldn't give to have seen the shock on Frame's snidey face. I want to savour every moment.

'What happened?'

'She was searched. We found a belt with five pockets sewn into it under her jumper, fifty grams of heroin split between each pocket.'

I let out a low whistle.

'She and Deano were frogmarched into a waiting police van in handcuffs.'

My mouth stretches into a smile but then freezes. 'What about Lena?'

'The police are waiting to question her. The governor's sending officers over to her cell now.'

We watch as a line of POs move along the ground floor as one, heading towards the landing stairs. 'Governor Cassidy's given them strict instructions. When they make their move, they're to go in mob-handed and loud, send out a message that dealers won't be tolerated.'

'What'll happen to Lena's brother?'

'He was caught on surveillance delivering the drugs to Frame's home, so he'll be getting a visit from the boys in blue right about now.'

The wing falls quiet as the officers reach our landing. Inmates turn to each other, intrigued by their presence. One woman slips quickly into a cell. The rest strain their necks to see where the convoy is heading.

'I'd better get back to the others,' I tell Officer Murdoch. I'm overcome with gratitude that he followed me that day. From what I've learned since, I could have ended up the same way as Tanya if he hadn't stepped in. 'Thanks for looking out for me,' I say.

His smile falls away leaving a grim line. 'I got into this lark to help folk turn their lives around, not to guard locked doors.

There aren't many days where I feel I've made a difference. This is one of them.'

I'm walking back to join the others when he calls out my name. I turn around.

'Have you heard from the parole board yet?' he asks.

I shake my head.

'It's in the bag, I'm sure of it,' he says, crossing his fingers. 'Promise me when the opportunity comes, you won't waste it.'

I can't remember the last time someone's asked me to promise something. Every promise made to me as a child was broken.

'I promise,' I tell him.

Just then an alarm rings out. The convoy of officers who've gone to collect Lena for questioning are backing away from her cell, coughing and spluttering. 'Mad cow has set fire to her mattress!' one of them calls out to Murdoch. He instructs them to withdraw, then unclips his radio to call for backup.

I crane my neck to see what's going on. Lena's standing in the doorway of her cell spitting and throwing objects at anyone close enough to be used as target practice. The burning mattress behind her fills the air with toxic smoke.

'Mercy, get back!' Murdoch shouts, and I do as I'm told, encouraging inmates standing nearby to leave the landing and return to their cells. I can't see Vonnie and the others.

Some prisoners won't budge – they're the ones who like inciting trouble. 'Fucking screws!' they yell, banging the landing rail with anything they can get their hands on. They're joined by others, buoyed on by their bravado. They jeer and throw glass bottles at the officers, which bounce off them and smash at their feet. The landing simmers with the threat of violence. Acrid smoke curls into the air making my throat sting. I look on as two women throw a burning mattress onto the landing as though forming a barricade. It doesn't take much to escalate a situation in jail, every wing operates in a state of permanent tension. How many would join in if they knew Lena was involved in Tanya's murder? I help an older woman into her cell and pull her door to. She's terrified and like most of us, doesn't want to get caught up in the crossfire. Riot officers dressed in blue protective suits, helmets and visors storm onto the landing, riot shields held in front of them. They bang on the shields with their batons, yelling at the rioters to return to their cells. The crowd starts to disperse, with only the most stubborn standing their ground.

'Mercy, over here!' I turn to see Debs beckoning me towards her cell. Vonnie and Lola stand in the doorway, arms outstretched ready to pull me in from the tide of women surging in the opposite direction.

'Thank Christ, I was getting worried for a minute,' says Vonnie, closing the door behind me.

'Me too,' I tell her, looking on as an inmate waving a chair at an officer is shoved to the floor.

'Frame's been arrested!' I tell her, raising my voice above the din outside. 'Lena must have got wind that they were coming for her.'

'WHAT?' ask Debs and Lola in unison.

'Say that again,' demands Lola. They stare at us goggle-eyed as Vonnie and I explain to them what's been going on.

'Looks like Lena was ready for them,' says Debs, when we've finished. That thought goes through my mind as a series of screams on the landing have us rushing to the door.

The riot officers have stormed Lena's cell. We look on as four of them drag her out and pin her down on the floor. Her screams peter out, replaced by the sound of several fire extinguishers trained on the furniture that's been set alight. Her supporters, subdued, start to withdraw.

Something about this tableau seems wrong. I look from Lena, spreadeagled on the floor, to the riot officers holding her down. Then back to Lena, whose soot-covered face resembles a nineteenth century chimney sweep. I regard the officers once more. They're not from this block; they're part of the rapid response team scrambled from the neighbouring block. They've been sent in to detain Lena but they don't know what she looks like. The woman they're pinning down isn't the same build as her. Doesn't have the names of the prisons she's served time in tattooed on her arms.

The inmate they're restraining isn't Lena.

I'm about to warn them that they've got the wrong person when I see Murdoch approach them from the other direction. Something feels badly wrong. 'Jack!' I yell but my voice bounces off the walls. A shadow jumps out from a cell door as he passes and squirts him with liquid. It gathers in his hair and runs into his eyes and his mouth and before I have a chance to tell him it's Lena, she throws a lighted match at him.

Those closest to him jump back in shock as his body sets alight. He cries for help but the accelerant has run into his eyes, has blinded him. He can't see which way to go and flails helplessly as the flames move over his body like angry tendrils. His scream, when it comes, is ragged, like an animal caught in a trap. The sound is loud, insistent, the kind that makes the hairs on the back of your neck stand on end. I run towards him, but an officer grabs me and holds me back. I look on as one of his colleagues knocks him onto the ground and attempts to smother the flames with a blanket.

'OFFICER DOWN!'

The sound of radio static fills the air as officers hit their emergency call buttons and shout for an ambulance.

Despite his colleague's attempt to put out the flames, the damage has been done. Murdoch's torso has blackened and his limbs have twisted in on themselves. I stare as tiny flames move around his crown like the wick on a candle.

Another minute ticks by and his colleague stops. Shakes his head. 'IT'S TOO LATE, HE'S GONE!' he yells angrily.

It's only then that I realise Lena has gone too.

The officer holding me loosens her grip, swipes a hand across her face. I take the opportunity to twist away from her and face her head on. 'YOU'VE GOT TO FIND LENA!' I yell, a sob forming in my throat at what she's done.

'Go to your cell!' she shouts at me but her heart isn't in it. She's more at risk than I am. Some lifers see injuring a PO as a trophy, an opportunity to enhance their status with other inmates without any detrimental effect to their term inside. She wants Lena caught but she isn't prepared to give chase. I run in the direction Lena was heading, trying not to think of the bottle of flammable liquid in her hand.

I come to a halt halfway along the landing and pivot round. None of the officers have followed me. 'SHE WENT DOWN HERE!' I yell but nobody moves. I look over at Murdoch smouldering where he fell and I don't blame them.

'WATCH OUT, MERCY!' Vonnie yells at me from the doorway of Deb's cell. Her eyes are wide as she scans the landing for signs of threat. 'What if she knows about you and Murdoch? She's killed him, what's to stop her coming for you too?'

Her warning fills me with dread. It hadn't occurred to me that she'd killed Murdoch out of revenge for what we'd done. Had she known Frame had been arrested and that she was next? Vonnie was right. If she knew about Murdoch then she'd know about me, about the recording I'd made, and that I'd taken it to the governor. But how? The only people who knew about it were me and Von and Governor Cassidy. And Murdoch, of course, and now he's dead.

And Magda.

Magda had been betrayed by Lena but what if she'd forgiven her? Had she thrown Officer Murdoch and me under the bus in a declaration of loyalty? But why now? Magda couldn't have tipped Lena off that she was about to be arrested as she wouldn't have known. Frame had only just been handcuffed and marched off the premises – nobody knew, except the officers who'd seen it happen... then again, what about the PO that Magda has on her payroll?

I shake my head in an attempt to make sense of it. Seeing Frame taken into custody would have put the fear of God into whoever it was. When they heard Lena was about to be arrested it made sense that they'd want to warn Magda. As far as everyone was aware she and Lena were still together. She'd had to maintain that front to avoid Lena realising we were onto her. Even so, it makes no sense that Magda would tip her off... unless she's willing to give Lena a second chance. People have done stranger things for love, I suppose.

A cold hard lump forms in my stomach. I look about the landing with fresh eyes. I've passed the only exit point, the corridor that acts as a slip road onto the landing from the stairwell below. Behind me a row of half-closed cell doors loom ominously. My fingers curl, digging my nails into the palms of my hands. This is the way Lena came, so she has to be hiding behind one of those doors. I recall the speed with which she jumped out at Murdoch. The sheen of the liquid as it ran down his face.

I need to get off this landing, and fast.

Sweat drips down my back as I weigh up my options. If I turn and run back in the direction I came, I am prey to Lena dousing me from behind, like she did with Murdoch. I decide to move ahead slowly, keeping my wits about me as I ease myself cautiously to safety.

POs are gathered by Lena's cell awaiting instructions. They'll have been told to stand down until backup comes. Their radios are silent. The frantic to and fro of messages with control have ceased. There's nothing they can do now but wait. 'The fire brigade are on their way!' one of them calls out to me, which brings no comfort at all. I've seen up close what damage liquid accelerant and a lighted match can do in a matter of seconds.

I turn slowly so my back is against the landing rail. From this vantage point I can see up and down the landing as I move tentatively along it. Each sideways step takes me away from Lena. Ten more steps and I'll have two options to choose from. Go straight ahead toward the POs or take the corridor leading to the stairwell. Sweat makes my clothing stick to my skin as I count down each step. Ten. Nine. Eight. The landing ahead of me is clear. I turn my head to check that no one has emerged from the cell doors behind me, in case Lena has slipped out noiselessly and is coming after me.

It's clear.

I blow out a breath. I turn my head the other way to check the cell doors I'm parallel with remain closed. I feel the threat of the space around me but no one jumps out.

I look over at the POs.

All clear.

I'm nearly there. Seven steps. Six...

A noise behind me sends me jumping into the air. Lena is standing there, arm raised, a yellow canister in her hand. 'You squealin' bitch!' she hisses.

I turn, ready to make a dash down the stairwell when a bulky frame emerges from it.

Magda.

I stare open-mouthed as she moves towards me. Her eyes are

wild and her hair is undone, moving around her face like deadly snakes. In her hand a silver blade catches the light. I falter, stumbling backwards. I grip on to the landing rail and brace myself for whatever is to come. Fire or knife, the outcome will be the same. I cower as the liquid hits the back of my neck and brace myself for the *whoosh* as the match Lena is reaching for ignites. She's about to strike it when Magda shoves me out of the way then leaps forward, sticking the blade into Lena's neck. An arc of blood gushes over me and suddenly Lena is upside down as Magda hauls her over the landing rail and lets go.

'You *disloyal* bitch!' she roars.

By the time backup arrives Magda is in handcuffs, the cell doors wide open as every inmate on the landing clamours to see Lena suspended face down on the safety mesh, bleeding out onto the floor below.

We're locked in our cells for the remainder of the day.

I pace what little floor space there is, wondering what I could have done differently to save Murdoch's life. Or rather, not to have put him in harm's way in the first place.

'It's not your fault,' Vonnie insists.

Like me, she's trying to come to terms with what we witnessed on the landing. The sheer brutality of it.

'This is all on Lena, Magda, and that fucking Frame. You're sure she's been arrested?'

I move my head up and down. 'Murdoch told me himself. He saw it with his own eyes.' I blink away the look on his face when he realised what Lena had done to him. The fear and resignation at the finality of it.

Vonnie keeps shaking her head, incredulous. 'How the hell did she manage to give the screws the slip like that?'

I exhale slowly. 'I wish I knew.'

'She used that burning mattress as a smokescreen, didn't she? Had them focusing on escaping the fire rather than dragging her out.'

'Seems that way.'

'Who's the woman she switched with?'

I hadn't been sure at the time. I thought she looked familiar but now it falls into place. 'One of Magda's minions,' I reply.

We exchange a look.

'For a while there, I was convinced Magda had forgiven Lena. That was the only reason I could think of as to why she'd have helped her give the POs the slip.'

Vonnie's forehead creases as she works it out. 'Magda didn't help Lena out of the kindness of her heart. You saw the state of her when she found out about Lena's deception. She was heartbroken.'

Or as heartbroken as someone like Magda can be.

I nod in agreement. 'She held off having it out with her because I didn't want Lena alerted to the fact we were onto her. I guess she's been biding her time to even the score ever since. Waiting for the right opportunity, and this was it. Hell hath no fury and all that...'

'What do you think will happened to Magda now?'

I shrug. 'A few more years added to her sentence. Transferred to another jail, I shouldn't wonder. None of the staff will want to go near her once it gets out that her tipping Lena off gave her the opportunity to kill Officer Murdoch.'

'What was she trying to achieve though? Either of them, for that matter?'

'Makes perfect sense in a twisted sort of way,' I say. 'Magda tips Lena off that the police are on their way on the back of the recording we took to the governor. Lena realises she's about to be boxed in, so creates a distraction.'

'So she could escape?'

That I'm not so sure about. Escapes don't happen on the spur of the moment. 'I think it was more about a cornered rat going down fighting. People like Lena, it's all about going out in a blaze of glory.'

Vonnie's face grows dark. 'Do you think Magda knew that Lena was going to... do what she did to Officer Murdoch, and then to you?'

I hesitate. 'I don't know,' I answer honestly. 'I think Magda's main concern was getting her hands on Lena. Once the police picked Lena up and charged her there was every chance she'd be re-remanded to a different prison for her own safety. Magda knew she didn't have long to make her move. Giving Lena that heads up – and knowing the most likely way she'd respond – gave her the opportunity she needed to punish her. I think to people like Magda, and Lena for that matter, the consequences of their actions don't concern them. Anyone that gets in the way of them achieving their goal is fair game.'

'That's horrible.'

'I know.'

We all operate on a continuum, a spectrum of depravity, even in prison. Some killers are contrite, full of remorse. Others are bewildered or downright deluded. Then there's the other kind. The hard-faced, cold-hearted monster that snuffs out life without breaking into a sweat. It's fair to say that Lena and Magda fall into that category. It doesn't pay to try to understand them, or rehabilitate them for that matter; they are already fully formed, their deficit already defines them.

I wonder if Officer Murdoch included them when he said he didn't want to guard locked doors.

I wonder if some people just can't be helped.

CHAPTER THIRTY

We've been let out of our cells for breakfast. The cordon put around the crime scene has been removed. All that remains of yesterday's carnage are two small lengths of police tape tied around the landing rail and blood stains on the safety netting that'll be a bugger to wash out.

The dining area is busier than normal. The women huddle in groups over coffee and cereal, second guessing the cause of Lena's and Officer Murdoch's murders. The rumour mill is already doing the rounds. Some are claiming it was a domestic that got out of hand, others claim Murdoch was the other man in a bizarre love triangle.

Around us, questions and opinions bounce of the walls:

'Why did the screws come for Lena before she killed Murdoch?'

'Since when do those fuckers need a reason?'

'I don't blame her for taking a screw out. I'd shake her hand if she was still alive.'

We sit at our table, subdued. I'm aware of the sidelong glances in my direction. Folk want to know what my involvement is but know I won't take kindly to their questions.

'It wasn't how I imagined my last night here would go,' says Vonnie.

I smile sympathetically. Today's her last day but none of us have the capacity to be cheerful.

One of Magda's minions saunters up to the serving hatch. Her hands are bandaged and there's a cut on her face. She swaggers over to her cronies' table, indicates the burnt toast on her tray. 'Just how I like my screws,' she sneers. I clench my fists but Debs places a hand on my arm. 'Remember what you once said to me. Don't show them how they can get to you,' she cautions.

'Why hasn't the governor put the record straight?' I hiss.

'There'll be someone much higher up pulling her strings,' Deb reasons, 'especially while an investigation's underway.'

My hands circle my mug as I ponder this. I try not to think of them circling that old crone's throat for what she just said, but it's a tall order.

'They'll need to put some sort of statement out, otherwise the press'll be all over it,' I say to no one in particular.

Two new POs enter the dining hall. A young, mixed-race officer, slim built with a neatly clipped beard. His female colleague is older, bottle blonde, stout, looks like she could hold her own in a wrestling match. Their shirts are spotless and the Fairmile epaulettes on their shoulders gleam.

'Replacement screws,' someone mutters behind me.

'They don't hang about, do they?' says Debs.

Life goes on, doll, I imagine Tanya saying.

'Hold on, has another of them croaked it?' someone asks. Her companion runs through a verbal roll call of officers on shift. She pauses when she gets to Frame. 'She was boasting she'd booked herself a fancy holiday,' another crony reasoned.

'There'll be no turn down service where she's going,' I say to the others, under my breath.

'I hope someone leaves a chocolate on her pillow though,' Lola says spitefully.

We all laugh.

We watch the new officers walk over to the PO standing by the hatch. They say something to him and in response he points to our table.

'I wonder what this is all about?' whispers Vonnie as they draw near.

'Mercy Reid.' The mixed-race officer states my name, the upward inflection at the end making it sound like a question.

'Yes,' I say to him.

'Governor wants to speak to you.'

I turn to Vonnie. 'Looks like I'm about to find out.'

CHAPTER THIRTY-ONE

Governor Cassidy looks drawn. There are sweat rings under the arms of her blouse and a tidemark around the neck of it that suggests she didn't go home last night. She looks up as I'm led in and there's a flicker in her eye. At last, something she can deal with.

The last few days have taken their toll on her. A murdered prisoner. A drug bust. Officer corruption. And now two more murders, one including the prison officer who'd helped blow the whistle. I'd heard from one of the POs that the inspection due at the end of the year has been brought forward. I'm no clairvoyant but I see a resignation on the cards.

Governor Cassidy motions for me to take a seat. She looks like an accident victim still in a state of shock. 'Times like this I wish I'd never given up smoking,' she says, scratching a patch of eczema on her arm, just above her watch.

'I won't tell if you won't.' I force out a laugh to show I'm joking.

She looks up at the ceiling, as though contemplating a way around the sprinkler system that will satisfy her nicotine craving without dropping her in it.

'Fuck it, come on,' she says, and I follow her into the corridor.

We're sitting on the galvanised iron steps behind the admin building, the wedged-open fire exit doors behind us in contravention of all manner of health, safety and security policies. She opens a pack of cigarettes that she informs me she keeps for emergencies and taps two out. She offers me one and even though I don't smoke, I accept it. I think of Lola taking that drink in the dry house because she wanted to join in. I tell myself this is different, but it isn't. At times we all need to feel a connection, to be part of something, however inconsequential.

'I've just got off the phone to Jack Murdoch's wife,' she tells me. She inhales deeply, like nicotine is the only thing that will keep her from screaming.

I swallow down the lump that forms in my throat. I've never really understood the appeal of nicotine until now. I take a deep drag on my cigarette, draw the smoke into my lungs, hold it there.

'I'm driving down to see her this evening.' A prospect she's clearly dreading.

'He was looking forward to his retirement,' I tell her, trying to recall the small talk we'd made that day walking back from the visitor centre. 'He mentioned a caravan, where he took his kids when they were little. Said he planned to take the grandkids.' I try to remember. 'Somewhere in Wales?'

The governor shrugs, this is news to her.

'What will happen to Officer Frame?' I ask.

This is easier for her to talk about. 'We're going to throw the book at her. Police searched her home and found several mobile phones, brand-new TVs, PlayStations, computers. She's clearly been at it for a while. There's a trail of texts between her and Lena. A damning one where she states she wanted Tanya dealt with.' She looks at me ominously. 'By any means necessary.'

'She actually put that in the text?' The governor nods and draws on her cigarette at the same time.

'Murder. Conspiracy to murder. Misconduct in a public office. Possessing drugs with intent. She's going down for a long time.'

I nod. Tanya deserves more though. I'm just not sure what.

'I wanted you to hear it from me. It'll all be made public soon enough.'

I smile in appreciation. 'Thank you. There are rumours going round. You know what it's like.'

She responds with a grimace.

I take another drag on my cigarette. 'What about Magda?'

This is where she loses it. 'If I'd known we had a leak... that she was going to use the information she was given to tip Lena off in order to get back at her...'

'You weren't to know.'

'I'm the governor, I'm supposed to know everything!'

She takes a long draw on her cigarette, blows out a smoke ring. 'Johnny bastard Daynes,' she says eventually. 'I never liked him.'

I look at her sharply. 'What?'

'The phones found in Magda's cell – and about her person,' she looks at me shrewdly, 'were sent to the anti-corruption unit for analysis. The information was downloaded and cross-referenced with their criminal database, which also has a record of all the prison staff's phone numbers. Daynes' number was there, along with a series of texts charting pickups from Magda's supplier and drop offs here.'

I'm still taking it in. '*Officer Daynes* is Magda's mule?'

Her nod is slow.

So, porcupine face was only a misogynist when it suited him.

'Greed is greed,' states the governor, as though I'd spoken aloud.

I tip my head in acknowledgement.

Cassidy takes another drag on her cigarette then exhales. 'I always knew he was a tosser, I just didn't have anything solid to go on to get rid of him. You know what it's like. As annoying as he is, he's never been daft enough to say anything within earshot of others, so if someone complained it was always his word against theirs. There are hundreds like him up and down every workplace in the country, like turds that won't flush away. The nation would come to a standstill if every prize prick got his comeuppance.'

I fix her with a look. 'He propositioned prisoners too. We didn't report it because no one listens to us.'

'I'm sorry,' she says, crestfallen.

'Has he been arrested?'

She nods. 'Police went to his home last night. I couldn't cope with any more drama unfolding on the premises.'

We lapse into silence. Behind us office phones ring and are answered. Someone informs a caller that the governor is unavailable at the moment. I smile at her. She smiles back, but then it drops away as though she's remembered that her career is a train wreck.

'There'll be plenty glad when I step down,' she admits. 'All those men I went through training with who called me hard-faced will be beside themselves.'

'A friend of mine reminded me not so long ago to stop caring what other people think. It's something I intend to work on if I ever get out of here.'

Her mouth turns down at the edges as she considers this. 'That reminds me...' she says, easing herself to her feet. She stubs out her cigarette, flicks it into a privet hedge that runs the length of the building. 'Don't get up,' she says, padding into her office before returning with a brown envelope that she hands to me. 'It arrived this morning,' she adds.

My heart thuds as I tear it open.

'It's from the parole board,' she tells me, although I've worked that much out from the postmark.

My hands tremble as I unfold the letter. I stare at it, too nervous to skip to the bottom but desperate to know the outcome.

Dear Miss Reid,

Thank you for your attendance...

To hell with it. I skim-read down the page impatiently:

After considering the circumstances of your offending, the progress you have made whilst in custody and the evidence presented at the hearing, the panel is satisfied that you are suitable for release.

Judge Double-Barrel's signature is at the bottom of it.

I read through it again before looking up at her. 'It's been approved. I'm to be released in seven days.' The words snag in my throat.

I picture Officer Murdoch on the landing, crossing his fingers for the right result.

Just make sure when the opportunity comes, you don't waste it, his words ring in my ears.

'Congratulations,' says Governor Cassidy, opening her

cigarette pack once more. 'I think a celebratory smoke is in order, don't you?'

I take another from her and use the dying embers from the one I'm currently smoking to light it. I stub it out on the step and flounder, unsure what I'm supposed to do with it.

'You know you want to,' she mocks, looking on amused when I flick it into the same hedge.

It's hard to take in that I'm finally going home. I feel a bubble of joy rise up in my chest, then blink. It doesn't take long for my overthinking to burst it.

'What's going to happen to Tanya?' I ask.

Governor Cassidy frowns. She knows we were friends; she's trying to choose her words carefully.

'Her family haven't claimed her body, so she'll be buried here, in an unmarked grave.'

'That's awful!'

'It's prison policy.'

I swipe a hand over my face.

Tanya spent sixteen years of her pitiful life here. The thought of her being stuck in these grounds for eternity is too much. 'I'll claim her body then. It's down to me to give her the send-off she deserves.'

Governor Cassidy looks sceptical.

'Why not?' I persist. 'I've got my parole. I've got a release date, what's stopping me?'

'Nothing,' she says eventually. 'Nothing at all.'

We sit quietly for the remainder of our smoke, each contemplating very different futures.

Vonnie is standing by her bunk when I return. She's wearing smarter clothes than she normally wears, the kind of clothes people wear on the outside. 'I was worried you weren't going to be back in time. I've got to go!'

'I hate goodbyes, Von,' I warn her.

We try to hug but it's awkward and hurried. 'Go on, don't keep your dad waiting,' I tell her.

'Mercy–'

'Don't say anything,' I tell her.

She narrows her eyes and wafts her hand in front of her nose. 'Have you been smoking?' she demands.

I hold up my hands in mock surrender. 'You got me,' I confess. 'I had a sly smoke with the governor round the back of the admin block.'

She grins and shakes her head. '*Whatever*. Seriously though, what did she want you for?'

'She wanted to give me this.' I hand my parole letter to her. She whoops when she sees it's been approved and punches the air.

'Oh, Mercy, that's brilliant!' Her grin slips momentarily and I know she's thinking about Tanya.

I give her an update on Frame's charges. 'And you'll never guess who Magda's mule is...'

She stares at me open-mouthed when I tell her.

The bottle-blonde PO pops her head around the cell door. 'Ready then, Yvonne?' she asks, using Vonnie's Sunday name. Vonnie picks up her bag of belongings.

'Here...' I scribble Clem's mobile number on a scrap of paper and press it into her hand. 'Call him. There's always a few shifts going spare if you're not afraid of hard work. It'll tide you over until something better comes along... Honestly, it's nothing,' I insist when she looks as though she's about to cry. The last thing I want is for her tears to set me off. If I start howling now, I'll never stop.

Dinnertime association

'At this rate we're going to need a smaller table,' observes Debs. We've spread ourselves out to try and fill the space left by Tanya and Vonnie's absence but that makes us feel worse. Just because they're gone doesn't mean they're not still here.

I look for something to lighten the mood. 'Wait till you read this.' I hand her my parole letter, which she reads out to Lola.

'Oh my God, oh my God, oh my God!' shrieks Lola, getting up from the table so she can hug me. 'This is the best news ever. Are you, like, totally excited?'

Her face reminds me of Hope on my wedding day. *Is this the happiest day of your life?*

Losing Tanya and then Vonnie – even for a good reason – has been tough. I need to navigate my way through it.

'Totally,' I reply because it's what she needs to hear.

Debs catches my eye over Lola's shoulder. Her look says she understands the remorse you feel when you get what you want. *It'll be okay,* she mouths.

I hope she's right.

News of both prison officers' arrests have spread through Fairmile like wildfire. The part Frame and Lena played in Tanya's murder is now common knowledge. Lena's notoriety has crashed and burned. The women who praised her for killing Officer Murdoch now despise her for her involvement in Tanya's death. If she's mentioned at all, it's in hushed tones of disapproval, the same way the public refer to celebrities outed for being sex pests.

I tell them that I've claimed Tanya's body. Neither bats an eyelid.

'What will you do?' Debs asks.

I feel less confident than I did before. 'Christ knows,' I admit, glumly. 'I suppose a cremation. At least me and Vonnie can be there.'

'Maybe we can do something together for her once we're all out?' Lola asks, returning to her seat.

'Like a memorial service, you mean?' asks Debs.

Lola nods. 'Yeah. We could all say a few words. Raise a glass to her. I think she'd like that.'

'She'd love it,' I say.

Lola picks up her fork. She pushes her food around her plate half-heartedly. Some people wear their heart on their sleeve, what you see is what you get, Lola is one of them. The world is wonderful or desolate with no in-between. In Lola's case it's mainly desolate but she tries so hard to find the good in it. It's the reason other people's joy matters to her. Gives her the opportunity to observe it up close, try it on for size, even if it's only for a while. She's pleased my parole has been approved, but it's bound to make her feel stuck in her own situation.

'You don't look yourself, Lola. I haven't forgotten what I said about helping you get Danny back. Your dad's a monster, there's no getting away from that. Your mum's done a great job of undermining you from the day Danny was born, probably long before that I shouldn't wonder. When I get out, I'll speak to Liam. He's been helping Debs apply for contact with her kids, maybe he can help you too.'

Lola smiles gratefully. 'He does a lot for you, that brief of yours,' she observes, gives me a cheeky look.

'She's right,' Debs says, catching Lola's eye. 'I reckon he's holding a bit of a torch for you.'

'I think it's more than a torch he's holding,' Lola shoots back.

I waft their comments away with my hand. 'Behave, you two. Anyway, those kinds of goings on aren't allowed between a solicitor and their client, you know that.'

Lola gives me the eye. 'Yeah, but you won't be his client for much longer, will you?'

'You know your trouble, don't you, Lola? You've got an overactive imagination.' I throw her a mock filthy look. 'I wouldn't mind but I've never even thought of him in that way.'

'Never?' they both chime.

I look away. 'Hardly ever,' I mumble. I mean, there was that time when he took off his jacket in the legal visits room, but I'd put that down to me having a moment rather than anything to do with *attraction*. I push the thought out of my head.

CHAPTER THIRTY-TWO

I walk out of Fairmile clutching a clear plastic bag of belongings and a cardboard box. Despite my protests, Lola and Debs waved me off from my cell. We've promised to keep in touch so we can give Tanya the send-off she deserves.

Clem is waiting for me in the car park. We hug awkwardly. For sixteen years our interactions have been watched over and controlled by the staff in the visitors' room. Now we can behave how we like I'm not sure what to do. Am I holding on too tight or for too long?

'I'm scared I'm going to hurt you,' Clem says, mirroring my fears.

I sit in the passenger seat gripping onto the seat belt. We're moving too fast and too close to the vehicle in front. We pass young men on electric bikes with insulated boxes on their backs. Deliveroo. Just Eat. Do people not pick up their own takeaways anymore? So many supermarket delivery vans on the road too, seems they don't go grocery shopping either. Small children on pavements ride motorised scooters. A teenager on a skateboard that resembles something out of *Back to the Future*. 'A hoverboard,' Clem informs me with a smile.

Clem's car is electric. He laughs off my concern, assuring me there's enough power in the battery to get us to John o' Groats, never mind the hour's drive home.

Home. My mouth stumbles on the word. The journey is unfamiliar: housing estates where green fields once stood; a high school converted into apartments. I feel as though I'm exploring alien terrain. 'Where have all the banks gone?' I ask.

'No one uses cash anymore,' he reminds me and with this I'm on familiar territory as prison operates a cashless system too.

There's a lot to learn. I feel like I'll need an induction into how to live on the outside. Clem describes Tap and Go, Contactless, Apple Pay, and power banks. I struggle to keep up.

He laughs good-naturedly. 'The girls will keep you right.'

'How are they doing?' I ask.

'They're great. They took the news about their mum badly at first, as you'd expect, but they're taking it in their stride now.'

'And Hope?' I've been dreading asking. Whenever I used to think of leaving Fairmile to come home, it was to return to everything as it was before. Now, with Hope's illness, home is like a shattered vase – all the pieces are there but no one knows where or how they fit.

Clem's doing his best to sound upbeat. 'Hope's good at the moment. She's been taking it easy for the last few days so that you'll get to see the best of her when we get back. She won't want you treating her like an invalid,' he warns. 'Trust me, I've had my head chewed off several times for trying to mollycoddle her. She'll let you know what she needs.'

We stop at a traffic light. The buildings on either side of the road loom impossibly tall. A stream of pedestrians cross the road in front of us. Mothers pushing prams. Men in suits with open neck shirts. Students with headphones clamped on their heads, like being outside in the fresh air is no big deal.

'I'm sorry about Tanya,' Clem says.

Tanya's belongings are contained in the cardboard box on the back seat. 'The governor thought you might want them,' said the PO behind the reception desk as he pushed the box towards me. I lifted the lid and peered inside. A hairbrush and a bar of chocolate. Clippings torn from magazines that she kept on the wall beside the photo of her kids: one is an advert for cosmetic dentistry, the model flashing a brilliant white smile towards the camera. The other had been taken from a travel supplement, a feature on a Turkish resort. One of those arty pictures: a row of sun loungers on a sandy beach, beyond them the crystal waters of the Aegean Sea. I replaced the lid quickly and nodded. Hugged the box to me as though Tanya herself was contained in there.

The lights change to green and Clem is off.

'I'm organising her funeral,' I tell him.

His gaze slides over me before returning to the road ahead. 'Isn't that something her family should do?'

'My thoughts exactly,' I tell him.

The Dog and Duck is a regular pub that I developed to serve great food. What I couldn't have accounted for during my time inside was the gentrification that took place around it. Five years into my sentence, the neighbouring office blocks built in the 70s were bulldozed during a major redevelopment. In their place stand glass-fronted office blocks and upmarket retail units set around a smart plaza. Private banking. Financial planning. Accountancy. Law, the commercial kind, not criminal justice and conveyancing. The open area has been landscaped with shrubs and benches. Communal seating areas are dotted here and there. It's a place for people to linger, rather than rush from

A to B. The people that work here dress up to go to work. They wear tailored clothing from high-end stores, have money to socialise with colleagues, not just friends.

All the usual big food chains are there, along with artisan stalls selling vegan burritos and cronuts, but if you're looking for quality food in an unpretentious atmosphere then the Dog and Duck is the place to go.

The pub itself looks different. Bigger than I remember it. The exterior walls have been repainted, a new sign – more contemporary-looking – has been placed above the entrance. Inside is more familiar. The décor has been refreshed but the layout is how I left it. Bunting has been placed over the bar. A home-made sign says: *Welcome home Auntie M*.

'It was the girls' idea,' Hope whispers as we hold on to each other. 'I'll make sure it's down before we open.'

I didn't want a fuss. Didn't want strangers gawping at me like a sideshow freak, but the gesture speaks volumes. 'Where are they, then?' I ask, looking around the dining area. Two athletic-looking teenagers step out from the kitchen carrying a large cake. 'They made it themselves,' Hope says, 'so apologies for the inappropriate humour.'

I can't take my eyes off them. The photos Hope kept sending me didn't do them justice. Long limbed, slender, a mass of curls dancing around identical faces. 'They're the spit of you when you were their age,' I say to her. 'And as for that cake...' It's square, covered in white icing, black lines across the top of it representing the bars over a prison cell window. 'Well, I'm not sure what to say...'

'Is it too soon?' one of them asks and I realise I'm going to have to learn how to tell them apart. The girl that's spoken turns to her double. 'I told you it was too soon, we should have gone with something more subtle.'

'I love it,' I tell them, suddenly overcome.

'Don't cry, Auntie M, you're home now.' They step forward in unison, circling their arms around me and I feel as though I'm unravelling. I disengage from their embrace and I'm met by a sudden wave of emotion that takes my breath away.

'How about we let Mercy go and freshen up. I think she needs time to acclimatise.' Hope looks at me and I smile gratefully.

'Thanks,' I say. 'I am feeling a bit wiped out to be honest.'

'When are we going shopping?' the quieter girl asks.

Hope has become their official interpreter. 'They thought you'd be keen to get some new clothes,' she explains. She looks at what I'm wearing. Over-washed leggings and her Christmas sweatshirt. 'Don't worry, your old stuff is where you left it. I'll warn you now though, the girls have got designs on bringing your wardrobe up to date.'

'That sounds like fun,' I say, reassuring them. 'Let me have a sort out first though, make room for something new.'

My room smells of fresh paint and fabric softener. The bedding looks new but apart from that everything is how I left it. A double bed with cabinets either side of it, even though one half of the bed remained empty the entire time I was here. An oak wardrobe and dressing table stands against one wall. I put Tanya's box on the dressing table before moving to the wardrobe to look inside. The clothing rail bulges with bright coloured outfits, reminding me how much I used to love attention. Designer handbags on the top shelf co-ordinate with the shoes stacked along the bottom.

I drop my prison issue bag on the floor. Its contents look tawdry and out of place in this room. I stare at my threadbare towel and tired clothes. The flip-flops I wore in the shower, the hair, dead skin and sweat of other inmates caked into the soles.

I return to Tanya's box of belongings and remove the lid. I

lift out the travel clipping and, recycling the Blu-Tack already on the back of it, I stick it on my wall. If I close my eyes, I can picture her staring transfixed at the sea from her bunk, imagining the feel of it lapping over her toes.

Another day in paradise, doll.

I hope the promise of it made her happy.

CHAPTER THIRTY-THREE

All those years of fantasising about sleeping in my own bed and it's the worst night I've had in a long time. I've been awake for hours, listening to the breath rising and falling in my throat. I pull on my old dressing gown and pad across the hall to the kitchen. Hope is sitting at the breakfast bar, an empty coffee cup in front of her.

'How did you sleep?' she asks.

'Like a log.'

She looks relieved. 'Bet it feels funny being in a proper bed after all this time.'

'Everything feels funny,' I admit.

'In a nice way, though?' She's anxious that I'm happy when all I feel is numb. I should be fussing over her, not the other way around.

'It'll take a bit of getting used to, that's all. But yes, funny in a nice way.' I smile at her.

'Is there anything you'd like to do today?' she asks.

There are things I *have* to do. Like check in with my probation officer and organise Tanya's funeral. Speaking of which, I add *See Liam* to my mental to-do list. 'I'm free this afternoon if those gorgeous girls of yours still want to take me shopping?'

Hope beams at me. 'They can't wait.'

I study her. 'Am I allowed to say you look tired?'

'Just this once,' she warns. 'Seriously, Mercy, I don't want a pity party.'

'I get that. But from now on in I want to be there for you.'

'You always were, Mercy, I've never forgotten that. And Clem's been brilliant. No matter what the news was from the hospital, he just got on with it, covering both our jobs while keeping an eye out for the girls.'

I nod my head in appreciation. 'He's a good bloke. I'm surprised women aren't beating a path to his door.'

'They'd have to knock Pete out of the way, first.' Hope smiles at me mischievously.

I look at her, dumbfounded. 'He never said.'

Clem shares very little of his life with me. It's as though an invisible barrier went up the moment he and Hope went to live with the Caplans. My brain dredges up the memory of us all outside the children's home. His sour expression as he waited in the back of their car. How he'd flinched when I kissed him goodbye.

Hope reads my expression. 'They've only been seeing each other for a few months. I don't think there'd been anyone before that.' She sounds like a lawyer submitting mitigating evidence to the court. 'I told him you'd be pleased for him but he kept putting off telling you until the time was right.'

'And when was that? Third of Never?' I snap. All those years of making small talk when we could have talked about what matters. *This*. This is what prison robs you of. I stretch my mouth into a smile to show no harm done. 'Has there ever been anyone special for you?' I ask.

'Not really. Twin girls are a handful and I didn't want to take my eye off the ball. Too late for me now.'

I'm about to contradict her when I remember she doesn't want soft-soaping.

'What about you?' she asks, breaking the silence. 'You've got a lot of living to catch up on.'

'I don't know,' I say, staring into the middle distance. 'The idea of getting close to someone...' I look away.

'He ruined everything, didn't he?' She jerks her head in a way that suggests she's seconds away from tears and I know the twins weren't the only reason she shied away from another relationship.

There's part of me that wishes I could take her by the hand and tell her that there are men out there who don't kill women when they're angry, but I can't. We can't embrace the future by eradicating the past. We're right to be wary.

She rips a sheet of absorbent kitchen paper from a roll and blows her nose in it. 'Promise me you won't live like a nun, though,' she says, as though her being beaten black and blue didn't alter the trajectory of my life.

'I'll promise no such thing,' I respond stubbornly.

She purses her lips at me. 'Can you remember what it's like to get butterflies in your stomach?'

'I've had my moments.' I jut out my chin.

This makes her smile. She dabs her eyes then leans back in her chair; arms folded. 'Go on then. Name them.'

I look at her askance. 'What?'

'Tell me about the men that came after Billy? The ones that set your world on fire,' she challenges.

'Well, there wasn't anyone specific.'

'Or anyone at all by my reckoning.'

'That's a bit harsh, Hope. You hungry or something?'

'Don't try and sidetrack me.'

'Wouldn't dream of it.' We laugh and suddenly it feels like there is a way back for all of us.

The taxi driver drops me outside the address on the business card I showed him when I flagged him down. 'Best o' luck,' he says to me before pulling away. I look at the sign above the entrance: *24hr Defence Lawyers.*

I climb two flights of wooden stairs to Liam's office, which bears his name on the door. Inside, the room is cheerful and tastefully furnished. I expect the law books, which are on bookshelves along one wall, what I don't expect are the fresh flowers displayed in a vase on his desk. I look at him and he turns pink. 'Thought I'd mark the occasion,' he says.

'Do that for all your clients, do you?' I ask, and he doesn't reply, no doubt exercising his right to remain silent.

'I've never actually been in here before,' I comment, looking around. Because I'd pleaded guilty to murder from the outset, my first meeting with Liam was when I was in police custody, just before I was remanded.

There's a TV on one wall, a cabinet that has tea and coffee making paraphernalia on top of it along with a selection of biscuits, good ones by the look of it. A pressed shirt and tie hang on the back of the door. 'I spend a lot of time here,' he says, shrugging.

'That your daughter?' I ask, pointing to a framed photo of a teenage girl on his desk. He nods. He doesn't see as much of her as he'd like since his wife moved away. Ex-wife, if I remember it right. 'You know it is, Mercy, which is why you knew fine well I'd help Debs.'

'I couldn't presume,' I say sweetly, 'but I thought you might consider it.' I wonder fleetingly if he has anyone new waiting for him at home.

He invites me to sit. Instead of moving to his side of the desk he stays on my side, perching his backside against the edge of it, folding his arms.

'How did your probation meeting go?'

I roll my eyes. 'Yeah, that was a right barrel of laughs.' My probation officer is a serious-faced woman with the demeanour of someone let down so many times she no longer trusts anyone. Maybe in time I can be a beacon of hope.

He smiles. 'Better than being inside, though.'

He has me there.

'I was surprised to get your call, to be honest. I thought you'd be wanting to spend every minute with your family.'

'I do, but Clem's warned me Hope doesn't want me fussing round her. She's keen for me to get to know my nieces better though, and what better way to do that than go shopping with them after this?' I tell him. 'I'm in need of a makeover, apparently.'

'You look great,' he says, his eyes travelling over my face in a way that makes me look away.

'Amazing what a bit of bronzer and a good shampoo can do.' I'm flustered and babbling. My hand automatically reaches for the scar on my chin; its ugliness reassures me. I move the conversation to the purpose of my visit.

'I've arranged a cremation for Tanya, tomorrow. It'll just be me and Vonnie there, but it seems like the right thing to do.'

'Would you like me to come?' he asks. 'I didn't know Tanya but you might be glad of the support.'

'Oh, no, you don't need to do that.' I'm touched by his thoughtfulness. 'Vonnie and I'll have a bit of Dutch courage at the pub before we set off. She's working there now, does a couple of shifts a week.'

Liam nods. 'So how can I help, then?'

'What happened to Tanya was terrible. You heard a prison officer was involved?'

I watch as he grimaces. 'It was front page news for a couple of days. Horrible, just horrible.'

'To be murdered by someone that's supposed to protect her. It got me thinking. Her family will be entitled to compensation, won't they?'

'Yes, of course.'

I reach into my pocket – using one of the many bags in my wardrobe after all this time seems unnecessary – and pull out a slip of paper I found in Tanya's belongings. I hand it to him. 'It's where Tanya's kids are living now. They're adults, but the money would come in handy, wouldn't it?'

'I'm sure it would,' he says carefully. He can see where this is going.

'Tanya regretted how much she'd let them down but this is something she can do for them, isn't it? A legacy, if you like, to help set them up. Would you be willing to speak to them, explain how it all works? Help them with the claim, even?'

Liam's mouth turns down at the corners, the way it always does when he's mulling something over. I stifle a smile.

'I suppose I could help them on a no-win no-fee basis,' he mutters to himself.

'That's the spirit,' I say, grinning.

I tell him about Lola and his view is the same as mine. Her father needs to be reported to the police. I'll broach the subject with her once she's released.

'If that's the business side of things taken care of, can I make you a tea?' he asks.

'I'd love that,' I tell him, 'as long as I get one of those posh biscuits.'

'Who do you think I bought them for?'

I study him as he sets about making our drinks. I'm touched that he thinks I'm good enough for fresh flowers and fancy biscuits. That he listens to me and has never yet baulked when I've asked something of him.

'Hope wants me to start dating,' I blurt out of nowhere. 'Like it's going to be that easy.'

He regards me as he hands over a steaming mug. 'You might be surprised.'

I raise an eyebrow at him. 'Oh, I'm sure the mechanics of it have stayed the same,' I say wryly, 'but the whole business of meeting someone compatible has completely changed. I mean, where do you even start?'

'A lot of people meet their partners in the workplace,' he says.

I consider this. 'I met my ex-husband at work,' I admit. 'In fact, that's how Hope met Gary.' I shudder. 'I think I can safely say they were epic fails.'

'You could always go online.'

'I'll stay away from dating sites, thank you very much,' I tell him. 'There's a huge gap in my profile that no amount of flannel will hide.'

'The right person will see beyond your past,' he says.

'You think?'

He looks a bit funny, as though he's sickening for something. I select a biscuit from the plate he's set down between us and peer at him closely. 'You okay?'

'Now that I don't represent you anymore, Mercy, there's something I've been meaning to ask.'

'Really?' I swallow down the mouthful of biscuit I've been chewing.

He shifts uncomfortably against the desk, as though his backside has gone numb. 'I was wondering if you'd consider coming out for a drink with me sometime.'

I widen my eyes at him. 'Like in a date?'

The skin around his eyes creases. 'Yes, definitely like a date.'

I break eye contact, searching the room for something I can focus on because his eyes right now resemble a puppy's, and that isn't helping. I try to analyse what I'm feeling. Shocked, obviously. Flattered, of course. I mean, he's a lovely bloke, not that I really know him. I mean, how do you really know anyone without letting them in? The question is, do I want to?

'You've just said you worry about the prospect of explaining your past to someone new. You wouldn't have that problem with me. I know everything about you!' He's smiling, like that's a good thing, and I almost get swept up in it.

That's when I realise the futility of what he's saying. Relationships require honesty to thrive – I've learned the hard way the importance of that – and anything less, with this good and decent man, prepared to take on a murderer for Christ's sake, just wouldn't be fair.

I shake my head at him. 'I'm sorry, Liam, I just don't think it'd work.'

I catch the cloud of disappointment before he shrugs it away. 'No of course, that's absolutely fine!' He throws his hands up and waves them around to show how fine it is.

'It's not you...' I falter. Did I really just say that? I'm so out of practice the only platitudes I can trot out are overused clichés.

'You don't have to explain yourself,' he says.

'No, I know that but what I meant to say is that I'm not ready to date anyone. I don't think I have it in me to open myself up like that.' I let out a sigh. 'It's too soon.'

Liam moves to the other side of his desk. He handles my rejection graciously, even asking if I'd like more tea. I tell him no thank you and he sighs with relief at my answer.

Vonnie is working a shift in the bar when I return from shopping with my nieces. She'd contacted Clem like I'd asked her to, following her release, and after a trial period he offered her a job. She's a natural, which is no surprise really, all she'd needed for her light to shine was to step out from behind the clouds.

The girls insist I change into one of the outfits I've bought and I do so to humour them. I stand in front of the mirror in my bedroom, turning this way and that. For sixteen years I've not cared how I look; all it's taken is the awe of two girls on the cusp of womanhood and I'm desperate to impress. They've a good eye, I'll give them that. It feels good to make an effort without the threat of someone on the wing wanting to take you down a peg because of it.

I've learned how to tell them apart. Physically the girls are identical but their temperaments are so different: Maisie is outgoing and exuberant, whereas Molly is quiet and introspective. Every shop we went into, Maisie ran around the clothing rails hauling gorgeous but impractical dresses into the air claiming that I'd look fabulous. Molly would sigh and say yes, but when will she wear them?

Vonnie turns to me as I step into the bar and I give her a twirl. 'Where have you been hiding?' she says as she gives me the once-over. 'Not the most practical of styles,' she states in a low voice. The girls have stayed upstairs in the flat and we're alone. Vonnie's right, the white broderie anglaise dress is more suited to a sun-kissed terrace than a backstreet pub, but the girls both loved it and I love them.

'How's it going?' she asks.

'Weird,' I tell her. 'How about you?'

'It's mental,' she agrees.

In the same way you need to acclimatise to life in jail, returning home requires a period of adjustment too. Taking as long as I like when I go to the bathroom. My showers are longer too. Prison leaves a stain on you that no amount of scrubbing will remove.

Vonnie's face brightens. 'I love it here though, chatting to the customers and listening to their stories. Clem and Hope have been brilliant,' she adds. 'It means the world to them that you're here, your family back together at last.'

She sees my smile slip and replaces her own with a frown.

'What is it?' Her voice is anxious.

'I'm fine, it's just that I've organised Tanya's cremation for tomorrow. Just you, me and the celebrant. How sad is that?'

'Her kids don't want to know, then?'

I shake my head. 'Said there wasn't much point now, and I can kind of understand it.'

Vonnie goes off to serve a man holding two pint glasses in the air. When she's done, she comes back. 'It doesn't matter that nobody else is going. We'll be there to pay our respects, and that's what matters. Agreed?'

'Agreed,' I say.

CHAPTER THIRTY-FOUR

The next day, Vonnie and I stand either side of Tanya's coffin as the celebrant reads out a version of her life that's close to the truth without sounding pitiful. When she's done, she looks over at me and opens her mouth, the way a parent might when coaxing a toddler to say Mummy or Daddy for the first time. She wants me to say something. She keeps nodding her encouragement and smiling, waiting for me to share anecdotes that will fill the awkward silence. I consider telling her that I met Tanya while waiting for the prison van to take us to jail and that her party piece was soaking a tampon with methadone to make it last longer, but you kind of have to have been there to get it.

'That was lovely,' I say instead, encouraging her to wrap it up.

Vonnie's made up a playlist that she's given to the funeral director. We stand sombrely while Tanya's coffin moves behind the curtain to the sound of 'Fix You'.

As we leave, I see Liam standing at the back of the chapel and though we don't speak the sight of him warms my soul.

Clem and Hope have put on a spread, which Maisie and Molly serve to us with sombre faces.

'Tan would hate this,' I whisper to Vonnie, and she nods.

I go upstairs. Stare at Tanya's clipping on the wall until sleep takes me.

CHAPTER THIRTY-FIVE

Deb's appeal was successful. She was released the same day as Lola, the remainder of her sentence suspended for two years. When I'm not accompanying Hope to medical appointments or cheering Maisie and Molly on from the sidelines at hockey matches, I accompany Debs on supervised visits to see her kids. Liam persuaded the family court to grant two hours of contact once a week, which leaves her diminished but not broken. She clung to me the first time we left the contact centre, but by the time I got her home she was already talking about her next visit. She isn't done yet. Her next step is to apply for custody. She's found another job so by the time her application's called she'll be able to show she's financially stable. The family social worker and school have promised to monitor her kids. It's far from perfect but for now it'll have to do. Liam's helping her fight on and I believe that one day she'll win. Either way I'll be by her side.

Lola's situation is problematic. She was placed in a bail hostel following her release from Fairmile – her recall to prison meant she lost the temporary accommodation she'd been staying in. This means she must report to the council's emergency housing team every morning to see if another room's available, which it never is. With only the hostel's address to give to prospective employers – which acts like a red flag – it's no wonder her search for employment has flatlined.

'I keep telling them I need somewhere I can bring Danny back to,' she tells me after another fruitless council visit. We've met up for coffee, our second meeting since her release. 'But then they want to know why I'm so bothered about my little brother living with me that I get all tongue-tied.'

I've been trying to come up with ways that can put things right for Lola, but none of them are easy. I can see from Debs' experience that resorting to the family court is protracted. When I spoke to Liam about her situation his advice was resolute: Lola must claim Danny as her son and report her father to the police. A course of action so much easier said than done.

I regard Lola as she sips her coffee; her clothes look slept in and her hair hasn't been washed for several days. She's not ready to take on Danny full time yet and she isn't equipped to deal with her parents. She knows this and this knowledge hinders her. She needs something to fill the void of Danny's absence, something to bring her into contact with people with a purpose. Vonnie's been offered a job in one of the city's hotels, on reception. They'll pay for her to study hospitality in the evenings, an opportunity to progress up the ladder if she shows potential. She's beside herself with excitement. I offer Lola Vonnie's old shifts and a meal in the restaurant for her and Danny next time she gets to take him out. She is so happy when we say goodbye, and I'm so relieved that she's happy, I ignore the fear gnawing away at me that warns it won't last.

My phone's shrill ring startles me awake, piercing the silence like a prison siren. My eyes snap open as I scramble to retrieve it: Lola's name flashes up on the screen. It's just after 4am; no good news arrives at this hour. I tap the 'answer' button with trepidation.

Lola's ragged breathing tumbles down the line: 'Mercy?' The tone of her voice makes me sit up straight and swing my legs over the edge of the bed in readiness.

'Lola, sweetheart, what's wrong?' I feel my pulse quicken.

Her answer is incoherent. A jumble of words and sobs that make no sense but I can feel the effort she's putting into making herself heard.

'Is it Danny?' I ask, then kick myself. Of course it's about Danny. 'Is he okay?' I'm standing now, pacing the floor as I wait for her answer. 'Lola, tell me!' I urge her when she doesn't reply. I wonder if she's been drinking. I strain my ear to listen for the slur in her words.

'He's fine.' Her words come out strangled, but clear. 'It's just me, as usual, making a mess of things. Mum says she's going to get a restraining order. That one call from her and I'll go back to prison... and I can kiss goodbye to ever seeing Danny again because they'll move and I'll never find them.'

Bastards.

'Are you at the hostel?' There's normally an echoey sound when she phones me from her room. This time I hear traffic, the wind buffeting her words as she moves. 'Tell me where you are and I'll come and get you.'

I hear the sound of an intercity train hurtling past. The proximity of it tells me she's at Pendleton station, ten minutes away at this time of night, five if I put my foot down. Thank God Clem put me on his insurance, persuaded me to use his car instead of getting taxis everywhere. He leaves the keys on the hall table so I can take them whenever I need to. 'I'm coming for you, Lola,' I tell her, throwing on yesterday's clothes.

'I can't do this anymore, Mercy...'

There's a whooshing noise as though she is running or the phone is falling.

'Lola!' I shout.

She doesn't reply.

CHAPTER THIRTY-SIX

As I approach Pendleton Bridge I see Lola cowering on the pavement like a frightened animal. I swerve the car onto the kerb then brake before throwing open the driver's door.

'Lola!' I call out as I run to her, dropping onto my knees so I can place my arms around her shoulders. She puts up no resistance. 'I've got you,' I tell her as I hold on tight. She's trembling and desperate but she is sober. Keeping one arm around her I reach for her phone, which is lying on the pavement beside her. A jagged crack runs along the screen where it clattered to the floor, but it's fixable. Like Lola, I hope, as I study her hunched profile. We stay huddled together until her trembling stops and dawn breaks across the sky.

I drop Lola back at her hostel. I have no choice, if she doesn't return she's in violation of her licence and she'll be back through Fairmile's gates before the day is out. She assures me that she's fine and I believe her. Last night was a one-off, a cry for help because what she's been doing isn't working and there are only so many times you can bang your head against a wall.

When I return to the flat, Hope is in the kitchen nursing a coffee. She nods when I ask if she'd like a refill. I set about making enough for two.

'What got you up and out so early in the morning?' She's eyeing yesterday's clothes. She gives me a sly smile, her thoughts already in the gutter.

'Lola needed my help,' I tell her, taking her mug and giving it a quick rinse before placing it beneath the coffee machine's nozzle.

'Is she okay?'

'She's fine. Just needed a shoulder to lean on.'

'You must be exhausted. Can you manage some breakfast?' She indicates the cereal laid out on the countertop in readiness for the girls but I'm already shaking my head. I splash milk into her coffee before passing it to her. Behind me the machine splutters frothy liquid into my mug.

'I'll get something later. I've only come back for a shower then I need to pop out again.'

I jump in the shower, then go through to my room, select one of the outfits the twins picked out for me on our shopping trip. A kick-ass trouser suit that I team with killer heels and a bag that was eye-wateringly expensive when I bought it back in the day. My bedroom door is open a crack and through it two pairs of deep brown eyes watch every move.

'Perfect timing,' I tell them. Holding the trouser suit aloft on its hanger I signal for Maisie and Molly to come in. I explain what I intend to do and that I need their help. They look at me, solemn-faced, before running back to their bedroom, returning with a state-of-the-art hairdryer and a beauty box packed with big brand make-up. They stand behind me at my dressing table as we study my reflection in the mirror. 'What look are you going for, Auntie M?' Molly asks. Maisie is ahead of her. She studies what I'm wearing and picks up on my vibe.

'How about bad-ass motherfucker?' she asks as she stares at me.

'That's the one,' I tell her, staring back.

CHAPTER THIRTY-SEVEN

Lola's parents live in a substantial detached property in a secluded development four miles from Delamere Forest. It's reached via a private, access-only road that opens out onto a gravel drive with ample room for their cars and mine, which I park facing out in case I need to make a rapid exit.

Established bay trees in matching pots stand either side of a double front door. Wisteria surrounds one of the large ground-floor bay windows like something out of *Country Life* magazine.

'Nice,' I mutter as I climb out of the car.

'You sure we've got the right address?' asks Von anxiously.

'I had no idea Lola's family lived here,' states Debs.

'Incest happens regardless of postcode,' I tell them as I ring the doorbell.

When I called Von and Debs first thing and told them Lola needed their help they didn't hesitate. Half an hour later they were standing on their doorsteps waiting for me to pick them up: Vonnie dressed in her hotel reception uniform with her name badge removed, Debs wearing the smart dress she wears for client meetings. They climbed in the car without asking where we were going or how long we'd be. I spent the rest of the journey filling them in on my plan.

I hear footsteps approaching the front door and mentally prepare myself. 'Remember, if it turns nasty you're to walk away. You're part of the clean-up operation, not the massacre.'

'Spoilsport,' Debs grumbles, but I sense her relief. What I'm about to do could land me in serious trouble if it goes wrong, there's no need to drag them down with me.

Deception is easy when you look the part. A quick flash of my expired gym membership card along with the voice I use when it's last orders and we're sitting in Lola's parents' living room declining tea and biscuits while I wait for her father to come through from the conservatory. Danny, I'm told, is having his nap.

Ours aren't the only appearances that are deceptive. If I didn't know the man who has joined his wife on the couch abused his daughter in the most appalling way, I could be forgiven for thinking he was an upstanding citizen, one of those pillars of the community referred to in obituaries. He wears a polo shirt tucked into beige chinos teamed with sheepskin moccasins to protect the carpet. The essence of propriety, rather than a dirty old man.

I uncross my legs, plant my killer heels into the insipid shag pile. Smile.

I can feel them assessing us. Trying to work out what we're doing in their home. I let the moment stretch out between us.

'You said you were here about Lola?' Lola's mother is the first to speak. Slim with pinched features, she has shoulder-length hair, which I imagine she ties back when she's working. She's unnerved by my silence. I file that away under *Good to know*.

'Mrs Shepherd? It's about Lola,' I'd said to her when she'd answered the door. I assume she thought the pass I held up was a warrant card, what with her daughter being on first name terms with the local constabulary.

She barely glanced at my companions as she ushered us in. 'Call me Sally, please. My husband, Neil, will be through in a moment,' she'd said.

I smile at them both now before answering. 'Yes, I did, *Sally*.' I guess she doesn't like the way I emphasise her name. She recoils, as though insulted by the word I've used.

'Where did you say you were from?' Neil isn't as gullible as his wife. Then again, I suppose years of raping his daughter has made him wily. As the saying goes, you can't bullshit a bullshitter.

I turn to Sally to see if she is able to enlighten him, but she frowns when she realises that I didn't actually say, and she didn't actually bother checking my card. Her face clouds over. It's her fault they are staring at three strangers who have entered their home and they're not quite sure what to do about it.

I put them out of their misery. 'I know Lola from Fairmile.' I watch the cogs move slowly as they process this information. 'From *prison*,' I add, enjoying their discomfort.

'Are you the new governor?' Sally asks, desperate for it to be true. I'm flattered that's where she's positioned me and I make a mental note to feed this back to my nieces.

'No. We were on the same wing.' I let that settle.

'Get the fuck out of my house!' Neil is on his feet, all civility gone. He points to the door in case we can't remember the way we came in.

'Now, now, someone's forgotten their manners,' I say to him, unfazed. I regard him as he hops from foot to foot, unsure what to do. He's working out whether he can drag us out of this room. Whether we'll let him, or whether he'll get hurt in the process. Men like him are terrified of women like us; that's why they hate us. I move my feet wide apart to take up as much room as possible, lift my chin so that he can see my scar. The sight of it stalls him. Despite the heavy make-up its edges are jagged, a warning that I've faced someone dangerous and come out the other side. 'The person who did that to me ended up in a coma,' I hiss, registering the alarm on his face.

'We don't want any trouble.' Sally's voice is quiet. She's an A&E nurse, used to dealing with people's rage but what I feel for this couple goes way beyond that. I get to my feet, though I'm not going anywhere. The adrenaline coursing through me makes every nerve end jangle and I wonder fleetingly if they have a cellar, and what Neil would look like lying at the bottom of it. I bat the image away. Getting recalled to prison won't help Lola, Hope, or the twins for that matter. I keep my hands by my sides and do my best to keep my head on straight. I know from bitter experience that acting on impulse can be deadly.

'Your old man's a piece of work,' I say to Sally. 'Brings guilty pleasures to a whole new level, doesn't he?'

I turn to look at him the way you might look at a favoured pet. 'For most of us it's a sneaky bar of chocolate when you're supposed to be on a diet. No real cause for concern, know what I'm saying?'

Sally's neck flushes pink. 'I think you should leave... *all* of you,' she adds, in case there's any misunderstanding.

My head snaps in her direction. 'And I think you should call the police, Sally. Report that sick fuck for what he did to Lola over and over and over again.'

Sally springs to her feet and moves so that she is standing beside Neil. I feel Debs tense but a side glance from Vonnie and she shrugs it away.

'I get it,' I say. 'It's not your fault you vowed to love a nonce in sickness and in health.'

'I don't know what lies Lola's been feeding you–' she states.

'Lies?' I cut her off. 'So a DNA test won't show this piece of filth fathered Danny?'

Sally blanches but says nothing. Beside her, Neil's moccasins squirm into the carpet.

I take a step towards her and narrow my eyes. 'Didn't it worry you when she was growing up? About how much time he spent reading her a bedtime story, or drying her after her bath?'

Sally shakes her head wildly. 'If you think I had any idea–'

I carry on as though she hasn't spoken. 'Weren't you ever curious? About what took him so long? About why he encouraged you to work nights?'

'I didn't have a clue, I swear...' She pauses as though trying to put her thoughts in order.

'Because men like him have an answer for everything, don't they?' I say.

She looks at me then looks away. I've hit a nerve and we both know it.

'You shouldn't believe a word that girl says!' Neil spits. 'She's a headcase! Needs therapy if you ask me.'

'Lola doesn't need therapy!' snaps Vonnie, unable to stay quiet.

'People go to therapy because there's someone in their life who *won't* go,' states Debs.

I signal for them to rein it in. I look at Sally and shake my head. 'How could you let your daughter down like that?'

She swallows before answering me. 'I really had no idea until she told me she was pregnant!' She looks away as she says this. She's lying and she knows I'm onto her. The things she could have done, could have said that would have made a terrified teenager feel less disgusted about herself. 'What do you want?' she says eventually.

'Why are you listening to her?' Neil's angry now and shouting. The male response to not getting his way.

I nod at Vonnie and Debs. They get to their feet.

'Sally, my friends are going to go upstairs with you and pack Danny's things while you bring him downstairs. You're then going to come with us, hand him over to your daughter and beg for her forgiveness. Then you and me are going to take a trip to the cop shop where you're going to throw *him* under the bus.' I jerk my thumb in daddy dearest's direction.

'I don't think so.' Sally stares at me defiantly.

I move uncomfortably close. Flash a smile that warns her not to fuck with me. 'Seems to me you're willing to give up a lot of things for a man who's convinced himself he's done nothing wrong.'

Sally's brow creases. 'What do you mean?'

'If you don't come with me to the police, then Lola will. Only you'll then be an accessory and believe me, women's prisons are no different to men's when it comes to the pecking order inside. Fraudsters look down on burglars and burglars look down on rapists and rapists are thrilled to high heaven when a nonce comes along. And a woman who lets a nonce abuse her child, well, that's right down there with sewer rats and sub-human forms of life that make amoebas look shrewd.' I stare her down. 'So, what's it to be?'

CHAPTER THIRTY-EIGHT

It's late when I get home. I've helped move an exhausted but ecstatic Lola from her hostel to Debs' place. Once her probation officer approved her change of address it was all systems go.

The second bedroom is hers – and Danny's – until Debs' kids move back. Debs is glad of the company, and Lola needs a positive role model to show her how to be a full-time mum, because that's what she is now. Her face when her mother handed Danny to her was a picture. The police will need to interview Lola, to corroborate what her mum confessed to when she accompanied me to the station and said she wanted to report a crime.

Now Lola has Danny I think she'll cope with anything.

Hope is resting in the living room when I return. I check she wants company then collapse onto the sofa beside her when she flashes me a smile. I lean back against the headrest. The TV is off and she offers me the remote control but I decline. I don't want to watch anything, just need a bit of time out to clear my head. I must have drifted off because when my eyes flutter open, she's watching me, an anxious look on her face.

'What's the matter?' I say to her, letting my eyelids droop once more.

'Seems to me you've been overdoing it lately.'

'I could say the same about you.' I turn to her and smile.

'I'm dying. I'm allowed to run myself ragged while I've still got the energy.'

She's already tiring more quickly than she did when I first came home, though it's not something she allows any of us to dwell on.

'You being here helps, Mercy. It helps a lot.'

'Good, because being back here means the world to me.'

'The girls love having you around. I've tried to keep their spirits up through all this but they're going to need you more than ever when the time comes.' Her cheeks are flushed, as though she's been building up to this.

'I know. Of course I'll be there for them. I always will. I couldn't love them any more than if they were my own, you know that.'

'Glad to hear it.' She points an accusing finger at me. 'Only the last couple of weeks you've hardly been here. You seem more interested in spending time with those friends of yours than you do with us.'

I sit up straight. 'That's not true! I love being with you, Clem and the girls, please don't think that isn't the case.'

'I don't get it,' she says, shaking her head. 'All that time you were forced to live together; I thought you'd be glad to see the back of them.'

'They're good people, Hope. Good people who happen to have gone through a rough time, like me. I don't turn my back on the people I care about. Never have, never will.' I fix her with a look. 'You should know that more than anyone.'

She looks away.

'The friendships I made in Fairmile kept me afloat all those years. So much so that I now look on Vonnie, Lola and Debs as part of my family, too.' I stroke the scar on my wrist absent-mindedly. 'They're not taking me away from you, Hope, they're the ones who brought me back.'

'Oh, Mercy, I'm so sorry!' She turns towards me, burrowing her head into my shoulder. 'I ruined your life that night, didn't I?'

I wrap my arms around her. 'Hush now,' I whisper into her hair. 'None of it matters.'

'How can you say that when it was me who pushed him!' Her body gives in to heaving sobs and as I hold her close, I'm taken back to that night.

Gary was in a terrible rage. The heroin he'd hidden behind the barrels in the cellar had gone. He blamed Hope because he blamed her for everything, she was a convenient punchbag that he'd begun to despise. In his mind, the only person who could have moved it was Hope – if I'd found it, he'd have had his marching orders and the police would be knocking his door down – so he set about teaching her a lesson.

Men like Gary don't change. Reporting him for assault would have provided Hope with a temporary respite but nothing more. As a first-time offender he wouldn't have served long, would have soon returned to the bosom of his loving family to belittle, bully and break them as he wished.

My appearance in the hallway must have put him off his stride because one minute he was throttling her and the next minute she'd pushed him away. Unlike the statements we gave, he didn't fall down the steps, merely teetered at the top of them. The drink he'd consumed earlier, adding to his unsteadiness. Before I could do anything to prevent it, Hope lunged forward, shoving him violently down the stairs.

'What the hell have you done?' I whispered. I sent her to call for help while I worked out what to do. Gary wasn't assaulting her when she pushed him the second time, in the eyes of the law it was murder, not self-defence. The babies she carried would be strangers to her by the time she was released. Her life, their lives, *in that moment mattered more than mine. I needed to concoct an alternative story. By the time she came back I had it all figured out.*

'I thought he was going to kill you,' I kept saying to her. 'I had to stop him.'

It had only taken a matter of moments to reframe the entire incident. Tell a story enough times and you believe it to be the truth.

It was the reason I was so fearful about Alice Maltby's threat. Hope wouldn't stand for Maltby's claim about drugs being the reason Gary's dead. I'd have lost the tariff I'd been given, compelling her to confess to what she'd done, and what would be achieved if she ended up in jail after all those years? Now, with her terminal diagnosis looming over her, I know I made the right choice.

Hope lifts her head and searches my face. 'Can you ever forgive me, Mercy?'

'What for?'

'For letting you take the blame.'

'I couldn't let you go to prison, could I? Besides, you were in fear of your life.'

'But I wasn't, was I? Not in that moment. In that moment I was angry and wanted to stop him hurting me ever again.' She shakes her head. 'The fact remains that he's dead because of me! I was grateful to you for taking the blame like that but I was selfish, too. You gave me a life with my girls I would never have had otherwise, but look what you lost.'

'Doesn't matter, love. All that matters is that he's gone. That you're safe and those little ones didn't have to grow up in fear.'

'But you gave up your freedom for me.'

'I'd do it again in a heartbeat.'

'I wouldn't let you. If I had my time again–'

'Enough!' I snap. 'Look, there's something about that night you need to know. When you pushed Gary and he fell. I went down into the cellar to check on him while you called for help.'

'Yes, I know that.'

'What you don't know is that I saw him move. I leaned in closer to take a better look and he opened his eyes. I got the shock of my life, I can tell you, but there he was, lying at my feet, nothing but hatred all over his face.

'I was glad you pushed him. He was no good for you or the family you were about to have. He was downright dangerous, which is why I lifted his head and banged it against the concrete steps. Once. Twice. Three times for good measure. The last thing I wanted was for the bastard to get to his feet like he was the fucking Terminator.'

I look at Hope. 'So you see, his death was down to me, after all, not you. The right person went to jail.'

She looks at me with wide eyes. 'Is that why you told me not to tell the police why Gary was so mad?'

I nod. 'Think about it. If the police had found out about Gary's heroin they'd have got it into their heads that the bar was a dealer's paradise, which it wasn't, and they'd have shut it down in no time. Then where would we all be?'

'Shit street without a paddle,' says Clem from the doorway.

I crane my neck to look at him. 'How long have you been standing there?'

'Long enough.' He steps into the room and flops down on the opposite sofa.

'Pete not with you?' I ask, giving him the eye. Clem's mentioned him several times over the last couple of weeks but I haven't had the pleasure of meeting him yet.

'Don't worry, he's just as curious about you,' he says, grinning, and it's lovely to know he's not keeping anything from me anymore.

He turns to his twin. 'Better not let the girls see you like that, Hope.'

She acknowledges him with a nod before pushing herself up off the settee. 'Think I'm going to have an early night anyway,' she says.

Clem waits until she's left the room. 'You can't keep doing that,' he hisses.

'What?'

'Trying to make everything better for us.' He lets out a sigh. 'You did a great job of protecting us when we were younger, but we're adults now. You don't need to keep shielding us from the truth.'

'What do you mean?'

Clem stares at me. 'I was there, Mercy! I came the moment I heard Hope scream. I stood at the top of the steps. I saw what you did when Hope ran for help. You checked Gary's pulse before shaking your head, nothing more. You didn't kill him; he was already dead.'

I grab his arm. 'Promise me you'll not tell her! You can see the turmoil she's in. Let me do this one last thing to ease her guilt before she leaves us. Please, Clem!'

'Like you let me believe you didn't want to come and live with us when in truth the Caplans didn't want you?'

I search his face for understanding. 'I didn't want you to blow your chance of a happy family by hating them.'

'I understand that now.' He eyes me steadily then sighs. 'I'll keep your secret if you promise me something in return.'

I narrow my eyes.

'I want you to start creating happy memories for *you*, Mercy. Do you think you can do that?'

'Why couldn't you pick something simple like eradicating poverty?' I grumble, then seeing the reprimand on his face, I promise I'll try.

'Think I'm going to call it a night, too,' I say, getting to my feet.

'Oh damn,' Clem calls when I reach the door. 'Someone from the funeral home phoned for you earlier. Asked me to pass on a message.'

I turn to look at him.

'Tanya's ashes are ready for collection.'

CHAPTER THIRTY-NINE

It's hard at first to get used to the sun. The sheer heat of it that hits you when you step off the plane. The sweat trickling down your back as you queue for a taxi. The exhaustion you feel as you check in to your hotel, even though it's only the middle of the afternoon.

I step into my room and look around. It's light and spacious and the view from the balcony is just like the travel agent's photo online. I nod appreciatively. I quickly unpack and change into something cooler. How did Maisie get it so right when she picked this dress out for me? I stare in wonder at the white cotton material that'll be impossible to keep clean but felt so summery when I'd tried it on it the changing room, I was unable to resist it.

Hope and the girls are coming over to join me next week while Clem looks after the bar. He doesn't know it yet, but I'll return the favour next month when Pete whisks him off to Paris to propose. It's all hush-hush so the girls have been sworn to secrecy. *Good luck with that*, I couldn't help but think when I saw the excitement on their faces. Pete's a good man and he makes my brother happy and that's enough, isn't it?

I think of Liam. It's been a month since we've spoken yet every day, I find myself wanting to share some aspect of it with him. Like Lola asking me shyly if I'd be Danny's godmother. Debs is helping her with the arrangements for the naming ceremony she never got to give him and I swear it's turning into a royal event. Lola's not religious but sees it as marking the start of a new phase in their lives, and she's right. She's sober and relishing being a mum. Her father's on remand and her mother's on bail, but her relationship with them is beyond repair. As Lola says, we're her family now.

Thanks to Liam, Debs has a custody hearing next month. Her contact with her children has increased considerably and their relationship is strong. She tells me that Liam is hopeful the outcome will be positive.

As for Vonnie, her confidence knows no bounds. When I told her what I had in mind for this break she insisted on making all the arrangements: booking the flights to Turkey, arranging accommodation, negotiating a group discount. When she puts her mind to something she's unstoppable.

She had the audacity to remind me of something the other day. That time in Fairmile when I told her she suffered from cherophobia. 'You were right of course, but I wasn't the only one who was frightened of happiness, was I? It's about time you started living your life.'

She's beginning to sound like Clem. Hope, too, for that matter.

I've been hard-wired for so long to fear good when it happens. I feel like a bird struggling to escape its cage, a cage I've built around myself. I want to tell Liam I was flattered when he asked me out. That I'd like to have said yes, but I'm just not brave enough.

My gaze falls onto the cardboard tube on top of the chest of drawers. When I collected Tanya's ashes, I had no idea what to do with them. I carried them home and put them on my bedside table, bereft. 'Tell me what I can do for you, Tanya,' I whispered. Then I looked at the magazine clipping stuck to my wall and realised I was staring at the answer.

I check the time on my watch. The others will be waiting for me. I pick up Tanya's ashes and head out to meet them.

We follow a path through the hotel's manicured lawns to a white picket fence that denotes the end of the hotel grounds and the start of the public beach. Vonnie has spoken with the hotel manager and he's drawn us a map of the cove we're to head out to, that will be secluded even at this time of day, where we can scatter Tanya's ashes and say our final goodbye.

'Mummy, paddle!' shrieks Danny and we remove our sandals before heading to the shoreline. Lola holds his hand tightly as he kicks and splashes. She swipes her face with her other hand but it isn't sea water she's wiping away. I catch her eye briefly and nod; I heard him say it, too.

I watch my friends as they step into the sea. The world encourages women to be wary of each other, yet I look at the group walking ahead of me and know they are my soul sisters. Each one of us has known what it's like to be broken but we've made it through. We're here.

This is what joy feels like and I lift my face to feel it.

That's when I realise that Liam makes my world better too. He sees me for what I am and that's enough for him. When I go back to the hotel I will ring him. I smile at my decision, at the anticipation of making the call.

The cove is in sight and I hold tightly on to Tanya's ashes as I hurry to keep up with the others.

Vonnie turns to me, grinning. 'Over here!' she calls excitedly.

'Oh my God, it's boiling!' shrieks Lola, adjusting Danny's sun hat to make sure the back of his neck is covered.

'It's roasting,' shrills Debs.

I take a deep breath in, exhaling slowly as I blow away the past.

'Just another day in paradise,' I say.

ALSO BY EMMA SALISBURY

One Good Reason

WRITING AS MAYA ROSS AND COMING IN 2026:

Blood Feud

Bad Blood

Blood Money

ACKNOWLEDGEMENTS

Grateful thanks to Betsy Reavley, Tara Lyons (especially for her patience!), Hannah Deuce, Lexi Curtis and everyone at Bloodhound Books for getting this book over the line, and for the awesome cover design. Particular thanks to Abbie Rutherford for her kind words and keen eye whilst working on copy edits.

Thanks to Lynn Osborne, friend and reader, for not batting an eyelid when I announced on a whim I wanted to write a novel in a different genre. Your encouragement in that moment was pivotal.

Thanks to my family for their continued support, in particular Stephen, who tirelessly puts up with my characters when they invade our home taking over the quiet spaces.

ABOUT THE AUTHOR

Emma writes gritty crime that challenges readers' perception of morality and justice.

Her previous work with socially excluded men and persistent offenders provides her with a lot of inspiration. When she's not writing she has been known to frequent bars of ill repute, where many a loose lip has provided the nugget of a storyline. Find out more about the author and her other books at: www.emmasalisbury.com

A NOTE FROM THE PUBLISHER

Thank you for reading this book. If you enjoyed it, please do consider leaving a review on Amazon to help others find it too.

Follow Bloodhound Books on your socials.

www.ingramcontent.com/pod-product-compliance
Ingram Content Group UK Ltd.
Pitfield, Milton Keynes, MK11 3LW, UK
UKHW041609060226
10553UKWH00033B/206

9 781917 705660